SHOPPING FOR WORLDS

On *Veldte* you will be an amphibian on a planet of islands; note the webbed foot and hand structures . . .

On *Diamond*—where your father is, Amber—you will be a sentient crystal: perfect and alone and immortal.

On *Chaos* nothing is certain—certainly not form. It is not even a planet, but a series of bubbles in the fabric of Space. . .

On *Deirdre* all is jungle and battle, but there is no sex— unlike *Veldte* which is all sex and no battle!

The counselor looked at the young couple sitting before her: the ungainly, unhappy woman; the earnest, retarded man. "There are no *human* colonists," she said. "And of course there is no return. These planets are your choices . . ."

SYMBIOTE'S CROWN

SYMBIOTE'S CROWN

SCOTT BAKER

A BERKLEY BOOK
published by
BERKLEY PUBLISHING CORPORATION

In Memory of Walter Scott Underwood

SYMBIOTES CROWN

CHAPTER ONE

HIS SKIN, cracked and scaled like peeling stucco, hung in loose folds over his lax muscles. A playsuit of soft blue velour concealed his bloated belly and protruding ribs, hid the match-stick thinness of his arms and legs, covered his swollen joints. His breathing was shallow, for it hurt to breathe, hurt as it hurt when he tried to move, but he was used to the pain. It had been with him all his life.

From the hand-carved mahogany infant seat strapped to the passenger's seat of his mother's sports car he stared with dull, dry, disinterested eyes at the highway visible through the plastic windshield. Four years and some months old, he seemed sexless, not with the virgin plasticity of a child, but with the exhausted hermaphroditism of an old man shrinking into death. He was very small for a child of four and he sat very still.

His mother's hoarse, crooning monologue rasped at him, incomprehensible, irritating, yet incapable of piercing his apathy. His skin itched but he had long ago given up making the effort to scratch himself.

"We're almost home, Amber. Almost home, darling, almost safe from those bad men and women who tried to take you away from me so they could feed you all their poisons—

"Look! Another deer, Amber! I didn't know there were so many of them this close to Chicago, did you? And they're herbivorous, HER-BIV-OR-OUS, just like rabbits. Would you like me to get you a rabbit for a pet when we get home?"

Without waiting for any sort of reply she uncapped a clear plastic canteen and took a measured sip of spring water from it, then reached across to Amber and held the canteen to his lips. A little made its way into his mouth but most of the water dribbled down his face.

His mother resealed the canteen and put it back on the floor of the car. Reaching down into a white paper sack on the floor of the car she took out a single grain of uncooked brown rice. Putting it into her mouth, she patiently chewed it a hundred times, then swallowed.

"They were trying to make you like them, stupid ugly little people, trying to destroy you like they almost destroyed me, but they'll never get to you again, I'll keep you safe and you'll have a better chance against them than I ever did."

She was tall and gaunt, sallow, with weary lines etched into her face, but she still retained much of the beauty that a decade before had made Angela Mallory the most sought-after model of the 1990's. She had been driving now for twenty-seven hours, pausing only when her electric car needed recharging, and she had already been two days without sleep when she had located Amber and stolen him back from the L.A. hospital where they had put him after taking him away from her.

She reached over to stroke Amber's fine, colorless hair—

And suddenly the roadway ahead of her was choked with milling, bleating deer. She swerved frantically to the left, across the median strip and into the path of an oncoming truck.

The woman died instantly, her neck broken, but the child was still alive when the police pulled his tiny body with its twisted, shattered legs from the wreckage.

"I'm Willard Bronson and I represent Baja Continental Life, Ms. Mallory's insurance company," the man in the candycane-striped suit said. "We still have a few questions about the accident report."

"Sit down, Mr. Bronson." The clerk motioned the insurance man to a chair beside his desk. "What can we do for you?"

Bronson looked at his notes. "Well, you must understand that we're a very old-fashioned company in many ways and that Ms. Mallory's insurance was void if she was under the influence of drugs at the time of her accident. That includes prescription drugs, stimulants, euphorics, alcohol—any drug at all with a mind-altering effect, whether legal or illegal. Now, according to the accident report, when you 'deadbrained' Ms. Mallory''—he spoke the word with a certain finicky distaste—''you discovered that she'd been hallucinating severely immediately prior to her death and that her hallucinations were the probable cause of her accident. Am I correct so far?''

''Yes, of course, but, uh, hasn't your computer verified all this for you already?''

''We employ no computers. It's a matter of religious principle with us, you understand. There are a great number of people who feel as we do and who are glad to pay a little extra to ensure that their affairs are handled by men and not by soulless machines.''

''I see.'' The clerk frowned, consulted his screen. ''Well, we're virtually certain that Angela Mallory saw a herd of deer on the highway in front of her car and that she swerved into the opposite lane to avoid hitting them. I can have the computer recreate the scene for you if you like.''

''I'm afraid that would be against company policy. We depend solely on human testimony and the written word.''

''But I'm only telling you what the computer tells me.''

''It's still a matter of company policy. You and I are both human beings and I can weigh your words and expressions and judge for myself whether or not I can trust what you say, but who can detect a machine in a lie? Better to deal with the men who work with the machines.''

''Well, anyway, the computer puts the probability of there actually having been a herd of deer on the highway as virtually nil.''

''Yet you deny the possibility that she was under the influence of drugs?''

''The autopsy showed no sign of any drugs, illegal or otherwise. And our autopsies are very thorough.''

''How, then, do you account for her hallucinations?''

The clerk felt suddenly tired. ''To her lack of sleep and the fact that she was suffering from an advanced case of pellagra.''

''Pellagra?'' The insurance man in the out-of-date gaudy clothes looked momentarily baffled. ''Wasn't that the disease blacks used to get before the melanin plagues wiped most of them out?''

''No. You're thinking of sickle cell anemia. Pellagra's a disease caused by a vitamin deficiency. Niacin, to be exact. And among the symptoms of an advanced case—as the autopsy showed Angela Mallory's most certainly was—are delirium and hallucinations of the sort that accompany uncompensated schizophrenia. The computer states that the known facts about Ms. Mallory's condition are sufficient to account for her accident without the necessity of dragging in some unknown drug which for some unknown reason the computer failed to detect.''

"I'm afraid, Mr. Mallory, that the clinic's confirmed your nephew's suffering from xeropthalmia (that's why his eyes are so dull), rickets, beriberi, pellagra, scurvy—just about every known disease caused by a vitamin deficiency—plus kwashiorkor. That's massive protein and caloric starvation. And we can't forget the multiple fractures in his legs. With intensive care we can eventually alleviate or compensate for most of the effects of the vitamin deficiencies but it's too late to undo the damage kwashiorkor has done to his brain and I'm afraid he'll never attain the size or strength he would have been able to look forward to if he'd been properly fed.''

"Just how retarded will he be?" Alfred asked.

"It's impossible to say. Despite her aberrations, your sister's IQ was well up in the genius range—" looking down at the clinic's report, the nurse missed Alfred Mallory's quickly suppressed scowl—"so he should have some genetic advantage over the average kwashiorkor victim, but even so you'll still be very lucky if his IQ is anything over seventy and if he ever learns to control his body very well. Very lucky indeed.

"The traumatic factors make it difficult to be completely positive," the social worker told Alfred, "but—to put it bluntly—the odds are he'll be a moron, Mr. Mallory. You're still sure you want to adopt him?"

"He doesn't have anyone else. His father left my sister to transfer to Diamond. Amber's alone in the world and he *is* my sister's child."

"Of course. Well, her estate will pay you eleven hundred dollars a month (that's New Dollars, of course) until he reaches legal age— sixteen in Michigan, isn't it?—and I believe you can expect some additional compensation from the Federal Government when he starts school. If you'll sign here . . . and here . . . and here. . . . Very good. Thank you very much, Mr. Mallory."

"When can we bring him home?" Alfred asked.

"I'm afraid there's no way we can answer that yet," the director of the clinic told him. "In his condition it'll take abnormally long for his legs to heal. How long, God only knows. But a matter of several months, at the very least. We'll make sure you're furnished with regular reports on his progress here and we'll be sure to inform you of the date of his release well enough ahead of time so you can get everything ready for his arrival. I'd strongly suggest you hire a professional nurse to help cushion his transition from the clinic to your home, but the final decision's up to you, of course."

"No, I agree with you. It sounds like an excellent idea."

They stood and shook hands. Alone in the descending elevator Alfred Mallory smiled, thinking that with Amber as well as Jane to take care of, Inez was less likely to want another child of her own. One child had already done irreparable damage to her figure and he had no desire to see the beautiful woman he had married turn into a brood sow like so many other women her age.

Especially if she were going to produce more children like Jane. Alfred knew he was handsome and he had married Inez for her beauty; how two such people had produced a skinny kid with a face like an Aztec mask. . . . He grimaced.

Then he smiled again. Eleven hundred dollars a month was a lot of money. There should be something left over, even after feeding both kids and paying for Amber's special schooling and medical costs.

Though there was no reason why Joseph Mallory, Alfred's father, need ever know that his son was making a profit from his apparent charity.

And Amber would get the care that Alfred's oh-so-beloved sister's child deserved.

CHAPTER TWO

IT WAS A CLEAR, unusually warm summer morning and Alfred, Inez and Jane were eating breakfast on the porch. Built in a straight line so that there was a view of Lake Huron from every room, their house was divided into two unequal sections by the enclosed porch in its center. One section contained two bedrooms and a bathroom connected by a short corridor; the other held the living and dining rooms and a small kitchen. The house had originally been intended only for summer use, and though the porch had been fitted with storm windows and baseboard heaters, it was usable only as storage space during Drummond Island's fifty-below winters. But in late spring, summer, and early fall it doubled as a dining room.

"Jane," Inez said firmly, distracting her daughter from her intense concentration on the problem of separating yellow raisins out of the oatmeal in her bowl. Alfred did not look up from his copy of *The Islander*.

"Jane, do you remember your Aunt Angela?"

"The pretty lady Daddy said was so—"

"Yes," Inez cut in hurriedly. Alfred did not like to hear himself quoted back to himself by his daughter. "Well, your aunt died a little while ago and her little boy is coming here to live with us. He'll be your new brother."

Jane thought a while, not at all sure she liked the idea. "How old is he?" she asked.

"Four."

"What's his name?"

"Amber."

"That's a silly name for a boy."

"His mother was a silly woman."

"She was an evil bitch," Alfred said without looking up from the paper at which he was scowling. His father's editorials always angered him and since there was far too little news, by any definition, to justify Drummond Island's daily paper, every issue of *The Islander* consisted primarily of pictures, fish maps and his father's editorials. This morning's issue decried the lower standards of sexual morality that vacationing tourists, "especially a certain couple from Chicago who need not be named but of whom we are well rid," were bringing to the island this summer.

"Are they building the new room for him?" Jane asked when it was clear her father was not going to say anything more.

"Yes."

"Why is it bigger than my room?"

"Amber's very sick. His mother was very bad to him so he'll need a nurse to help me take care of him until he's better."

"Then he'll have the room to himself?"

"I suppose so."

"That's not fair. I'm older than he is."

"He's going to be sick a long time."

"How long?"

"We don't know."

"Then how do you know it will be a long time?"

Alfred threw down his paper. "Quit interrogating your mother and finish your oatmeal!" he commanded. Jane slowly began to mix the raisins back into the rest of her breakfast but her father snapped "Now!" and after a quick glance at his dark glowering face she began to eat hurriedly.

After breakfast, when Alfred had taken the boat to work, Jane asked her mother, "Will I be able to play with him?"

"I doubt it," Inez said. "Not until he's much better and then he probably won't be much fun. His mother made him very stupid. Now go out and play." She kissed Jane and turned back to her holovision program—*Snow White Meets Casanova in the Guise of a Dwarf,* the latest erotic satire out of Detroit—and lost herself in the glowing three-dimensional images. Jane went outside to play until her school-preparatory program came on.

• • •

The Mallory house was located on a small cove on the southwestern shore of Drummond Island, close enough to Espanore Island that Alfred had no trouble commuting to work at the Espanore Island Dimensional Transfer Institute, where he worked as an electronics engineer, by boat in summer and by snowmobile in winter. In late fall and early spring, when the ice was too chancy for his snowmobile, he caught a ride on the company's ground-effect vehicle, but he much preferred the freedom that his own vehicle gave him.

Alfred's house had been built in the early 1970's, when wood was still relatively cheap, but now, some thirty years later, with Drummond Island's building codes among the strictest and most archaic in North America (demanding, for example, wood for jobs done everywhere else with plastics), the price of new construction was incredible. If the bank administering Amber's trust had not been willing to pay for the new bedroom, Alfred would never have been able to afford to have it built, but as it was, he had been able to work out a deal with a mainland contractor which promised him the opportunity to siphon off some of the bank-administered monies for himself. Unfortunately, such an arrangement had necessitated dealing with a contractor of less than perfect honesty and that, in turn, was now causing problems.

"I'm sorry"—the building inspector, a gnarled old man who must have been eighty-five, was unyielding—"but it's not built according to code. You'll have to rip it out and replace it."

"But, Mr. Gantry," Evans, the contractor, protested without hope, "this spray-on insulation—"

"The law says you can't use it here. You should know that; you've built houses here before. As long as I'm building inspector you'll have to obey the code to the letter. You'll have to redo it."

"But, Mr. Gantry," Alfred protested weakly, entering the conversation for the first time, "my adopted son and his nurse are due to move into this room in less than a week. He's retarded and very sick and we have no other place to put him. The room *has* to be finished by then."

"That's no business of mine," the inspector said. "I'm merely here to see that the law's obeyed."

"How long until you can redo it to satisfy him?" Alfred asked Evans.

"Probably at least ten days. And I'll have to pay my men overtime, maybe hire a couple of others to get it done that soon."

"But I don't have ten days. I've only got six."

"The two of you will have to settle this between yourselves," the building inspector said. "Like I said, it's no business of mine." He got into his car and drove off.

"That asshole!" Evans said as soon as the inspector was gone. "If I'd just been able to get the panels in and painted he would never've been able to tell the difference."

"But why the hell did you take the chance?" Alfred demanded. "You ought to know what he's like. You've built houses here before."

"And I've gotten away with stuff before. Gantry's old; he doesn't usually check things very carefully. The spray-on stuff's better anyway; they've been using it everywhere for twenty years. But what with Gantry and all, you may as well forget about getting any money out of this deal. There won't be any profits in this job for either one of us now. I'll be lucky to break even."

"OK, forget the kickback," Alfred conceded reluctantly. "But what about the room? I need it in six days."

"Impossible. Tell the hospital to keep the kid another week."

"I can't. I've already collected the money for his upkeep and paid for his nurse. Besides, if the bank and my father see that I can't take care of him like I promised to—"

"That's your problem, not mine."

"Maybe so, but it's your fault. So what do I do with the kid and his nurse?"

"Put them in with your other kid?"

"Jane's bedroom's not big enough."

"So move Jane in with you and Inez."

"Inez won't like it."

"So? It'll save your ass, won't it?"

Amber's new nurse, Mary Sorenson, a slim but strong-looking blonde woman in her early thirties, arrived early on a Tuesday afternoon. Alfred was still at work over on Espanore and would be until five-thirty, though he'd arranged to take Wednesday off and pick Amber up at the airport. Jane was off at her swimming lesson, so only Inez was home to greet the nurse.

Mary had only that morning received Alfred's letter describing the makeshift arrangements she would have to endure for her first week of employment (Evans had fallen behind schedule) and she was somewhat anxious, but after seeing that the self-cleaning and baby-monitoring crib was in working order and that her own living arrangements would be endurable for the week, she relaxed.

"Your husband didn't give me many details in the letter and I was afraid, you know, that I'd be cleaning the child and changing diapers or bedsheets in the middle of the night. . . ."

"Of course," Inez said. "But though the construction people let us down, we *have* bought all the toys and other things you suggested. The sandbox is in the backyard in a sunny spot you can watch from the porch and, well, . . ."

"I'm sure everything will work out fine," the nurse assured her. "But I'm afraid there's one rather major matter we'll have to get straight as soon as possible, and that's the question of just how long you're going to want my services. We originally agreed that I'd work until August sixth, but in your husband's last letter he mentioned the possibility that you might want me to stay on until the beginning of September. But he wasn't very definite . . ."

"*Are* you free to work until September?" Inez asked.

"I've been offered another position but I haven't accepted it yet. You do want me to stay on, then?"

"It's a bit complicated. You see, I do but Alfred doesn't. In September the child'll be starting in that special school the Fellowship of Prismatic Light runs near Cedarville—you know about it?"

"Of course. Everybody who's worked with educable retarded children in this area is familiar with it. The school has a fine reputation, no matter what one may think personally about the, well, the rather childlike views the Fellowship's members hold."

"I agree with you. But perhaps that's why they get along so well with the children. Anyway, Alfred wants me to take over caring for the child in three weeks, just as soon as the period we originally agreed on for your employment is up. Now, frankly, adopting the child was Alfred's idea—it was *his* sister's child, after all, and I've already got Jane—and while I agreed that we should adopt him and while I'm sure that in time I'll learn to love him like he was my own son—like I love Jane—well, I still don't think three weeks is long enough to develop the proper attitude.''

Inez's patently insincere smile irritated Mary. ''All it takes is patience and compassion,'' she said.

''Yes, of course, but''—Inez's smug smile and fleshy face irritated Mary anew—''don't you see, I don't *feel* like he's mine yet. How could I? I've only seen him once and then he was in a hospital bed. It's not that I lack compassion, but neither Alfred nor I is overlong on patience and, well, I just need some more time to get used to the idea of caring for a retarded child.''

''If that's how you feel about it''—the nurse kept her voice expressionless—''you're probably right. The child probably could use some additional care. And you're right, a retarded child *is* quite a responsibility,'' she admitted, forcing herself to be fair, ''so if your husband agrees I'll stay the extra weeks. I could use some time away from the city and it's certainly beautiful up here.''

''Yes, it is,'' Inez agreed, though she herself had never been overly taken with Drummond Island's rustic charm.

Alfred and Mary picked Amber up at the airport the next day. Tiny and unhealthy looking, his legs bowed from rickets despite his casts, his hair colorless and mussed, his pale skin blotchy, the boy was reluctant to part from the nurse who had brought him from the clinic in Chicago. He began to wail as soon as she deposited him in the back seat of Alfred's car and he continued to cry all the way back to the Mallory house. Huddled against the window, as far away from the two adults as he could get, he ignored Mary's smiles and soothing words and would not accept the sweets she offered him.

Fuck, he's going to be hard to live with, Alfred thought.

Mary helped the boy out of the car in front of the house and led him firmly by the hand up to the door. His walk was only slightly clumsy despite the plastic braces on his legs, but he had difficulty managing the three short steps up to the door.

Once inside the living room he confronted the waiting Inez and Jane with the look of a frightened animal. Jane thought he looked dwarfish and ugly, not like a human being at all. She wondered what his mother had done to him. What if her mother decided to do the same things to her? She parted her lips to ask what Amber had done to make his mother punish him so terribly but she was afraid to ask.

Amber continued to sob. "He's probably not used to strangers," Mary said after attempting without success to calm him down. "Why don't you leave me alone with him for a while? Then you can come in one at a time and let him get used to you gradually."

The family filed out gratefully.

Jane was the last to return, called in from the new sandbox with its multicolored sand some two hours later. Holding a finger to her lips, the nurse ushered the five-year-old girl into the living room.

Alfred and Inez were seated in their customary chairs, watching with expressions alternately bored and pained while Amber tried to pile three brightly-colored blocks on top of each other. When his tower collapsed the boy threw a red block in the direction of the wall and began to cry again. He had taken no notice of Jane's entrance.

Jane stood silent a moment, watching him as he hit a green and yellow block with his tiny fist and sent it scuttering a few inches across the floor. Then she went over to the cupboard where she was allowed to store her toys and took out her favorite doll.

"Amber did something so awful his mother hit him over the head with a hammer and broke him into little pieces," she whispered to the doll, holding it close to her. "And when his mother tried to put him back together she lost some of the pieces. That's why he's so little and stupid and ugly."

Amber was babbling happily to himself, his anger forgotten, as he piled up more blocks. This time the tower was five blocks high and did not collapse.

The doorbell rang, a soft double chime. Alfred opened the door and gestured his parents, Joseph and Paula Mallory, into the room. The strong-featured old man helped his frail, cancer-ridden wife seat herself on the couch, then sat down beside her.

"How do you feel, Mother?" Alfred asked.

"As well as can be expected," Joseph said, answering for her. "Neither better nor worse."

"I'm glad it's not worse," Inez said.

"Thank you," Paula told her.

"Hello, Amber!" Joseph said in a loud, bluff voice, startling

Amber. He began to wail again. Paula winced, started to say something, then thought better of it.

"Can't he do anything but cry?" Jane demanded scornfully. Her father gave her a dirty look but said nothing.

"Don't you think it's perhaps time for his nap?" Inez asked uncertainly. "I mean, I really don't know anything about—"

"No, you're right," Mary said. "I'll take him to our room and stay there with him until he's asleep."

It's my room! Jane thought fiercely as the nurse led Amber away.

"Jane, why don't you go outside and play in your new sandbox?" Alfred asked. When she was gone he told his parents, "The people at the hospital estimate his mental age as a little over two and his IQ at about sixty, though they think the traumatic effects of the accident and a lifetime of Angela's tender loving care may be masking a little of his intelligence."

"Now Angela meant well—" the elder Mrs. Mallory began uncertainly.

"By starving the child, Mother?" Alfred demanded, his eyes on Joseph. "We're going to have to keep Ms. Sorenson on to help us until he starts school this fall. It's going to take a long time to cope with the damage Angela did to him. Even if her intentions *were* good."

"We've got to look beyond the immediate future," Joseph declared. "School's fine for now but he'll be a man someday and a man needs a job. I don't want my grandson living on public charity. I've been thinking of creating a job for him at the paper. . . . What'll he be like when he's grown?"

"It's too early to tell. He'll be clumsy, of course, and he'll probably never develop beyond, say, third or fourth grade level."

"If I get rid of the automated machinery in the mailroom and replace it with hand-operated machinery—He'll be able to read, won't he?"

"Some. Probably not much."

"All right. Everybody's been automated for forty years but I should be able to find an old Addressograph and plate-maker somewhere. If I can't I can have them made. But we've got years to work on that. Right now, I'm worried about this Fellowship of Prismatic Light."

"Cranks," Alfred admitted. "But not at all dangerous. Quite the contrary. And very good with children. You won't find a school for educable retarded children in the United States that can match theirs. They have complete computerized supervision of each child at all times."

"Are you sure he'll be educable?" Paula asked.

"Almost positive," Alfred said.

"But that, that phony religious service of theirs with the mechanical whatever it is—" Joseph protested.

"Harmless. And perfectly legal. Don't worry; I checked them out very thoroughly. Anyway, they don't use their machine on the kids. I made very sure of that. And did you know that no member of their organization—that is, their local organization—has *ever* been arrested for anything more serious than a traffic ticket?"

"No, I didn't. It's a relief to hear it. You seem to have done a fairly good job of looking into things; I guess I better trust your judgment on this. Though I must admit I'm a bit surprised to see you coming through so well for the family after Angela failed us all so grievously. I think perhaps we were wrong to pin our hopes on her."

Inez kept her features respectfully attentive, needing all the control her early training as a model had given her to keep from betraying the excitement she felt at the chance that Alfred might be reinstated as the old man's heir. *It's too early to tell,* she cautioned herself, but her heart leaped within her.

Perhaps her marriage would be the road to success she had hoped it would be after all.

We'll have to pretend to love the little monster, Alfred thought with distaste.

For the next week Jane slept in her parents' room, kept awake on the nights Alfred and Inez spent together by their arguments and loveless bouts of lovemaking, awakened at some time every night by the sound of Amber crying or screaming in the next room. Now that the curtain of apathy separating the boy from the world had been rent he was always angry, irritated or afraid—irritated at his inability to grasp the smooth plastic sides of his crib with his clumsy little hands, frightened by the shocks the crib gave him whenever he lost control of his bladder or bowels, frightened of the dark and terrified by the nightmares in which he relived the accident, the collision and the never ending pain in his legs.

Jane bitterly resented her foster brother's occupation of her—her!—room. And though she soon learned that she would be punished severely if she said such things herself, she agreed inwardly with her parents whenever, careful not to be overheard by the nurse, they complained to each other about what a stupid, ugly, deformed little bedwetting monster Angela's son was.

CHAPTER THREE

MARY AWAKENED to soft Vivaldi, opened her eyes to glorious cascades of golden light. Two yards away from her Amber slept undisturbed, unable to hear the music sounding in the surgically implanted speakers beneath her skin, unaffected by the holographic projections playing around her head. It was seven o'clock on the morning of Mary's twelfth day in the Mallory household.

She held the dream from which she'd awakened in her mind for a moment but decided it was of no particular significance and let it slip away from her. In Detroit she would have held onto it longer, saving it for discussion at breakfast, but though Alfred and Inez thought of themselves as cosmopolitan, they set no portion of their morning meal aside for dream exchange.

Memories of the night before swam into consciousness and she found herself frowning. Not that Alfred was physically unattractive or incompetent in bed, quite the contrary, but she regretted the fact that Drummond Island's medieval mores made it inadvisable for her to seek out a sexual partner more to her taste.

Once out of bed she automatically checked the monitor screens showing the living and dining rooms. As she had expected, she was the first one up.

She stepped into the shower cabinet and let the ultrasonic vibrations cleanse her body and hair. She had showered after Alfred had left her to return to Inez, of course, but almost eight hours had passed since then and as always upon awakening she felt herself soiled by the accumulated residues of sleep.

Alfred and Inez were awakened by a chorus of twenty-some

angels wearing green satin gowns and singing minstrel songs. The angels all had golden wings, green eyes that matched their gowns, and delicate white skin. Halos floated over their heads. Though they all appeared female, somebody in the chorus was singing a raspy negro bass.

Alfred cursed the psychodecorator who had charged him so much for this month's sequence of individually tailored holographic awakening scenarios. *This* was supposed to stir his unconscious creativity? *This* was supposed to give him the proper outlook for the day ahead?

Inez rather liked the angels.

Jane was awakened by Dippy Duck, as she had been, every morning since she could remember and, as it had been every morning for at least the last year and a half, her first reaction was embarrassment: she was too old for Dippy. But she'd been promised a new sequence for her birthday, now only two weeks away.

Jane cleaned herself in her shower booth, then examined the clothing set out for her. Like everyone else, she owned only a single outfit, but that outfit was infinitely protean, capable of changing shape, color, texture and size. Today, she saw with distress, it had become a fancy cowboy suit with high-heeled, leather-looking boots—not that a cowboy suit would have been so bad in itself, but the material of this suit looked like satin and changed color as she watched, flowing from fluorescent orange to a pointillistic melange of lavender, beige and white, then shading into a blue disfigured by irregular white splotches. She hated to put the clothes on but she dared not be late for breakfast.

It was a warm day and Inez had decided to serve breakfast on the porch. Her hair rose in a silver and jade cone above her head and she was dressed in a body stocking of what looked like canary yellow mink.

Doesn't she realize how fat she's getting? Alfred thought. *She looks like a hairy ice cream cone.* He himself was dressed as a nineteenth-century British undertaker—he liked to dress in black; he felt it emphasized his dark coloring—while Mary had chosen to outfit herself in what looked like a sari made of tin foil and scarlet lace.

During the course of the meal Inez noticed a stout brown water snake sunning itself on the dock.

"A snake," she said, pointing it out to Mary. "I hope it'll eat some of those damned toads. The way they squish under your feet when you step on them—"

"What kind of snake is it?" Mary asked.

"A water snake," Jane offered.

"You know, I'd never seen a snake or toad before I came here," Mary said. "Wild, that is: I saw some in zoos, of course. And I like the way the deer come right into your yard." She activated the EEG monitor in Amber's crib, listened to the tone for a second, then switched it off, satisfied he was still asleep. She ate another spoon-full of cereal.

"Not just the deer," Inez said. "Neighbors too. Poaching."

"Still," Mary said. "I like the fact you've got all these animals running wild around here. I even like the toads."

"In the Middle Ages," Alfred said, looking up from his copy of *The Islander,* "people believed that toads had jewels hidden in their foreheads and that you could use the jewels to neutralize any sort of poison."

"Oh," Mary said.

"Alfred knows a lot of stuff like that," Inez said. "He used to want to be a writer."

"No. My late sister—No. Maybe I'll tell you about it some other time. Better yet, let Inez tell you. I don't want to think about it. Ever." He lowered his head and began to reread the editorial which had been angering him only a moment before.

Jane broke the deepening silence. "Mommy," she asked, "will you make my clothes look like they did yesterday? Nobody else has to wear clothes that change color." While she was speaking her cowboy suit faded from apple green to a dark mahogany and her boots turned yellow.

"I think you look very pretty," Inez said. "Don't you, Mary?"

"But I don't want—"

"No!" Alfred said, dropping his paper and glowering at his daughter. "What's wrong with the way you look?"

"None of the other kids—"

"Quite right. None of the other kids. You're *my* daughter, not some idiot Drummond Islander's, and it's up to me to see that you're dressed properly. I spent good money on the computer chip for that color sequence and you'll wear it and like wearing it.''

"Alfred," Inez said, "couldn't she save it for some other time and wear a more normal sequence today?''

"No. She's going to wear that sequence and she's going to wear it today. Period.''

"Alfred," Mary said hurriedly, "do you have time to tell me something about your work over at the Institute? I don't know anything about dimensional transfer.''

"Why ask me?" Alfred demanded, watching Inez. "I do electronics work there but I don't know anything about the alternate worlds. Father refused to help me through postgraduate schoo , so I never got the certification I need to do design and research. Which leaves me building what other people with more expensive degrees tell me to build. I'm just a glorified handyman: they don't tell me anything.''

"Alfred!" Inez protested. "Don't listen to him," she said, turning to Mary. "He gets these self-destructive moods sometimes but he's an electronics engineer, not just an electrician or—''

"Bullshit. They treat me like the holo repairman. Worse. Like a plumber.''

"Alfred! That's not true!''

Sincerity now, he decided. *Make her feel guilty.*

"I'm sorry," he said. "It's not all that bad. Look, Mary, dimensional transfer's all neurochemistry. The only reason you're here talking to me now is because you perceive yourself as here—and because you've got an innate, genetically determined perception of yourself as a part of this world's ecological system. Does that make it any clearer?''

"I'm not sure. I mean, I'm not sure I understand what you said.''

"All right: at the Institute we change people's reality by changing their conscious and unconscious perceptions of reality.''

"You mean, all I have to do is *really* believe I'm somewhere else and—Poof!—I vanish in a cloud of smoke?''

"Wrong. What you think of as you, your mind or whatever, just isn't all that important. The tip of the tip of the tip of the iceberg. It's your perceptions on the cellular level that're important and the only way to change those types of perceptions is through neurochemistry. About which I know nothing. I just build supplemental gadgetry."

"No puff of smoke?"

"Look, you wouldn't even vanish. Your body's part of everybody else's reality. It stays behind, dead, while your consciousness fashions itself a new body in some alternative NeverNeverLand.

"And the way things are going they're going to be asking me to help them dispose of the bodies in my spare time. Without pay, of course: another strictly fun extracurricular activity for the employees."

Amber was playing in the sandbox, digging holes in the multicolored sand, pushing and patting it into mounds and letting it run between his fingers. Mary watched him from the porch.

"Do you use holo-emph?" Inez asked Mary. "I haven't asked you before because I didn't know you well enough and, well, people around here don't approve of it. Even Alfred doesn't know I use it very often. But now that I've gotten to know you a little better and because we're going to be spending a lot of time together for a while I thought I'd better find out what you think about it."

"I *have* tried it, of course," the nurse admitted. "Only once or twice, though it's becoming quite popular in Detroit. But I didn't really like the way it made me feel and I doubt if I'll ever take any again. And certainly not when I'm taking care of a child."

"Of course not," Inez said. "I certainly wasn't suggesting you should. But would you mind very much if I took some myself today? Timed, of course—you won't have to worry about fixing yourself lunch. You see, my favorite program's on today. It's only on once a month and I've never missed an episode.

"I'm Queen Elizabeth," she added.

"The virgin queen?" Mary asked. "I'm surprised. I wouldn't have thought that was your style."

"You must not know the program," Inez said. "I—the Queen had quite a few affairs. She had to keep them secret, that's all."

"Go ahead," Mary said reluctantly. "I won't tell your husband. But what are you going to do when you have to take care of Amber on your own?"

"I'll only take emph when he's away at school," Inez promised. She took two tiny red pills from a flat black pillbox and swallowed them without water. A few minutes later she was Elizabeth Tudor, Queen of England.

Mary kept an eye on her. People on holo-emph were nasty if anything disturbed them.

At work that day one of the technicians called Alfred a glorified electrician, not for the first time. Alfred hit the man.

Alfred had been thinking about the last story he'd ever written. The story that had won the Bennet prize. The prize that had been taken away from him when Angela convinced the judges that she'd been the one who'd really written the story that Alfred had submitted.

Nobody had believed Alfred's denial.

"Mommy, can I watch my program again. I didn't understand everything."

"No. You're not stupid; I'm sure you understood enough. Hurry up and finish your lunch. I have a program coming on in five minutes."

After Jane had finished eating Inez sent her out to play with the other children in the neighborhood, warning her not to come back before dinner time. Then Inez took nine emph pills and returned to her holovision. This time she became Judy Osborne, black police-woman in the New York City of the 1980's, just prior to the time when the Arch Boerbishop of the Church of the White Christ loosed the first of the melanin viruses. The series would follow her career until after her election as the first black mayor of New York City, but the present episode showed her dealing with a clinic peddling phony cancer cures.

Jane came running and stumbling into the room. Her cowboy suit was dull black, all color fled. Only one of her many bruises showed on her face but her right nostril was rimmed with drying blood.

"Mommy, mommy!" She tugged desperately at Inez's arm, half-blinded by tears and too caught up in her own misery to take warning from her mother's slumped motionlessness.

Out in the yard Mary was sitting on the edge of the sandbox, watching as Amber buried his toy train in the sand.

"Train under," Amber said smiling.

"They all hit me and then they knocked me down—Mommy!" Jane tugged harder at her mother's arm, finally bringing her back to consciousness of herself and her surroundings.

The first thing a person using holo-emph feels when the trance is broken is blind, murderous rage.

Mary heard Jane's cries and over them, drowning them out, Inez screaming with rage. She ran for the house. Jane lay curled on the floor, her hands raised in an attempt to protect her face, while Inez kicked her again and again.

"Leave her alone!" Mary shouted, trying to pull Inez away from her daughter.

Inez hit the nurse in the face and stomach before Mary caught her hands. Eyes bulging, her face red and distorted, Inez tried to bite Mary's hands but Mary managed to keep them away from her. Then Inez began kicking Mary in the shins. The nurse tightened her grip on Inez's wrists, enduring the pain, waiting.

Suddenly the rage drained from Inez's face. Mary let her collapse to the floor.

The second effect of a broken holo-emph trance is unconsciousness.

Leaving Inez lying blank-faced on the floor, Mary helped Jane to her feet and led her back to her own room. The nurse put her arms around the child and held her until her sobs subsided.

"What happened to you?" Mary asked quietly.

"Mommy kicked me—" Jane began crying again. Her nose was bleeding.

Mary dabbed at the blood with a cloth. "Before that. Why did you disturb her?"

"Jimmy pushed me and Bobby was down on the ground behind me and I fell over him and hit my head on a rock and then they all kicked me and when I tried to stand up Jimmy knocked me down again—"

"Why did they want to hurt you?" Mary asked.

"I didn't know the rules of the new game because Mommy wouldn't let me watch the program again and Jimmy said I was too stupid and ugly to ever do anything right just like my idiot brother and I said he's not my brother— He's not my real brother! Not my real brother!''

"No," the nurse agreed quietly, "he's not really your brother."

"I hate him! They said, yes, he really was my brother and I was just like him and did I think I could lie to them and Jimmy pushed me—"

"I don't think you're stupid and ugly. I like you," Mary said.

"I am so stupid and ugly!" Jane stared defiantly at Mary. "You're lying! Daddy says I am. And Mommy kicked me. She hates me."

"Your mother was angry about something else. She doesn't really hate you," Mary said but she could see her words were making no impression on Jane.

"Why did your father say that?" Mary asked.

"I don't know. He always says it. And now Mommy hates me." Jane's control gave way completely. The nurse did her best to comfort her.

When Alfred returned from Espanore ("And don't come back until you can find it in you to get along with the rest of us") Mary showed him Inez's unconscious body and told him what happened.

"I can't continue to work here if there's any danger of this sort of thing ever happening again," she said. "And, frankly, if I thought I'd be leaving the boy in a household where—"

"Where this sort of thing was likely to happen to him you'd alert the authorities and see that he was given another home?"

"Yes."

"You'd only be doing what's right. But give us another chance. I'll make sure that nothing like this ever happens again. I'll make sure that Inez never does *anything* like this again, I'll make sure there's *no* danger of anything like this ever—The problem's not Inez, it's holo-emph, and if I tell her to stop taking it she will. She does what I tell her to."

Had he convinced her? If the trustees ever heard about this—

"How is Jane doing?" he asked. "Is she OK?"

"Yes, luckily. She's sleeping now."

"Are you sure we shouldn't take her to a doctor?"

"I don't think that's necessary. But if I hadn't been there—"

"We're all just lucky you were. And it'll never happen again."

Outside in the cooling afternoon sun Amber reburied the train he had just dug up for the nineteenth time.

"Train under," he said happily. "My train under."

CHAPTER FOUR

"CAN'T YOU even remember how to open a car door?" Inez demanded, momentarily amused by the sight of Amber struggling futilely with the dials and buttons of the child-proof opening mechanism. Her short-lived amusement died. "If you waste any more of my time I won't have a chance to pick you up a cake for your party," she threatened. "You understand? Never mind. Let me open it!"

She leaned across the seat and shoved Amber's fumbling fingers away from the three dials and five buttons. They were too much for Amber but no problem for Inez: the door swung open.

Amber scrambled clumsily out of the red car onto the rainbow plaza from which the differently colored paths led to the various domes of the school. The door swung shut and the red car sped silently off down the snow-free pavement of the drive, disappearing behind a snowbank at the first curve.

Snow rose in nine-foot banks on either side of the yellow path leading to Amber's dome. He clutched the bag of sweetprotes Mary had sent him for his birthday and started up the path. Like the roads and plaza, the path was heated to keep it snowfree, but the air above it was almost thirty below. Amber's clothing, however, was thermostatically controlled and his face and hands had been treated with winterspray to protect them from the cold. The wind brushed against his face but only his untreated eyeballs felt the chill and he blinked often to keep them warm.

He reached the yellow dome. Beside the featureless white rectangle of the door a red button was set into the wall. Amber pressed it eagerly, his anticipation tinged as always with a faint anxiety. What if nothing happened?

"Hello, Amber," the door said in its bluff, friendly voice and he relaxed. Today would be like every other day; he would not be denied entrance.

"Hello, door," he replied. "Can I come in please?"

"What day is it today?" the door countered but its questions no longer worried Amber. They were always questions he could answer.

"My birthday," he said.

"Right you are," the door chortled. "And how old are you?"

"Six."

"Right again, Amber," the door said happily. "Very good!" Six trumpeters in red coats appeared on the door's surface. They were only two dimensional images without the reality of holograms but when they raised their trumpets to their lips the proud sound of their birthday salute thrilled Amber.

"Happy birthday, Amber!" they called out to him, lowering their instruments and waving out to him from their two-dimensional world. Still waving and smiling, they faded to transparent mist and were gone, leaving the door once again featureless.

After a few seconds the door's opaque surface began to take on a shimmering translucence. Though he could never have described it, Amber knew what was going to happen next—by now he had seen it happen hundreds of times—but his foreknowledge only added to his pleasure. He watched the door. It began.

Like something rising toward him through waters not blue but white . . . at first invisible, then a faint tinge of gray shadow in the milky depths, a shadow slowly taking on form, becoming more distinct as it grows larger, taking on color as it approaches the sunlit surface . . . he can see that it is yellow, a pale yellow growing ever richer as it comes nearer and nearer to the surface where he waits entranced—

A tiny pillar of sculptured gold, so much smaller than he had expected it to be but so exquisite he cannot look away from it, it thrusts itself out of the white water, flaming into the crystal air, shining with the light of a newborn sun, yet its radiance is somehow gentle and does not blind him as it begins to melt, liquid gold flowing towards him in faery evolutions, neither metal nor flame but both, and each transient glory, each living form is only the chrysalis from which a creature yet more glorious will emerge—

And then, just as Amber found himself tiring of its wonder, its brilliance began to diminish, not dying away but only becoming less and less perceptible, and like the dome's cat curling up to go to sleep, the form shifted one last time and settled into a final shape, becoming an exquisitely sculpted gold doorknob protruding from the door at just the right height for Amber to grasp it.

To Mary, who had accompanied Amber on the boy's first few visits to the school, the knowledge that what she was watching was only a memory-plastic door extruding a doorknob of its own infinitely protean substance had rendered the sight trivial. Alfred had appreciated the complexity of the programming involved in the door's transformations and had been appalled at the wasted money. But for Amber the doorknob was a living thing and the fact that he could manipulate it himself so as to open the door did nothing to detract from its fascination.

"Hello, doorknob," he said.

"Hello, Amber," the doorknob answered. "Happy birthday!" The master computer had endowed the doorknob with a distinctly masculine but melodic voice in keeping with its massy elegance. "You can come in now," the doorknob added. Amber grasped it and twisted it carefully, then pushed the door open and stepped into the dome's interior.

"Good morning, Amber, and happy birthday!" A human voice this time, warm and somehow liquid despite the trained precision that kept each syllable sharp and distinct: the voice of Brother Percival, Amber's teacher. Dressed as always in the silver-gray trousers and long rainbow tunic of the Fellowship, he was a lean, unusually dark-skinned man with a long mild face and bright eyes. He was smiling.

Behind Brother Percival stood the seven other students in the class. "Happy birthday, Amber!" they chorused in response to a signal from the teacher. Amber smiled shyly back at them and held out the bag of sweetprotes.

●　●　●

"The tumor doesn't seem to have grown any since your last examination," the specialist told Paula Mallory. "With luck, you can forget about it."

"It's benign then?"

"I don't know if I'd say that any tumor's really benign. And with this particular kind of growth you can never be sure. *But,* as far as we can tell it's not actively malignant."

"You can't . . . cut it out of me, burn it up with a laser or something. . . ."

"No. Not without destroying a good part of your brain. And as long as it's not actively menacing you any more it's not worth the risk of killing you. Which the surgery might well do."

"But . . . just to know it's there, sitting inside me, like it's waiting. . . ."

"Some of the current research in recombinant DNA *may* result in techniques that would be helpful in your case. And they're starting to get better results with some of the newer approaches to chemotherapy. Perhaps in time. . . ."

Inez loved driving out in the country, where there were no people, where she could put the car on automatic and watch the pure, white snowbanks glide by on either side, demanding nothing of her, giving her nothing she didn't choose to accept, chill but clean. . . .

Everybody but Amber was already wearing one of the headbands that allowed Brother Percival and the master computer to monitor the frequency and amplitude of their brainwaves. Amber took the headband Brother Percival offered him and slipped it onto his head, adjusting it to fit snugly against his temples. It began to flicker with violet light, showing his excitement.

"Today," Brother Percival told the class, "is Amber's birthday. Today we do whatever Amber wants us to do."

Amber thought a moment. "I want to bake a cake," he decided. "But I want to take it home."

"I want to bake a cake too!"

"Me too!"

"Fine," Brother Percival said. "Today we'll have a bakery. But not everyone in a bakery bakes cakes. Some people make other things, like bread and cookies. Somebody else arranges things in the window for customers to look at. Somebody else sells the cakes, bread and cookies to the customers and of course that means we'll need customers as well.

"Amber, you want to bake yourself a cake, right? Fine. Who else wants to bake a cake? How about you, Jenny? And Robert? Fine! Who wants to bake bread and cookies? Michelle? Good! How about arranging the cakes and cookies in the window? You, Eddie? All right. Now, who would like to sell the bakery goods? Abner? Of course—

"What's wrong, Amber?"

"I've got to take my cake home," Amber said, his headband indicating the intensity of his feeling.

"Don't worry," the teacher reassured him. "We won't sell *your* cake. But you don't mind if we sell the others, do you?"

Amber shook his head.

"Now, Kevin and Roberta, would you like to be customers and buy the cakes and cookies and bread?"

Roberta looked indecisive but Kevin said, "No! I want to drive a train."

"Me too!" Roberta said.

"How about a delivery truck?" Brother Percival asked. Roberta looked at Kevin.

"Sure," Kevin said.

"Fine. You can take turns driving the truck that delivers the flour and eggs and milk and sugar to the bakery. All right? Good! And when you get paid for your driving you can spend the money you make at the bakery. OK? Excellent!

"Ready, computer?" Brother Percival asked subvocally into the microphone implanted in his throat.

"Three more minutes," the computer answered, speaking to him through a surgically implanted radio receiver.

Brother Percival kept the children amused in the anteroom for the three minutes the computer required to finish molding the memory plastic interior of the dome into a bakery.

● ● ●

Since older students attended school on the mainland, Drummond Island boasted only an elementary school. And since, despite the wealth of a few of the newer residents such as Joseph Mallory (who had been a year-round resident less than twenty years, after all), most of the islanders were both poor and deeply conservative, the school was extremely old fashioned. The teaching machines were primitive and seldom used; the holovision was a standard home model, not only unable to utilize cassettes but broken and unrepaired now for over three years; there was only a single movie projector; and there was no computer. The seven teachers were old men and women who had retreated to the security of a backwater school to avoid dealing with the successive revolutions that had taken place in teaching methods since they had received their training in the fifties and sixties of the previous century.

Jane fidgeted at her desk, unable to keep her attention on the old woman scrawling math problems on the blackboard. Jane was the worst student in the class and well aware of it, just as she was well aware that she was hopelessly ugly: tall, skinny, with lank brown hair framing a face all ridges and crevices. She had no friends.

A song was running through her head, a song that had been sung to her on her last birthday, a half year past:

> Happy birthday to you.
> You belong in a zoo.
> You look like a monkey
> And smell like one too.

She would sing it to Amber when she got home from school.

"Now stir me!" the blue bowl cried in a piping voice. "Mix me all up. Around and around and around and around. . . ."

"My turn again!" the yellow bowl yelled. "Pour some of the batter in me into the blue bowl. That's right, pick me up with both hands. . . . Careful now! Not too much. . . . There! Perfect!"

"I bet you don't know what you just poured into me," the blue bowl challenged.

"Sure I do," Amber said. "Eggs and milk and shortening."

"You forgot the vanilla," the yellow bowl snickered.

"There was only a little vanilla," the blue bowl said, coming to Amber's defence. "But it's time to stir me again. Around and around and around and around. . . ."

"What are we supposed to do with the damn thing?" Inez asked. "It's not big enough to feed all the kids and their parents and it's probably not very good. What if it's awful? It *looks* awful."

Alfred sipped at his drink, frowned, added another pinch of mojo powder to it. "We've got to serve it," he decided reluctantly. "His teacher and all his little friends'll be expecting it. But—Why don't you put two slices of cake on each plate, a little slice of the cake he made and a bigger piece from one of the cakes you bought? That way everybody gets enough cake and if they don't like his cake they don't have to eat it."

Jane waited until her parents were distracted, then sneaked into the kitchen. There were three cakes on the counter but she had no trouble distinguishing Amber's single-layered cake with its plain frosting from the gaudily decorated store-bought products sitting beside it.

Taking the salt shaker, she sprinkled a few grains of salt onto one corner of Amber's cake. The salt dissolved on the moist white surface, leaving almost invisible pock marks where the granules had fallen.

Jane hesitated a moment, then carefully sprinkled a thin layer of salt over the whole cake.

CHAPTER FIVE

ALFRED AND INEZ met Brother Percival at the door. All the other guests had already arrived. The adults were standing around with drinks or sniff-pipes in their hands and the children were on the floor playing with Amber's toys. Jane was leaning against a wall, watching everyone.

"Come in, Brother Percival," Inez said, smiling. The teacher stepped inside.

"Good evening," Alfred said, shaking Brother Percival's hand. "Where's Brother Ashoka?"

"Sick, I'm afraid. He said to give you his regrets."

"I'm sorry to hear that. Father," Alfred called out to an older man with shrewd eyes beneath heavy gray brows, "come here for a second. I want you to meet Brother Percival, Amber's teacher. And Brother Percival, this is my father, Joseph Mallory. He publishes *The Islander*."

"Print and edit it as well," Joseph said. "Not to mention writing all the editorials and most of the copy. I even take some of the pictures."

"I've been curious about your paper for some time," Brother Percival said. "How do you make it pay for itself with such a limited circulation?"

"I don't," Joseph admitted. "Oh, I do do some other printing, brochures for the Institute and stuff like that, but I still end up losing money. But— Before I start I better ask you, were you just being polite or are you really curious?"

"Some of both," Brother Percival said.

"A good answer," Joseph said, nodding. "Well. . . . Back, oh, in the early eighties I was publishing a newspaper in Chicago. *The Chicago MidAmerican*. I was doing quite well financially and starting to get pretty influential but it looked to me like the country was just about ready for a civil war. Black against white. And Chicago would have been no place to be if that'd happened.

"So I sold the paper and came up here where I thought Paula and I'd be safer. I thought a press might be useful during the period of anarchy I was expecting to follow the civil war. So I had it built and was even able to use some of my government connections to get a fusion plant for it. The first one in this area.

"But the melanin plagues prevented—No. A civil war would have been better. And I still think there would have been one. But as it was, when the epidemics died down I found myself here with a functioning press and more money than I knew what to do with. I'd always been a newspaper man and here I had a chance to make a paper exactly what I wanted it to be with no need to compete for readers or placate advertisers. Except influential, of course: you can't have much effect on the country as a whole from an island in Upper Michigan. But I was old enough so that was OK: I'd already *been* influential.

"So, anyway, here I am with a paper with which I can do whatever I want. Call it a hobby or a rich man's folly if you want. I don't mind. You might even be right."

Jenny, one of the children from Amber's class, had been tugging on the green gossamer of Inez's sleeve for some time. "Do you need some help with something, dear?" Inez asked her when Joseph finished.

"Can we have the cake now, Mrs. Mallory?"

"Of course, dear," Inez said, flashing her an automatic smile. "We were just waiting for Brother Percival. Would you like to help me serve it to everybody?"

"Uh-huh. Can I help cut it too? I cut the cake this afternoon. At school."

"Of course. Excuse me, Brother Percival," Inez said and led Jenny through the party back to the kitchen.

"Sorry to be so late," Brother Percival said to Alfred, "but I'd forgotten we were Opening one of my former pupils tonight. You should have started without me.''

"Nonsense," Alfred said heartily. "No harm done. It's still early."

"Excuse me for prying into what very well may be none of my business," Joseph told Brother Percival, "but what exactly did you mean when you said you were 'opening' one of your pupils tonight?"

He looks like he can barely wait to pounce, Alfred thought. *But more like a vulture than a hawk. Why doesn't he get a hair transplant?*

"A *former* pupil," Brother Percival said. "Jerome's sixteen now. But in answer to your question, we initiated Jerome into the Fellowship of Prismatic Light tonight and he participated in the Latihan for the first time."

"The Latihan?" Joseph queried.

"Our group spiritual exercise."

"And, if you don't mind me asking, what's the connection between this 'group spiritual exercise' and those hypnotic machines you use?"

"None, because the Inductor is not a hypnotic machine. To understand what it *really* is, though—Do you mind listening to a little of *our* history?"

"Not at all. I'd be fascinated."

"Can I get you another whiskey, Father?" Alfred cut in.

"Yes. A double. No water. And no mojo powder either. And see if your mother needs anything. Now, Brother Percival, as you were saying. . . ."

"Have you ever heard of Subud or The Church of the One Sermon, Mr. Mallory?"

"No. I've never been interested in things like that. My family's always been Catholic."

"Well, Subud was a religion—or perhaps a religious discipline would be a better description—that originated in Java around 1930 and spread from there to most parts of the world. It's not really very surprising that you never heard of it: Subud was never a proselytizing sect and its membership declined rapidly after the death of its founder.

"Anyway, Subud had almost no dogma of its own and many of its members were Christians and Muslims. There were even a few Catholic priests and monks. Members practiced a group spiritual exercise, the Latihan, in which, as they believed, they opened their souls to God. It was as if they made of themselves cups into which God poured the divine wine of His presence. And, carrying the cup analogy a bit further, just as a cup may have its own unique shape which will enable it to contain a different amount of wine than a cup of another shape could contain, so God seemed to manifest Himself in different ways to each individual Subud member.

"A person being Opened stood in the midst of a group practicing the Latihan and 'surrendered.' And though not everyone initiated experienced anything immediately, if a new member continued with the group he would eventually learn to experience the Latihan's effects for himself. In time he would even be able to do the Latihan without the aid of the group. Are you still with me?"

"Yes." Joseph sipped at his drink. "After enough city council meetings you can listen to anybody. Without having trouble following what they're saying, I mean."

"Of course. The Church of the One Sermon was founded by some Subud members who believed in the use of psychedelic drugs in conjunction with the practice of the Latihan. But, more importantly, they thought that the Latihan could be explained in purely physiological terms. We of the Fellowship of Prismatic Light are the spiritual descendants, if you will, of a group of members of The Church of the One Sermon who rejected the use of drugs while retaining the belief that the Latihan was a purely physiological phenomenon."

"So you *don't* approve of the use of psychedelic drugs?"

"No. Despite our origin, we're rather puritanical on the subject."

"Good. So am I."

"A few years after the Fellowship was founded, research proved that a person doing the Latihan radiated a complex array of microwaves which, while very weak by ordinary standards, were nonetheless powerful enough at close range to trigger the Latihan phenomenon in persons in a state of relaxed surrender—"

"Meaning what?"

"Persons whose brainwaves had a frequency of between eight and thirteen cycles per second."

"OK."

"What the Inductor does is reproduce these triggering microwaves. The Latihan phenomenon itself has been found to consist of a specific type of pulsed electrical wave in the solid-state plasma of the semiconducting neurons of the brain stem."

"Is there any reason I need to understand that?" Joseph asked.

"Not really."

"Good. Then my question is, what does all this physiology have to do with God?"

"We believe that the Latihan state is a state of truly expanded consciousness, nothing more or less. What one perceives in this state—whether or not the person doing the Latihan attains some awareness of God—is between that individual and God. You can teach a man to read and show him the Bible, but he must read and understand it for himself. And even then, without God's assistance he will never truly attain understanding and faith."

"You're a Christian, then?" Joseph asked.

"Yes." Joseph looked satisfied.

Jenny appeared holding two cake plates. She gave one to Joseph, who shook his head and directed her over to his wife, and one to Brother Percival. She was serving the adults first, the teacher noted with approval, and the children were keeping their impatience under control. Good. He took a bite from the piece of Amber's cake on his plate.

And was shocked by the taste of salt. He *knew* the master computer had supervised every step of the cake's production; there was no way Amber could have ruined his cake without his teacher being aware of the fact. And all the other cakes had been perfect.

He looked closely at the small square of cake, noticed for the first time the pitted surface of the frosting. Amber must have sprinkled it with salt after he'd taken it home, and the salt had left little pits behind in the frosting when it dissolved. But why?

Or—somebody else had sprinkled the cake with salt. But in that case, who? And again, why?

He surveyed the room. Those adults who had tried their pieces of the cake Amber had made had taken only single bites; he noticed that a few of them were talking in low voices while darting occasional guarded glances at Amber and himself.

Probably wondering what kind of school would teach a child to make a cake with salt instead of sugar, he thought.

Alone among the children Amber had chosen to try his own cake before devouring the larger pink and white wedge of store-bought cake. He looked confused and ashamed, as though he were trying not to cry, but he seemed to have himself under control, Brother Percival was thankful to note.

Something about Jane's posture attracted the teacher's attention. She was standing alone near one wall watching Amber and the other children, a lonely malicious smile twisting the corners of her mouth.

Brother Percival knew children, could recognize gloating when he saw it. Jane had been the one who had salted the cake. But why? And what could he do about it?

She looked so unhappy.

Kevin finished his wedge of store-bought cake and took a bite of Amber's production. He spat it out onto the carpet.

"Hey Amber!" he yelled. "Your cake really stinks!"

Jane was trying to suppress her smirk. Brother Percival noticed a hint of—could it be satisfaction?—on Alfred's face. Alfred and Inez exchanged resigned glances.

"I'm afraid this is all my fault," Brother Percival said loudly enough to catch everyone's attention. Conversation stopped; people turned towards him. "For those of you who haven't tried Amber's cake yet, I suggest you don't try it at all. There's salt on it. But Amber didn't put the salt on it. I did."

Jane's face expressed a cringing certainty of punishment; Amber looked confused but trusting.

"You see," the teacher continued, "after Amber finished his cake I tasted a bit of the frosting and decided it could use a little more sugar. So I sprinkled some on. That is, I thought I was sprinkling on sugar, but the computer doesn't bother to keep track of me as carefully as it keeps track of the kids and, well, it seems I got the salt by mistake. So it's not Amber's fault at all. It's mine."

Somewhat later, when the incident had faded from the forefront of the guest's minds, the teacher approached Jane.

"Would you mind coming into the kitchen and talking with me

for a while?'' he asked. ''There's something I think we should discuss.''

''I don't want to,'' she said, looking about her for an excuse to escape.

''Please. It's important.'' She came with him unwillingly, like a dog expecting to be punished.

In the kitchen he said, ''Jane, you're not going to be punished because of what I know. I'm not going to tell anyone. But I know you put salt on Amber's cake.

''I didn't do anything.''

''Jane, I know the cake was all right when Amber took it home. And I saw the expression on your face when Kevin yelled at Amber.''

''Then you lied to everybody.''

''Yes. I didn't want to see Amber hurt and I didn't want to say anything that would get you punished.''

''So then how do I know you're not lying when you say you're not going to tell anybody?''

''If I was going to tell on you why would I have lied to everybody for you?''

She thought about that for a moment, nodded reluctantly.

''Why do you want to hurt him so badly?''

''I don't want to hurt anybody.''

''Jane, I *saw* the way you were looking at him when Kevin yelled at him. You looked like you hated him.''

''You won't tell on me?''

''No. I'd like to become your friend.''

''I don't need a friend like you! I'm not a, a—''

''No, you're not retarded. And you don't need me in the same way as Amber needs me. But I think you're very unhappy and I think you could use a friend. Just a friend.''

''I am too happy.'' But her face, her craggy, woebegone face, denied it.

''Perhaps you think you're happy,'' he said gently. ''And perhaps you *are* happy sometimes. But you must have been very unhappy to think it would make you happier to ruin Amber's birthday for him.

''Listen: whenever you hurt someone else—anyone else—you

hurt yourself too. But you hurt yourself deep down inside, so deep down inside that sometimes you don't even know that that's what's hurting you. You may think it makes you feel good to hurt somebody else and it may seem like fun when you do it. True. Sometimes it *does* feel good. For a little while. Just a little while. And then, Jane, then you feel unhappy. You feel unhappy a lot, don't you?''

Jane nodded her head.

''And you keep on feeling unhappy and it gets worse and worse and you don't know what to do about it. All you know is that you're miserable. So you try to hurt people more because you think it'll make you feel better. But it's as if you were taking a butcher knife and cutting away at your soul—''

''Daddy says nobody has a soul. He says there aren't any souls.''

''Soul is just a word, Jane. Think about what makes you really you. That's your soul and it's real. And hell—Did your father tell you there wasn't any hell?''

Jane nodded again.

''But there *is* a hell, Jane. If you keep on hurting Amber someday you'll have hurt *yourself* so badly deep down inside that nothing can ever make you happy again, not even for a moment. And that's what hell is, hurting yourself so badly that nothing can ever make you happy again.''

''I don't want. . . .'' She trailed off.

How much does she understand? Brother Percival asked himself. But she seemed to be understanding most of what he was saying.

''What *do* you want, Jane?'' he asked softly.

''I want to be happy and, and have lots of friends and not have everybody be so mean to me all the time and, and—''

''I'll be your friend. If you want me to. And Amber will learn to love you if you're kind to him.''

''What good is he? Everybody laughs at him! He's stupid! And they all say that I'm stupid like him, and Daddy said I was even uglier than him and—''

Brother Percival listened as the frustrations and miseries of her short lifetime came pouring out, listened as she told him all the things she had never been able to tell anyone.

Later, much later, he brought the conversation back to Amber.

''He's smarter than anyone else in his class—''

"Yeah, at the moron school!"

"Jane, *I* think he's worth having as a friend and I'm not mentally retarded. You're much smarter than he is, true, but he's kind and gentle and loyal. . . . But because you're so much smarter than he is he wouldn't be just an ordinary friend. He could be something more, almost like a child of your own."

And later still: "I'd like you and Amber to come to my house sometime for dinner. Would you like that?"

"Maybe."

"And afterwards you could come to the school—"

"No! I'm not stupid like him—"

"Of course you're not," the teacher agreed. "Neither am I. But I go to the school, don't I? Because I'm a teacher. And that's why I'd like you to come. So you could learn how to help take care of Amber. We need your help. But you don't have to come if you don't want to.

"Some of the other boys and girls with brothers and sisters at the school also come in on Wednesday nights," he continued. "You'd have something in common with them and maybe you'd make new friends. . . ."

When Brother Percival broached the idea to Inez, she was only too happy at the prospect of having Jane relieve her of some of the responsibility for Amber. And Alfred had no objections.

On Amber's seventh birthday Jane baked him a cake.

CHAPTER SIX

AT SIXTEEN Amber stood only five foot two. Twelve years of being treated by Alfred and Inez as a mental and physical incompetent who was in some unstated fashion morally responsible for his own deficiencies had stamped his face with hesitation; his gestures were diffident and he hunched his shoulders forward when he walked.

Though it had been six months since the birthday that had rendered him a legal adult, he still lived with Jane and his foster parents and still attended the Fellowship's school weekday mornings. But his schooling would be over within the month and then six days out of every month would be as dreary as the afternoons he now put in working by himself in the windowless room that housed *The Islander*'s fully automated presses and incidentally served the paper as a mail room.

The sound of the presses was deafening.

The job Amber's grandfather had created for him would perhaps have been suitable for a low grade moron, but it bored Amber, whose IQ had turned out to be just below eighty, making him almost borderline normal: smart enough to be fully aware of the chasm separating him from normal humanity, not smart enough to bridge it.

And the job itself—His grandfather had taught him to value useful work. But he could take neither pride nor pleasure in the accomplishment of tasks he was intelligent enough to realize could have been done more cheaply and efficiently by machine alone.

I need the money, he reminded himself. Inflation and mismanagement of his trust fund (neither of which he understood, though

41

Joseph had taken him aside and tried to explain them to him once) had reduced his independent income to less than Alfred now demanded of him for room and board. And though he dreamed of escaping from Alfred and Inez, there was nowhere else on the island where he and Jane could live.

He'd passed the morning pleasantly enough in Brother Ashoka's class, but the afternoon at the paper had been so far drearily typical, enlivened only by his anticipation of the Tuesday night Latihan. One new subscriber to deal with, Mrs. Donna Lee Something out on Cream Point, and two people who'd let their subscriptions lapse. Spinning the wheel of the eighty-year old machine that engraved subscribers' names and addresses onto the metal plates for the addressograph, he lined the pointer up with what he hoped were the correct letters of Mrs. Donna Lee's last name. If he'd guessed wrong, he could expect his grandfather to pass an irate letter on to him within the week.

He slipped the completed name plate onto a blank addressograph card, used the new card to print itself a label, slipped the label into place above the name plate, then filed the card. After pulling the two lapsed subscribers' cards from the appropriate drawers and throwing away their labels and name plates, he fed the remaining cards a drawer at a time into the ancient grey addressograph. But there were only three short drawers of cards and despite the time he wasted placing the printed address with unnecessary precision on exactly the same spot on each paper, he'd addressed, bundled, labeled and bagged all the papers before two-thirty. He still had three and a half hours to go before he could leave the concrete-floored room in the fortresslike building, six hours till Latihan.

He picked up a copy of the day's paper and leafed through it examining the pictures. There was a photo of a Sunday School picnic in the woods, a picture of two bears going through the garbage at the dump, another of the night sky glowing red and green with the Northern Lights, and a final picture of a sunset reflected rippling across the surface of Lake Huron.

The phone rang. Amber picked it up. It was Joseph.

"Everything all right, Amber?"

"Yes. I'm doing fine."

"Nothing too difficult for you?"

"No, grandfather. Everything's fine."

"I'm glad to hear it, boy. Call me if anything comes up."

"I will, grandfather."

"Goodbye, Amber."

"Goodbye."

He returned to the paper. Though Amber had no interest in the fishing maps and had long since given up trying to read his grandfather's editorials, he loved the pictures, just as he loved the country they depicted. He had tried to take some pictures for the paper himself with the camera his grandmother had given him but somehow they never came out the way he wanted them to and he had eventually given the camera to one of his classmates.

Though Amber had only been to Detroit a few times, he had learned a lot about the world in school. Enough to know he could never be happy in the urban megalopolis that covered most of the North American continent, even if he could find a job that would provide him with more than bare subsistence, more than an empty life in a bleak cubicle of an apartment in a welfare ghetto. Many people chose the simplicity of welfare life of their own free will, opting out of the struggle for economic survival so as to be better able to pursue other options: art, music, meditation, culture—options which had nothing to offer Amber. Despite his sham of a job, despite Alfred's petty cruelties and Inez's blind rages, at least here on Drummond he had Jane, the woods and the lake, and the twice-a-week ecstasy of the Latihan. He was not happy, but there was no place on earth where he would be any happier.

No place on Earth. But there were other worlds.

He took from his pocket one of the brochures his grandfather had printed up for the Espanore Island Dimensional Transfer Institute. Amber had nothing to do with the brochures—they were shipped directly to a mailing house in Detroit and sent out from there—but they fascinated him despite the difficulty he had reading them even with the help of his computer dictionary.

The cover of this particular brochure showed a forest of yellow-leaved trees with scarlet trunks and branches. Through the forest a pioneer settlement of scarlet log cabins could be glimpsed. The picture was only an artist's conception, of course—nothing physical, not even light, could pass from one dimension to another.

Amber opened the brochure. It was an old favorite of his and Jane had long since given him the help he needed to grasp the more difficult concepts. Long ago he had memorized the meanings of all the words the brochure used which were not part of his everyday speaking vocabulary.

He skipped over the early pages ("an analogous place in a different ecological framework. . . . The chance to participate in any one of a number of different Utopian experiments. . . ."), came to the part that he wanted to look at. Paragraphs leaped out at him:

Have you seen everything this world has to offer? We can show you something new. Or is your body maimed, mutilated, damaged beyond repair? If your problem is genetic or the result of natural aging there is little we can do for you—YET— but if you have suffered some form of crippling damage at any time after your conception we may very well be able to offer you a second chance. Your personality can be transferred intact to a new body in a new world. . . .

A new life—new in EVERY aspect, for even your body's genetic pattern will have been not replicated, but TRANS- LATED into other-dimensional terms so as to fit your new self for life in a world unlike our own. . . .

On Alter you can become an entity with a physical body almost identical with that of an Earth-Standard human but with all the advantages of a fresh start in a wilderness paradise. On Petrovich II you would find yourself with a body equally at home on dry land and in the depths of the sea. On Diamond you would live a life of solitary bliss as a sentient crystal.

We have gained access to scores of alternate worlds, some much like our own, some so different that their natural laws are as yet still incomprehensible. Perhaps in one of these worlds or in one as yet undiscovered you can find the life for which you've always yearned, your fantasy come true. . . .

We desperately need explorers and communicators who can live simultaneously in this world and in those we have discov- ered. We have openings for men and women of all sorts who want to escape the limitations of their mundane existence here

on earth and become colonists in worlds they can make their
own. . . .

A long time ago Amber had realized what transfer would mean to
him: a body perhaps new and strange but no weaker than that of his
fellow colonists and a fresh start with a new unstunted brain in
which his mind could attain the brilliance that he knew should have
been his by right of birth.

But unless you had the special mental abilities required to become
an explorer or communicator or had some vitally needed skill it cost
a fortune to become a colonist, more money than Amber and Jane
together would ever be able to save, far more than remained in
Amber's trust. Escape was reserved for the rich, denied to those
who had the most need of it.

Joseph could have paid their way but Joseph would never have
financed them. Ever since Amber's father had deserted his wife to
transfer to Diamond, Joseph had detested the Institute and all it
stood for—though naturally he had never allowed his feelings to
prevent him from making a profit by doing business with them.

Amber felt in his pocket for his two tickets for this month's
National Sweepstakes. The Sweepstakes were the only hope Amber
and Jane would ever have of affording transfer.

Even Amber knew how slim that hope was.

They wanted Alfred to stay late on Espanore to help with the new
simulator for the center in the Soo but as always he managed to find
a convincing reason to leave. The boat gave him a little trouble on
the way back but he found the loose connection and repaired it easily
enough and he made it home with time to spare.

He tied up at the dock and went inside. As he had expected, Inez
was sitting entranced before the holovision. Her skin showed none
of the flush characteristic of Newemph, the drug developed to
replace holo-emph after the widely publicized killing of a nurse and
two orderlies in a rest home where it was used to keep senile patients
occupied had resulted in the government declaring its use illegal:
she had obviously located another illicit source. The drug was far
more satisfying to the user in its original form and Inez used it
whenever she could get it.

When Alfred roused her she would come out of her trance in a killing rage. Luckily, her muscles had atrophied so much from lack of exercise—all she did was take emph in one form or another and sit—that there was little chance she would manage to lay a hand on her husband before she went comatose.

Alfred looked at the clock: five ten. Joseph wouldn't be back with Amber until six fifteen or twenty. Plenty of time.

But if they were early for some reason . . . Alfred shuddered, appalled as he thought of what would happen to his plans for the future if his father found out about Inez. *No,* he told himself, *it's insane to pretend you're going to be able to keep him from ever finding out. Not if he finds out. When he finds out. I've got to protect myself. Get a divorce—*

But that was no solution: as a good Catholic his father did not approve of divorce. And if Alfred tried to get a divorce Inez might well tell his father that he was a member of the Scarlet Monk Club. And then Alfred could kiss all hope of inheriting the family money goodbye.

Alfred reached into the hologram, found the on/off switch, and turned off the set. The three-dimensional images winked out of existence; the dialogue was cut off, yet Inez still sat staring blankly into space.

Alfred grabbed her by the wrists, yanked her to her feet. She came awake fighting him but she was so weak and her period of consciousness was so short that he had no trouble protecting himself from her.

Not a bruise on me, he thought with satisfaction as he carried her to the bedroom and stretched her out on the bed. If Joseph looked in on her she would appear to be taking a nap. *At least I've learned how to handle her.*

She would sleep for a while, then awaken in plenty of time to make herself presentable for dinner. After dinner, with Amber and Jane gone for the evening, she would of course return to her holovision. Let her. She wouldn't even realize her husband was at the Scarlet Monk Club again.

Not that it made any difference to Alfred if she did know, as long as she kept quiet. And both Amber and Jane knew better than to question his activities or talk about him outside the immediate family.

Which emphatically did not include Alfred's father or mother.

Jane worked near the Drummond Island Ferry Dock in DeTour, in the Paul Bunyan Café. Her boss was a grossly fat man six feet eight inches tall who had had his name legally changed to Paul Bunyan fifteen years previously, when he first opened the cafe. The café's specialties were its twenty-seven varieties of flapjacks and its Babeburgers of bright blue soy protein; the waitresses—Jane and a girl named Anne Marie—wore shoes with nonfunctional wheels on them. The wheels were supposed to make the shoes look like roller skates.

At eighteen, Jane was six feet three inches tall and though her face was as forbidding as ever, her body had developed a gaunt beauty somewhat reminiscent of that of her late Aunt Angela.

Once she had heard Paul tell a customer, "Put a plastic bag over her head—not clear plastic, of course, one of those brown trash bags would be more like it—and she wouldn't be half bad. Of course, she might suffocate, but that wouldn't be all that great a loss now, would it?"

The customer had laughed. He was a Drummonder about five years older than Jane, a commercial fisherman, and two nights later he had asked her to spend the night with him.

It had been the fourth such proposition she had ever received, the fourth such she had declined. Like the three others it had come from a man dead drunk, from a man who would not have been caught dead propositioning her sober.

As some comments she'd overheard him making to Paul a few nights later had made abundantly clear.

Made it clear that she was as ugly as her father had always said she was. Made it clear that she had no hope of ever finding a man who would love her as a woman.

So at eighteen Jane was still a virgin. She had some friends, a few of the Brothers and Sisters at the Fellowship's school and two or three other people she had met through them, no enemies if you discounted her parents, but only one person whom she really loved, only one person who really loved her. Amber.

It was five-thirty, but there were only three customers in the café, all seated in Anne Marie's section. Which was fine with Jane: her feet hurt from the idiotic shoes Paul made her wear and she would have liked nothing better than to sit alone, earning nothing but bothered by no one, until Sister Leila picked her up.

Two summer people whom Jane vaguely recognized came in and sat down in her section. This year the woman sported a moustache and eyebrows of green feathers; her head was shaved bald and she wore a blouse with electrostatically puffed balloon sleeves that stood out a foot from her arms. Her companion was dressed in black and wore a matching hood with the number of his license to conceal his identity printed on the forehead in yellow. Their hands moved in elaborate stylized gestures, sometimes touching, as they murmured to each other.

Whenever Inez came out of her trance and was feeling friendly toward her daughter she would promise to try to talk Alfred into paying for cosmetic surgery "so you can look like my real daughter, Jane." Jane longed for the surgery, though if she stayed on Drummond Island afterwards she knew she'd always be known as the girl who was so ugly she had to get a new face. But Inez never asked Alfred about it and Jane knew it would do *her* no good to ask; she had once hesitantly approached her grandmother but had been told it wasn't right to try to change the face God had given her ("We've all got our burdens to bear, dear. And we love you anyway,") and there was no way she would ever be able to save enough money from work to pay for the surgery herself; besides—

Looking at the two summer people Jane knew that no amount of cosmetic surgery would be enough, that neither she nor Amber could ever adjust to life in the megalopolis, that neither of them could ever become satisfied, successful members of the urban society whose members, in the words of one of her grandfather's editorials, "despised religion but admired martyrs for their style, living lives of elaborately patterned courtesy and calculated crudity, empty of all but a fantastical devotion to style." No. She and Amber were hicks, and perhaps they were better off so, though it meant they were stuck on Drummond, stuck with Alfred and Inez, with *The Islander* and the Paul Bunyan Cafe.

Jane bought two sweepstakes tickets a month to please Amber but though she too dreamed of transfer she knew better than to believe either of them had any chance of ever winning the lottery.

No chance of escape. Still— She lost herself for a moment in a dream of a world where Amber was strong and brilliant (uneducated, but she would teach him) and where everyone was strange-looking, where there was no fluctuating but rigid standard of beauty by which she would be judged and found wanting.

"Hey, Jane! Move your ass! Customers!" Paul yelled at her. She twisted her features into a weary smile and got to her feet.

"Ah ha! I know who *you* are!" the man in the concealment hood said. "Do you remember me? Bet you don't know who I am."

Jane couldn't wait for Latihan.

CHAPTER SEVEN

IN THE first decades of the Twenty-First Century only rare individuals faced the same group of people over the supper table as they had seen at breakfast. The family was whole and solitary at breakfast time but for dinner it fragmented or was incorporated into larger units. Supper clubs and associations of all sorts, ranging from those priding themselves on strict exclusivity to those matching people at random, were universal, and most North Americans belonged to several. Even on Drummond Island one either ate at a friend's or had friends over for dinner.

But Alfred despised his fellow Drummonders and was heartily disliked by them in turn, while Inez was wholly absorbed in her holovision and could not care less about the social amenities. So except for those rare occasions when they ate with Joseph or Paula or when Amber was invited out by one of his schoolmates, the Mallorys ate together, with no other company. And since Jane usually ate at the cafe and the remaining members of the family had few interests in common and no liking for each other, dinner usually went by in dull silence.

After a dinner during which she had eaten without pleasure the prepackaged food Alfred had heated while she slept, Inez stationed herself in front of the holovision and took four three-hour Newemph pills, each a little six-pointed star embedded in a globe of transparent gel. Sitting on the couch with his hands folded over his small but developing paunch, Alfred found it almost impossible to see any resemblance between the lax-faced, slump-bodied matron in the green dress that covered her from throat to ankle and the ambitious, body-conscious girl he had married, the girl he was well aware had married him in the hope that becoming Angela Mallory's sister-in-law would advance her modeling career. In which hope Alfred had encouraged her until she realized that Angela Mallory hated Alfred and that her marriage to him had been the kiss of death to her career.

Alfred felt an unaccustomed surge of sympathy for his wife. Neither he nor she had gotten what they wanted out of life.

But I haven't given up, he reminded himself. It was a pity about Inez, but he couldn't allow his sympathy for her to drag him down. *If I can just keep father from finding out about her until I've figured out a way to free myself from her that won't involve too many complications.* . . . He reached for the sniff-pipe on the table by the couch.

The doorbell chimed. "Come in!" Alfred yelled. He put the nozzle of the sniff-pipe to his left nostril and pushed the button that activated the spray. The alkaloid-laden mist felt cool and refreshing.

He put the pipe down and glanced over at the stocky woman framed in the doorway.

"Come in, Sister Leila," he said cordially. "Amber should be out—Ah, here he is now."

Amber came running into the living room and hugged the woman. Both he and she wore the rainbow-colored tunics of the Fellowship; she wore a long, straight silver skirt while he wore loose silver trousers. She was much taller than Amber, perhaps a little heavier than Inez.

A thoroughly unattractive pair, Alfred thought.

"Good night, Mr. Mallory," Sister Leila said, polite as ever.

"Good night," Alfred echoed. The woman closed the door.

Alfred looked at the clock: seven-ten. They would make the seven-thirty ferry; he would be able to take the eight o'clock without fear of being recognized. No one but Amber or Jane was likely to know his license number or recognize his car.

Making his way through the porch to his bedroom, he made a mental note to try to get around to taking down the storm windows over the weekend. In the bedroom he stripped and fed his clothing to the alterator, punching the proper code for a suit of anonymous

black and the matching concealment hood he always wore on his
visits to the Scarlet Monk Club. He put on the suit but hesitated
before donning the hood. Better to wait until he was on the road,
safely away from the house. That way no one would learn to connect
the number on his hood with his house.

Back in the living room he took the scenarios he had ready to
submit from their hiding place behind the bookcase. He knew they
were good, even better than the last ones he had submitted. There
was a fairly good chance, in fact, that he would find that he himself
had plotted his encounter for tonight, though the anonymity and
amnesia drugs would keep him from realizing it until the encounter
was over.

Another sniff for the drive up? he asked himself. No, it would be
better to arrive in as virgin a condition as possible.

As virgin a condition as possible. . . . He smiled, well pleased
with himself, as he closed the door behind him, leaving Inez
entranced before the holovision.

Some kids twelve to fourteen years old were hanging out on the
pavement outside the Paul Bunyan Café. Jane watched them idly
through the window. She had already cleansed herself and used the
alterator in the cafe's bathroom. Her feet still hurt and she was
massaging them while she waited for Sister Leila.

She didn't notice the car pulling up outside but she heard a kid
yell "Hey dwarf!" She straightened abruptly, stared out the window, saw Amber slowly turning to face his tormentor.

"Dwarf, mind telling me something?" Though the kid was at
least six feet tall he couldn't have been over thirteen.

"I guess not," Amber said with a visible effort at control.

"Dwarf, is your sister as stupid as you are? Because you're as
ugly as she is."

But by then Jane had pushed her way through the kids to Amber.

In the car Sister Leila said, "You did very well, Amber."

"Somebody should keep them from doing that," Jane said.
"From doing things like that."

"God," Amber said. "God will take care of them."

Jane wondered what he meant by that.

Once at the school they separated. Male and female neophytes did the Latihan in separate domes while the more experienced members of the Fellowship practiced the Latihan together in a third, larger, dome.

Amber followed the crimson path to the appropriate dome. Entering, he removed his shoes and put them on a rack by the door, then slipped on his EEG monitor. He walked across the room, deviating only slightly from a straight line in order to keep from brushing against the gray metal sphere of the Inductor which rose on its coiled stalk from the center of the room. He took an unoccupied seat on the bench against the far wall.

Some of the neophytes were talking to each other in low tones but Amber sat silently, not really looking at the ten or so men and boys who sat around the periphery of the dome.

Brother Percival and Brother Ashoka, the guides for the session, came in and seated themselves. A moment later Amber heard a single pure tone. His eyes closed of their own accord and he began to relax, sinking further and further into his own depths.

Scenes flashed before him, dissolved and were gone. The kids jeering at him. Prying loose a card jammed in the addressograph. Inez sitting silent at dinner, Alfred saying something which she was not deigning to notice. A white flower—

The scene took on reality, becoming almost as vivid as it had been when he'd experienced it. He was standing springsprayfooted beside Jane on the cool moist ground, small sticks and a single sharp stone digging into his feet, staring down at a timber lily—its long slender stalk rising twelve inches from the ground to the three broad leaves, light with darker green veins, and then another inch or so up to the erect flower: the three green sepals below the three fleshy white petals and in the center the six yellow stamens. He could almost hear the creek gurgling off to the right, feel the cedar-scented breeze. . . .

But he relinquished that scene as well and it too dissolved. He sank deeper and deeper into the calm ocean.

Another pure tone. The Latihan had begun.

Alfred saw the lights of the Soo gleaming ahead of him. He would be at the club soon.

• • •

Inez sat entranced before the flowing three-dimensional images, feeling as never before the joy that came from having her kitchen truly clean.

The Latihan had begun—

Jane felt herself seized by a tremendous impersonal force. Her eyes opened—it felt as though her lids had been peeled back by rough hands—and she sprang to her feet. Obeying a will not her own her arms extended from her sides and she began to spin wildly while she stared out at the Latihan dome and its occupants.

Green walls, blue carpeting, the gray metal ball of the Inductor in the center of the room. Two women sitting quietly, blissful smiles on their faces. A girl Jane's age marching around the room: her eyes were closed yet she lengthened her stride at the proper moment to step over the women lying weeping on the floor. Sister Katherine singing while a girl chanted nonsense syllables in harmony.

To her right a woman was arguing with herself in two voices:

Deep voice: "Big. Gibb, Gibb, Gahl, Gahr!"

High voice: "No! No, no!"

Deep voice: "Gahl, Ghar, Gish, Ghak!"

High voice: "Ghak-ghish? No, Arp-Art! Ash, Alp, Infinite Arch, Absolute Arg!"

Deep voice: "Arf? Yes! Arf Arf!"

Both voices: "Arf Arf Arf!"

The force holding Jane rigid suddenly left her unsupported and she collapsed on the floor, racked by slow convulsions. But Sister Katherine and Sister Judith were by her side, singing, singing. . . . Their voices were so beautiful. Jane followed them up and out of her body and into the infinite blue of the sky.

Though Amber was sitting with his eyes closed he could see the Latihan dome around him as clearly as if his eyes had been open. A soft round ball of light was approaching him, sinking into him, becoming part of him. . . .

He was covered with soft glowing fur. He was a luminous rabbit. . . .

Alfred and the kid who had jeered at him outside the café attacked each other with knives and fell to the ground dead. Their bodies rotted and out of their mouths and noses and ears and empty eye sockets tiny deer came streaming. The deer gamboled and frolicked, singing in high sweet voices.

The Latihan dome was opening to the sky like a flower as the mountain that had formed beneath it pushed it higher and higher, ever closer to Heaven. . . .

The Latihan Flower swayed gently on its mountain stalk. Its petals were arcs of rainbow, its center was a parquet floor of celestial oak and mahogany whose inlaid pattern danced like the sparkling water of a fast-running stream. . . .

The other neophytes were standing rapt, their arms outstretched, singing hymns of joy which became flowering vines growing from their hands, stretching upward and twining round the beams of light from their eyes, vines growing toward God. . . .

The music swelled and became God's face, flowing young-old, bearded bald feathered covered with grass, His Eyes green gold blue flaming icy, swelling as they descended, coming closer, closer—

A single pure tone, piercing, the blast on an angelic trumpet| "Finish!" God cried, his voice diminishing to that of Brother Percival by word's end. Amber found himself sitting with his eyes closed on the padded bench. The Latihan was over.

Brother Ashoka caught up with Amber on the path. "Can you come to dinner with my wife and myself this Sunday?" he asked.

"I hope so," Amber said. "I'll try."

"Please come. And could you find out when Jane will have a night off? We'd like to have her over sometime soon too."

"I will," Amber promised.

The Boer who had been Alfred Mallory and who would be Alfred Mallory again stared at the dark-skinned man and at the two naked native girls who were undressing man. He shifted the whip he held from his right to his left hand so that the younger woman could ease his ruffled shirt off him.

He did not know who he was or who they were and he did not much care. He knew what he was going to do.

Back at the house Inez sat entranced in front of the holovision.

CHAPTER EIGHT

AMBER ALWAYS stayed for the Question Session that followed the regular Friday night Latihans. Tonight only two of the other neophytes had chosen to join him. Amber knew them both slightly: John Underhill, a plump man in his early twenties who worked for the park service on Drummond Island, and Joseph Henry Thomas Thompson, a harsh-faced old Treaty Indian who had lost his first wife to the melanin plagues.

"Do you have your question formulated, John?" Brother Ashoka asked.

"Yes." John blinked, rubbed at his left eye.

"Do you wish to ask it in privacy?"

"No. I'd rather have all your help."

"What about you, Joseph Henry?"

"I've got my question ready. I don't want any help but I don't care if you hear what I have to say."

"All right. Amber? Your usual question?" Brother Ashoka smiled.

"Yes."

"All right. Close your eyes, please, and relax. . . . I've activated the Inductor. John, state your question."

"My wife doesn't approve of me attending Latihan," John said slowly. "She says the Fellowship is for mental defectives, not grown men. How can I get her to change her mind?"

In the silence that followed John's question Amber felt a surge of utter joy pass through him.

"Finish," Brother Ashoka stated. "John, are you satisfied with the answer you received?"

John shook his head. "No. . . . I got something but I can't make sense of it. A fish floating dead on the surface of the water. . . . What did the rest of you receive?"

"Nothing," Joseph Henry snapped.

"I felt really good, like a good Latihan," Amber said. "Maybe she should come too."

"But she doesn't even want *me* to come," John said. "Brother Ashoka? You're my last hope."

"You can always pose your question again some other night," Brother Ashoka said. "But I did get something that might be useful. I saw what seemed to be a dinner party, with lots of people there: my wife and myself, you and a woman I assume to be your wife, Dr. Mulbry and his daughter, Brother Percival and Sister Angela, plus some others who weren't clear. To me this means you should make an effort to ensure that your wife gets to know some of us as people, away from the school and the Fellowship, before you try to get her to change her mind. Is that any help?"

"Maybe," John said. "I'll think about it. But it still doesn't explain my dead fish."

"Now close your eyes again and relax," Brother Ashoka said. "I've activated the Inductor. Joseph Henry, state your question."

"Both of my sons by my first wife died with her in the plagues," the old Indian said, "and my son by my present wife was born deformed and an idiot. The doctors told me it was because of what happened to me in the plagues, but they also said there was a chance I could have a normal child and that there was little chance of another outbreak of the plague. I am rich; I want a son. Should my wife and I take the risk?"

Amber felt a jagged purple pain dissolving into joyous warmth, then freezing into a straining rigidity.

"Finish," Brother Ashoka said and Amber felt his muscles go limp. "Joseph Henry, are you satisfied with the answer you received?"

"Yes." The old man was elated.

"All right. Now please close your eyes again and relax once more. . . . I've activated the Inductor. Amber, state your question."

"Which sweepstakes tickets should I buy this week?" Amber

asked. He waited until the ticket numbers swam into his field of vision: NJ76902 and PB00531, and slightly behind them the alternates: DD10444 and AU66611.

"Finish," Brother Ashoka said. "Amber, are you satisfied with the answer you received?"

"Yes," Amber said.

The antidotes in the six four-hour Newemph pills Inez had taken after dinner jolted her back to reality. The brightly-colored images the holovision projected were shrunken and garish; the sound rasped at her ears. She reached into the images and turned the set off.

The living room was in darkness. Inez got unsteadily to her feet and felt her way along the wall to the light switch. Turning on the light, she noted with stale disgust the dusty room and bulky furniture, the bookcases against two walls.

"Alfred?" she called. "Amber? Jane?" She waited a moment. She was the only one home. Good.

She crossed the room and took a book out of the bookcase against the far wall. The book was a collection of photographs from the height of Angela Mallory's career which Alfred kept on prominent display for Joseph's benefit. Inez bent the covers back, squeezed the pages away from the spine. A number of tiny red pills dropped into her hand. She counted them: thirteen. Probably enough. She put the book back on the shelf and went into the kitchen for a glass of water.

A moment later she turned the holovision back on. Sitting in front of it, she once again became someone else.

In his privacy cubicle at the Scarlet Monk Club, Alfred tried vainly to remember the features of the people who had participated in the encounter with him. It was no use, his returning memory told him: their every action was clear in his mind but he would never learn their identities. The anonymity drugs took care of that.

What if that old woman really was Mother? he asked himself. But part of the thrill was the knowledge that he would never find out.

He punched for his bill and looked it over. Though the encounter he himself had participated in had been plotted by someone else, he was credited with three of the scenarios that had been used tonight, so he was only being charged eighty dollars. He could afford another session, even taking into account the surcharge on the special stimulants he would need this late at night.

I'll do it, he decided, punching the proper code for the type of experience he wanted into the console. A moment later a plastic envelope containing five white pills and two green spansules fell out of the delivery slot.

The doorbell chimed insistently twice, four times, twelve times. Through the living room window Joseph could see Inez sitting oblivious, her still form illuminated by the light from the program she was watching.

"Inez! Let me in! Please let me in!" His finger jabbed the bell. "Paula's dying, she's dying and she wants to talk to all of you before—Goddamn it! Open up! Hurry, damn you! Let me in!"

He saw her get up, leave the circle of light around the set. A moment later the door opened.

As he was stepping over the threshhold Inez brought a heavy brass lamp down on his head. He fell, struck the floor heavily, blood matting the thick grey hair of his new scalp transplant.

The lamp had fallen from Inez's hands. She picked it up, smiled, brought it down once again on his head. The sound the lamp made when it struck delighted her. She was smiling when her legs gave way and she fell across his still body.

Amber and Jane found the two bodies in the doorway. Jane called the doctor. The doctor called the police. Inez came to in DeTour's one-room jail, charged with murder.

"Win the hand of my daughter and my kingdom shall be yours," the old king, resplendent in robes of velvet and ermine, his scepter gleaming in his hand, promised the prince who had once been and would soon again be Alfred Mallory.

CHAPTER NINE

THE TINY CELL in the Sault St. Marie jail was gray plastic, window-less, furnished with only a toilet and a bed with sheets and blanket of institutional green.

Inez was sitting on the bed, her eyes closed. The prisoner's advocate sat down beside her.

She opened her eyes, looked at him. "What are they going to do to me?" she asked. Her voice was flat.

"You'll be tried for the murder of Joseph Mallory," the advocate said. "He's being dead-brained now. And the part of his brain they use was almost intact. So if you did kill him they'll know about it soon. Did you?"

Inez hesitated.

"I'm here as your friend," the advocate said. "All the recording devices are turned off for as long as I'm in your cell. You don't have to say anything you don't want to, but nothing you say to me will ever be used against you."

Inez still said nothing.

"*If* you killed him—and I'm not saying you did—but if the evidence *seems* to prove you killed him, are there any extenuating circumstances you'd like to claim?"

"Holo-emph. Not Newemph. I'd taken nineteen or twenty pills. I wasn't in my right mind."

"So the police report says," the advocate agreed. "Unfortunate-ly, the U. S. Supreme Court ruled some time back that you're legally responsible for any action you commit while under the influence of any drug you take knowingly and of your own free will.

You *did* take the holo-emph knowingly and of your own free will?''

"Obviously." Then, retreating, "What are they going to do to me?''

"You'll have a trial, of course, due process of law and all that, but I'm afraid the outcome's pretty certain. Judge abu-Bakr's not known for his leniency, especially in drug cases. He's what they used to call a 'hanging judge,' only of course we don't hang anybody anymore. So—I expect you'll be turned over to the Michigan Colonial Authority for a lifetime of involuntary servitude. And that means you'll probably be assigned to the Sahara Reclamation Project. I'm afraid Michigan didn't do all that well in the Big Grab.''

"I don't want to spend the rest of my life as a slave." Decision firmed her voice. "I want euthanasia.''

"Impossible.''

"But every citizen—''

"Criminals aren't citizens.''

"I haven't been convicted.''

"You can put in a request for euthanasia. But they won't even process it until after your trial's over.''

"You're my advocate. Help me.''

"In your case there's nothing much I can do. But if you can think of something—''

"Thanks. How long until they try me?''

"Six to eight weeks. Do you want to spend the time awake or asleep?''

"Asleep.''

"Would you like to see anybody before they put you out? A lawyer, your family, maybe a priest? You're listed as Catholic.''

"No. I don't want to see anybody.''

"Amber," Alfred said, "you can't spend every day playing in the woods like some sort of overgrown kid. You've got to find yourself a new job. How are you going to pay next month's room and board if you don't bring in any money? I can't afford to support you.''

"There isn't any work.''

Alfred smiled. "Not around here, perhaps. You may have to go somewhere else."

"Where?"

"How should I know?" Alfred snapped. "You're an adult now, aren't you? Make your own decisions. But if you can't pay rent I'll have to kick you out."

"Maybe grandfather left me some money."

"Maybe. But your grandfather didn't believe in just giving people things. He thought you should work for a living."

Since space was at a premium in the jail, most of the prisoners awaiting trial were asleep. Like the rest of them Inez lay unconscious in a small, coffinlike compartment, her body massaged regularly by machines designed to maintain her muscle tone over long periods of inactivity. She was fed intravenously once a day.

She did not dream.

Since Alfred showed no interest in attending his parents' funeral, Amber and Jane caught a ride to the church with a neighbor, Trudy Gaskell, who, although she was not a Catholic, and had had only a nodding acquaintance with Joseph and Paula, never missed a funeral or a wedding.

Joseph and Paula shared a plot of earth in the center of the churchyard, beneath a nine-foot granite angel that towered above the plain crosses of weathered wood and crumbling cement that marked the old indian graves on the right side of the cemetery. The grass was uncut and in the fields around milkweed, red clover, and purple vervain bloomed.

The ceremony was performed. An electric winch lowered the two coffins into the ground. Trudy wept. Amber and Jane returned home.

Alfred was gone. He stayed gone two days, missing a day of work, and when he returned the right side of his face was badly bruised. He refused to tell anyone where he had been.

It was not yet noon. Jane had called in sick and Amber had decided they should spend the day in the woods. They sat together on a spongy birch log, their bare feet resting on the soft moss of the glade. Sunlight filtering through the branches above flecked their faces.

He looks so frail, Jane thought. *Like a child. A beautiful awkward child.*

"What're you going to do now that Grandfather's gone?" she asked aloud.

Amber thought a moment, finally shrugged. "I don't know." He picked up a twig and used its pointed tip to scratch a clumsy oval into the sticky red surface of a mushroom growing from the moss by his feet. "Do you think he's in Heaven?" he asked.

"Like they said at the funeral?"

"Yes."

"If there really is a Heaven—"

"There is." The certainty in his voice!

"Maybe. He tried to be a good man."

"I asked if he was there Friday."

"At the Question Session?" Though Jane herself had little faith in the answers received in Question Session, she knew Amber believed that God answered the questions he asked there.

"Yes."

"What did you receive?"

"A picture of his face. His eyes were closed."

"Like he was asleep?"

"Yes."

"Did he look happy?"

"I don't know. Maybe. I only saw him a second. Then I fell asleep."

The silence went on and on, broken only by the sound of the wind. Then, "You're not looking for work any more, are you?" Jane asked.

"No. Nobody needs me for anything."

"Maybe somebody'll buy the paper," Jane offered.

Amber thought a moment, shook his head slowly. "Grandfather didn't really need me either."

"I need you," Jane said. "You're the only brother I've got."

"Not your real brother."

"Real enough for me to love you."

"Yes, but—" He thrust his little stick into the mushroom and twisted it. The mushroom disintegrated into sticky fragments. "I've got to go to a welfare ghetto."

"Don't go. Stay here with me."

"Father's going to kick me out. I can't pay rent."

"How long can you stay?"

"Three weeks."

"Can you stay with someone else? Maybe someone from the Fellowship?"

"No. Brother Percival said he asked everybody."

"The Fellowship's got a center in Detroit. If you have to go somewhere, maybe you can go there."

Amber nodded, said nothing.

"I'll go there with you," Jane said. "I've got some money I saved up for, for medical reasons. In case I got sick. We can live on it for a while."

The office of Abraham Random, senior partner of Random, Isley, Murphy, Stonehut and Seaman, was large and square and paneled in oak, though most of the paneling was hidden behind bookshelves overflowing with old lawbooks. The chairs in which the Mallorys sat were upholstered in what appeared to be cracked brown cowhide. Mr. Random himself wore glasses and looked like a survivor from the Nineteenth Century. Everything in the office suggested age, venerability—and to Alfred, affectation.

"Joseph Mallory predeceased his wife by about an hour and a half," the lawyer told them. "His will can be disposed of quite simply, as he left everything he owned to his wife, Paula Nelson Mallory. It's her will that we're concerned with today. With your permission I'd like to read it to you. You can ask me questions later if you'd like.

"I, Paula Nelson Mallory, being of sound mind and body, do hereby will and bequeath my—"

"Excuse me, sir," Amber said.

The lawyer looked up from the will, obviously annoyed at having been interrupted. "Yes?" he asked testily.

"I'm not very bright," Amber said. "I don't understand words like bequeath. Could you tell me what it says in simple words?"

"I think I'd like that too," Jane said.

"It's already very simple, but—Well. Your grandmother has left you and your sister each five hundred thousand New Dollars, the remainder of her liquid assets—that's money, stocks, bonds, things like that—to go to the Fellowship of Prismatic Light. Her real property—her house and its contents, the two cars, and the grounds and physical plant of *The Islander*—she left to you, Mr. Mallory."

"Just the goddamn paper?" Alfred demanded.

"Plus the house and its contents. Quite a valuable house, from what I understand."

"Of course. The house and its contents. What if my mother really died first?"

"Then, Mr. Mallory, your adopted son and your daughter would each receive five hundred thousand New Dollars, to be given them on their twenty-fifth birthdays, and the rest of the estate would go to the Catholic Church. There's no provision for you at all in your father's will, I'm afraid."

"We don't get the money until we're twenty-five?" Amber asked.

"No. That would have been the case only if your grandmother had predeceased your grandfather."

"I don't understand."

"He means we get the money right away," Jane said.

As they were driving back Alfred said, "I want you out at the end of the month. Both of you."

He glared at Jane. She stared back, suppressing a smile. Happy with the knowledge that neither she nor Amber would ever have to be afraid of him again.

CHAPTER TEN

"STATE YOUR QUESTION," Brother Ashoka said.

"What will happen to me if I transfer?" Amber asked.

"Trans. . . ." Brother Ashoka's voice echoed. The voice faded, was gone. Amber opened his eyes.

He was alone. The Latihan dome was gone, replaced by a hall of mirrors. In each mirror Amber saw himself reflected as he knew himself to be: diminutive, his undistinguished face resting on narrow shoulders, his stance somehow awkward, his ill-fitting clothes betraying his clumsiness with the alterator. He felt trapped, imprisoned by the images in the mirrors.

He felt suddenly dizzy, nauseated. The hall of mirrors was swaying, shifting, whirling around him. And he was free. Suddenly free, no longer imprisoned by the mirrors. In total control of himself and everything around him.

And because he wanted them to, the images in the mirrors were changing. Now his face was framed by shifting configurations of yellow and black feathers. Now he was bald, his massive green-skinned head resting on broad shoulders as white as ivory. Now his slim body and narrow triangular face were crimson; his eyes were yellow and his long hair was glossy black, as black as the ends of the slender palps that ringed his tiny mouth. Now he moved slowly on jointed legs across the bottom of a sea of molten metal. Now he was tall, tall and strong, his four black arms outstretched to the four corners of the world as he swayed on his stalk to the slow rhythm of the phases of the third moon. . . .

Joy, building, resonating, increasing with every transformation he willed himself to experience . . .

Until he found himself back in the Latihan dome, shrunken small and awkward again, yet still free of the mirrors in his mind.

"Are you satisfied with the answer you received?" Brother Ashoka asked him.

"Yes," Amber said, still overwhelmed. "Oh, yes. . . ."

Brother Ashoka frowned.

"You're both determined to transfer?" Brother Ashoka asked. They were standing by the rail on the ferry back to Drummond Island. Though Brother Ashoka was not a Drummonder he had gotten into the habit of giving Amber and Jane a ride home after Latihan.

"Yes," Jane said.

"And you, Amber?"

"Yes."

"I know quite a bit about transfer and translation. I've been interested in it for some time, even studied up on it a bit. And when you asked your question tonight, Amber, everything I knew about it came together in my head. And I thought of some things that I think you should think about before you make a decision to go.

"The first thing is that if you transfer you'll find yourself housed in a new brain."

"I want a new brain," Amber said.

"I know. But your new brain will never have been exposed to the Inductor. And it's the physical change the Inductor makes in your brain that gives you the ability to do the Latihan. And *that* physical change won't translate when you transfer. It's not part of your genetic matrix."

"What you're trying to say is that we won't be able to do the Latihan after we transfer," Jane said.

"I don't know for certain but that's what I think. Perhaps the memory of having done the Latihan which you'd take with you would be enough. I can't say for certain that it wouldn't be. But.

"Your new brains wouldn't even be human brains. Not really, not even on Alter. There'd be differences, and maybe those differences would make it impossible for you to do the Latihan."

"So you're saying we'll have to give up the Latihan if we transfer," Jane said. "You're just giving more reasons."

She's acting different, Amber thought. *Like she was arguing. She never used to argue with anyone.*

"I'm saying you're going to be taking the risk of never being able to do the Latihan again and I think it's a pretty big risk. You've got to ask yourself, is it worth the risk?"

"And you don't think it is?"

"I don't know."

"Has anybody in the Fellowship ever been translated?"

"Not that I know of."

"So you don't *know* we won't be able to do the Latihan. It might even be easier or better somehow. We won't lose any of our other mental abilities, so why should we lose the ability to do the Latihan?"

"If you think of the Latihan as, well, as an ability that comes from a certain kind of brain damage—"

"Would you deny Amber the mind and body he was cheated out of on a possibility?" Jane asked.

She's arguing because she wants to help me, Amber realized. Aloud he said, "Please don't argue. I'll be all right."

"But how will you feel if you find out after transfer that you can't do the Latihan anymore?" Brother Ashoka asked him.

Amber thought a moment, started to say something, thought some more. "I'll trust God," he said finally. "He won't abandon me unless I do something wrong."

"But the Latihan isn't like any other way of opening yourself to God," Brother Ashoka said. "And if you lose that—"

"I'll trust God," Amber said again and once again Jane heard that utter certainty in his voice.

"I hope you're right," Brother Ashoka said. "And I guess the rest of us will learn from you whether or not the ability to experience the Latihan does translate."

He looked out at the dark water. "We can move your things to my house this weekend," he added.

Though the primary work of the Espanore Island Dimensional Transfer Institute—dimensional transfer—took place, predictably enough, on Espanore Island, persons wishing to apply for transfer had to do so at the Institute's administrative center outside the Soo.

Amber and Jane's preliminary interview was set for three o'clock on a Wednesday afternoon. They ate breakfast with Brother Ashoka, then took a morning plane from Drummond to the Soo and a bus from the airport out to the Center.

The land which the Institute had acquired for the Center had originally been laid out as an eighteen-hole golf course. Offices, laboratories, and accommodations for the people being evaluated and trained there had spread out around the area once graced by the clubhouse. A twisting path led from the built-up area through more than two dozen holographic recreations of other-dimensional landscapes. The grounds were open to the public and had, in fact, become Sault St. Marie's primary tourist attraction.

"What if they don't want us?" Amber asked. Angular chocolate clouds whirled through the pink sky overhead; on either side of the white pebble path blue growths like broomsticks sporting clusters of jutting, right-angle fishhooks blocked the view. Small, birdlike creatures, their wings mere blurs, darted around in the geometric tangle.

"They've got to take us," Jane said, trying to sound more confident that she felt. A cluster of fishhooks to her right writhed suddenly and snared an unwary pseudobird.

"I don't like this world," Amber said. "What time is it?"

"A little after two thirty," Jane said, looking at her watch. "Let's go back."

A few yards back along the path and the sky overhead was suddenly cloud-flecked blue. The barbed growths were gone, replaced by more conventional plants: trees and shrubs and beds of flowers. In the distance the administrative center was visible.

"We better hurry," Amber said, quickening his pace. Jane had no trouble keeping up with him: even at his fastest he walked slowly and she usually had to make a conscious effort not to outdistance him.

By the time they reached the building where their interviews were scheduled to take place Amber was panting. A flight of gray granite steps led up to the front door. He paused a moment on the first step, then struggled up the rest of them. Jane held the heavy glass door open for him. Once within the waiting room he collapsed thankfully into an overstuffed chair while Jane gave their names to the receptionist.

There was a painting on the wall behind the receptionist's desk, a swirling confusion of brilliant purples and pinks that disturbed Amber.

Is that one of the other dimensions? he wondered, trying to imagine what it would be like to live in a world where everything looked like it did in the picture.

"Mr. Adamaski will see you," the receptionist announced, ushering them into the next room.

"Hello. I'm Curtis Adamaski," the man behind the desk announced, rising and offering them his hand. "Please sit down." He was tall, slim, gray-haired; he would have looked distinguished but for his bulging eyes.

"Now." He sounded brisk, efficient. "I've studied your applications and I think I've got a fairly good idea why the two of you would like to transfer. But I'd appreciate it if you could tell me yourselves, in your own words. Before you start, though, let me warn you that everything you say will be weighed and evaluated by our computers: this conversation is an integral part of our testing procedures. Mr. Mallory?"

"Amber's mother—" Jane began but Adamaski held up his hand and said, "Excuse me, but we'd prefer it if Mr. Mallory told his own story."

Amber remained silent a moment, collecting his thoughts, then said, "I don't have the—I'm not like I should be." He paused a moment, looking at Adamaski, then continued. "My mother didn't give me the right kinds of food when I was a baby so I got kwashiorkor and beriberi and—Do you know what kwashiorkor is?" he asked, suddenly anxious.

"I read up on it while processing your application."

"I had kwashiorkor and all the vitamin diseases. That's why I'm so small and clumsy and not very smart. But my real father and mother were very smart. And they were strong and healthy. My father transferred when I was a baby."

"To Diamond," the interviewer said. "I looked up his test results. They were quite impressive."

Encouraged, Amber continued, "I wouldn't be stupid and clumsy if my mother'd fed me the right foods when I was a baby. I want a new body and a new brain so I can be smart and healthy. That's all.''

"What about the Fellowship of Prismatic Light?" Adamaski asked.

"We're members," Jane said quickly. "We said so in our applications."

"I know that. What I don't know is, how do you see yourselves? Do you want to be missionaries spreading your faith to new worlds?"

"Us?" Jane asked.

"It's not like that," Amber said. "We just do the Latihan."

"If somebody asked us, we'd tell them about the Latihan," Jane said. "We wouldn't try to hide the fact we did it or anything. But we're not out to convert people. Is that what you're worried about?"

"It's what we need to know, yes. There are some colonies, of course, where missionaries of any and all sorts are welcome, but most of our secular colonies want no evangelists or prophets and almost none of the religious colonies want immigrants who aren't ready to embrace their faith."

"It's all right that we do the Latihan?" Amber asked.

"As far as I know. You may not be able to do it in some of the parallel worlds, though. The brain structures may not be similar enough."

"We've already been warned about that," Jane said. "Amber?"

He thought a moment. "We'll have to trust God," he said finally.

Adamaski scribbled a note on a piece of paper. "And why do you want to transfer, Ms. Mallory?" he asked Jane.

"There's no place for us here," she said. "Nothing to do with our lives. We've got money now but it can't do anything to help Amber with his real problems. I want him to be happy and I want to be there with him sharing his happiness."

"I see. Forgive me for asking you this if you find it embarrassing, but are you lovers?"

"Of course not," Amber said immediately. "She's my sister!"

"We're cousins, really," Jane said. "But I think of him as my brother and he thinks of me as his sister."

"All right. But now, can you tell me what you want for yourself from transfer, Ms. Mallory? *Other* than to make your cousin happy?"

"A chance to start over again. Where things'll be different."

"If you're accepted you'll probably get that chance. Now, what can the two of you contribute to a colony?"

"We don't have many skills but we can work hard," Jane said.

"When I get a new body I'll be smarter and stronger," Amber said. "I'll be able to learn to do all kinds of things."

"What if you don't get any smarter?" Adamaski asked.

"What?" Amber asked.

"What if you transfer and then find out that you aren't any smarter or stronger than you were here?"

"I—I wouldn't have a new brain?"

"Yes. But we still don't know all that much about the relationship between the mind and the brain. Perhaps your new brain wouldn't make any difference.

"And I'd like you to think about this. If you stay here you've got the money to live comfortably the rest of your life. You've got friends, holovision, recorded music, and the Fellowship of Prismatic Light. You've got your religious exercise, the Latihan, and it gives you a great deal of satisfaction. Now think: how would you feel if you discovered you'd traded all the advantages you have here for a lifetime of back-breaking labor under primitive conditions without getting any smarter?"

"But he'd be stronger, wouldn't he?" Jane asked. "Physically healthy?"

"He should be."

"We don't want to go to a place like Alter, where it's really civilized already," Jane said. "We want to go to a pioneer world, someplace where everything's simpler and what counts is how hard we work, not how sophisticated we are."

"Even if I don't get smart, I can work hard," Amber said. "We want to go someplace where they'll want us if we work hard."

"What kind of society did you have in mind?" Adamaski asked Jane.

"Someplace where we can be together, not like on Diamond. And someplace where it doesn't really matter too much if we're smart and educated. Simple, not a lot of big cities or complicated ways of doing things—''

''A pioneer world, as you said a while back.''

''Yes.''

''But what *kind* of pioneer world? We've got religious dictatorships, participatory democracies, anarchies, aristocracies, kingdoms, all sorts of socialisms and communisms—We've got examples of almost every kind of society man has every attempted to devise and most of them are still early in the process of getting themselves established: pioneer worlds. So what, specifically, are you looking for?''

''Someplace where people are close to each other and it's sort of free. Where nobody can tell you to do something just because *he* wants you to do it and it doesn't matter whether you want to or not.''

''No specific form of government, then?''

''No.''

''Someplace where there aren't too many people,'' Amber said. ''Where it's not too complicated yet.''

''All right,'' Adamaski said. ''I don't have any more questions for you today.''

''Do you want us?'' Amber asked.

Adamaski glanced down at the television screen set into his desk. ''Well, you're past the first barrier. The Institute'll accept you for testing. Though to be frank, we probably wouldn't have accepted you if we didn't have hopes of learning something if you transfer.''

''What happens next?'' Jane asked.

''Well, we'll assign you rooms in one of the dormitories. The tests'll take about two weeks. Less if you fail them completely in some way or another early in the process. Then, if you've shown yourselves able to adapt to a new existence as part of a new society and ecological matrix we'll match you with colonies where you'd be able to fit in.''

''And then we decide which one we want to go to?'' Jane asked.

''No. Then *they* decide if they want *you*. If more than one colony's willing to accept you you get to choose between them. And you can always choose not to transfer if you don't like any of the colonies that are willing to accept you. But in any case your testing fee's nonrefundable.''

"What if no one wants me?" Amber said.

"*Then* we'll refund your fee. But that doesn't happen very often. And there are quite a few colonies that've told us what they want in the way of new colonists and now leave the actual selection up to us. If we match you with one of them you'll be accepted automatically. And of course there's Diamond—"

"No."

"We don't want to go there," Jane said. "We want to go somewhere where we can be together."

"Are you going to tell them that I might stay—"

"That you might not get any smarter?"

"Yes."

"Of course. We're not in the business of fooling anybody. And there are a lot of alternates where anyone willing to work hard who can adjust to the world and society is welcome, even if he's not all that smart. There's an awful lot of physical labor to building a society from scratch."

CHAPTER ELEVEN

THE PHYSICAL examinations came first. Over almost immediately were the tests which proved neither of them had any serious allergies to the drugs used in translation; over a few hours later were the tests proving them neither too frail or debilitated by disease to survive the rigors of the translation process.

A battery of computers studied tissue samples each of them had painlessly, if nonetheless somewhat reluctantly, contributed. Relevant genes were mapped; their chromosomes' abilities to repair themselves when damaged were determined; the extranuclear material of their cells was examined for wild genes which might make them cancer-prone (cancer-prone subjects had a tendency to die during translation). But both Amber and Jane had clean gene charts.

After lunch the intelligence tests began. They took four days.

"What we'll call your IQ (thought it's not exactly what standard psychology means when it talks of IQ) is too low for any world that demands rapid adaptation for survival," Amber was told by a balding psychologist. "Take Thorntree, for example. A bluebarb bush would skewer you before you could master the maneuvers necessary to steal pseudopollen."

"But I'd be smarter," Amber protested, though he had no desire to transfer to any world like Thorntree.

"Probably. Not positively. And it would undoubtedly take you some time to learn to utilize your new brain capacity, longer probably than it'll take you to master your new body—and even on Alter new colonists start out as clumsy as babies. Clumsier, even, because most babies don't have wrong habits to unlearn. So put you

on a world like Thorntree, where you'd not only have to learn to use
a new body but you'd have to learn a whole new way of thinking and
learn it immediately if you wanted to survive and, well— You
wouldn't have a chance.''

"I don't want to go there anyway."

"It's just as well."

"Are there—How many are left? For me?"

"Worlds? Scores. You don't have anything to worry about."

"How many is a score?"

"Twenty."

"And some of them will want me?"

"That I don't know."

During the next phase of testing, computers posed them questions
while a multitude of sophisticated measuring devices analyzed their
reactions. As the questions grew more specific, more pointed,
Amber found himself feeling increasingly embarrassed and often
ashamed, but soon the computers had passed beyond the point
where he could figure out what it was they were trying to discover
and he regained his composure: it made you feel much more naked
to be asked about your reactions to naked women than it did to be
asked which of two angles felt more comfortable or what color you
associated with danger.

Then came holographic simulations of real-life situations. A drug
related to Newemph made them identify completely with the
simulated situations in which they were placed, while leaving them
free to determine their own courses of action within the framework
of the illusions; and this was coupled with computers capable of
keeping the simulated situations consonant with any responses they
might make.

A cliff crumpled beneath Amber's feet and he fell to his death.

Jane pronounced sentence on the man who had murdered her
daughter. She gave him life imprisonment instead of death.

Amber broke the shovel he was using on a stone. He was fined
three days extra labor for his negligence.

A great hairy spider crawled up Jane's leg. She stood frozen,
unable to move, afraid that the slightest twitch or tremor would
cause it to sink its fangs into her.

Amber was a member of the jury presiding at Jane's wedding ceremony. The other eleven members voted to deny her the right to wed.

The Prophet Elias announced to his flock that henceforth all the work of the colony would be done by the women, while the men passed their days in serving him and in the singing of hymns.

The crowd jeered at Amber, crying "Dwarf!" and "Idiot!" at him.

Somebody called her a dirty name and the next thing Jane knew she'd picked up a kitchen knife and stabbed him. She stared at the knife in her hands.

As the days passed the situations grew stranger:

A cliff crumpled beneath Amber's feet but he spread his great wings and soared off unharmed.

Jane cast her vote in the case of a colonist accused of hatching his wife's egg prematurely.

The crowd laughed at Amber's small hairy body. "Six-legs," they called him. "Mosquito monkey! Bloodsucker!"

A great hairy spider crawled up Jane's leg, enticed by the dew she was secreting from her underarm pouches. She ate its body but saved one of its eyeclusters to replace one of her own failing eyes.

Amber watched as the two hermaphrodites impregnated each other in an attempt to give birth to a shovel to replace the one he had ruined.

Jane killed Amber and planted him, then stood guard over the grave so that no one could dig him up before he sprouted.

"Of the thirty-eight worlds in which both of you would have a fair chance of physical survival, twenty-seven have some important feature or features which would make it psychologically impossible for the two of you to ever be happy there."

"Like what?" Jane asked.

Vittoria Johnson flicked a switch, consulted her desk screen. "Well, Diamond's the obvious example. Your survival there would be assured—nobody we've sent there's died yet and we *think* the sentient crystals there are immortal or the next thing to it—but though you'd be aware of each other you'd never be able to communicate. You'd live completely solitary existences."

"We want to be together." Amber said.

"And that's why Diamond wouldn't be suitable for you. And then, look at Rossini. The world is idyllic but the colonists resemble giant fourteen-legged spiders. That wouldn't bother you too badly after the first few weeks, Mr. Mallory, but you, Ms. Mallory, have too deep-seated an aversion to spiders to ever be happy as one."

Jane nodded, memories of spiders she had thought to be real still far too vivid for comfort. "What about the worlds we could adjust to?" she asked.

"Unfortunately, there are only four possibilities open to you: the other colonies have given us preliminary specifications for new immigrants which exclude you."

"Four's OK," Amber said.

"Wait," Jane said. "Which four? And what're they like?"

"Chaos, Deirdre, Oneness, and Veldte's Paradise."

"Veldte's Paradise?" Jane asked. "Can you tell us about that one first?"

"Of course." The counselor pressed some buttons on her desk and a landscape replaced the wall behind her. A wide beach of shiny black sand fronted a purple sea; on the low hills beyond the beach a village of rounded front huts sheltered under huge white-leaved trees. The sky was a shimmering pewter grey.

"This is Veldte's Paradise. It's one of our most popular worlds and they've left selection completely up to us, so if you decide you want to go there you can."

Amber smiled at Jane. She smiled back at him.

"There are no continents. The colonists live on innumerable tiny islands in the midst of a planet-wide freshwater sea. Life is paradisical: fruit, pseudomolluscs and edible seaweeds abound and in the seventeen years since the colony was founded no colonist has taken sick or died of old age, though a few have drowned. There are no dangerous land or sea animals; the air and water are always warm, though never excessively so, and though there are occasional storms they are never of any great severity. The colonists, in fact, look forward to them and celebrate them with feasts. All in all, a gentle pleasant world."

"Is that why you call it a paradise?" Jane asked.

"In a way. The first explorer to investigate it was a man called

Veldte and he refused to return. He told the people we sent in to find out what happened to him that there was no way we would be able to convince him to come back. So we named it Veldte's Paradise. And as far as we know Veldte's still there.''

Her hands flicked another button. The landscape winked out and was replaced by two glittering red-scaled figures, sinuous and reptilian but man-erect, with heavy bone ridges around large eyes, no visible ears and slightly protruding snouts.

"The colonists are not truly amphibious but they are perfectly at home in the water. Like seals, perhaps, or sea otters. Note the webbed hands and feet and the deep chests: they can stay under water for the equivalent of twenty minutes at a time.''

"The equivalent of twenty minutes at a time?'' Jane asked.

"Time rates differ in different dimensions. That's what makes them different dimensions. Living in two dimensions simultaneously, our explorers are able to determine equivalencies. But, to return to my lecture, the colonists on Veldte's Paradise frequently travel between islands in boats they carve from the soft wood of the giant trees. Islands are very close together, close enough so that it's rare that a colonist on the shore of one island can't see at least one other island in any direction he or she chooses to look. The average colonist rarely spends much time on any one island before wandering on to another.

"Life is easy and they spend most of their time either swimming and spear-fishing or engaging in sex and conversation. The figure on the right's male''—she pointed—"you can see the slightly larger ridges around the eyes and the heavier tail. The other figure's female. None of the other sexual differences are readily apparent except when a Paradisian's actually engaged in the sexual act.''

Sex with something that looks like that? Jane thought. But the red-scaled figures had their own alien beauty.

"The Paradisians have no written literature,'' the counselor continued, "but their memories are eidetic and they've revived the art of oral storytelling. And they spend much of their time in philosophical speculation and debate. Sex, however, occupies most of their attention.

"Though the Paradisian body is so constructed that reproduction occurs only rarely (we know of only thirty-some infants born in the seventeen years the colony has been in existence), it nevertheless has a much wider range of sexual responses and the Paradisian colonist finds him or herself with a much greater urge towards sexual expression than he or she had as a human being. Paradisian society is already far more sexually oriented than any human society on record has ever been and it is rapidly developing a highly stylized sexual etiquette, almost a language, that has no human parallel.''

''But what do they *do?*'' Amber asked. Jane wondered how much of what the counselor'd said he'd understood.

''Do? Not much in the conventional sense. They don't erect skyscrapers, build roads, dam rivers, fly planes. They talk and play and enjoy each others' company. Remember, life is so easy for them that no one need work to provide himself with food or shelter and sexuality has become a way of life, not something sublimated into the urge to accomplish or dominate. There is no property to protect and no government or police force. A boat or frond hut can be constructed in a few hours, a fishing spear in a few minutes. Why should they try to alter their natural environment? It's already perfect for their needs.''

''It doesn't sound right,'' Amber said. ''Not for us.''

''Everyone there seems quite happy with it,'' Vittoria Johnson told him. ''The two of you would need a little conditioning—or deconditioning, if that sounds less threatening—to overcome some of the sexual prejudices and inhibitions you're carrying around with you, but once you've overcome them you'd adjust very well to the Paradisian style of life. Your psychological profiles make that very clear.''

''I don't want to be conditioned,'' Amber said.

''We would do nothing to interfere with your free will or basic personality structure,'' the counselor said. ''We'd just open up a few options for you that your upbringing has sealed off.''

''What about the other worlds?'' Jane asked.

''Well, the first one's Chaos. It's a personal favorite of mine; I've put in an application for transfer there when my retirement takes effect.

''Chaos isn't actually a world at all, at least not like the Earth. It's not a planet. What it is is, well, a multitude of tiny environments, sort of like bubbles, each of which can accommodate between three and nine colonists. We call them bubble worlds. And the actual physical characteristics of each bubble world are determined by the desires and needs of the people inside it.

"For example, let's say that everybody in one bubble world wanted to live outdoors. Then the environment would be such that they would seem to be living outdoors. Or say they all wanted to live inside a big house. Then the bubble world would turn into the inside of a big house. And if everybody inside that particular bubble world wanted things painted black and white, with locked doors between all the rooms and lots of staircases and no bright lights, well, that's the way things would be. But if somebody wanted his or her room bright red, then that's how it would be—with maybe a very long staircase separating it from the black and white rooms. That's a very oversimplified example, of course: if there was any sort of major conflict—if, say, half the people wanted to live in bright red rooms where they could always hear loud orchestral music while the other half wanted to live in dull green waters where it was absolutely silent—then their combined needs and desires would manifest themselves in some more complex fashion. Maybe a seashore, with red sand and loud music out of the water and everything green and silent under the surface. Or maybe everything would turn yellow and there'd be earphones people could put on if they wanted to listen to music. Or maybe half the people would have ears and the other half wouldn't but everybody'd be able to fly. And so on."

"It sounds—I don't know," Jane said. "Do you get to choose who you're with?"

"No. Not that it would make any difference if you did: the bubble worlds are *always* merging and dividing again. Sometimes every few minutes.

"When two normal bubble worlds merge they form a new bubble world for a while, a much bigger one with twice as many people in it to determine its characteristics. But pretty soon the big bubble world divides back into two normal bubble worlds. And when it divides some of the people from each of the two previous bubble worlds go into each of the new bubble worlds. So you're constantly finding yourself in new worlds with characteristics determined by new sets of people."

"And what decides who ends up in which world?" Jane asked.

"Where you are at the moment the big world divides. If you and Amber stayed together you'd probably end up in the same world. And even if you lost each other you'd be bound to find each other again."

"It sounds frightening," Jane said.

"Things there are always highly unstable, to be sure. That's why it's called Chaos. And a lot of people would find it terrifying. You yourself, Ms. Mallory, could adjust to it, though it would take quite a bit of effort on your part at first. The reason, we suggest it is that there's a chance that it would be the ideal environment for Mr. Mallory to learn to use his new capabilities."

"But Amber and I might be separated?"

"For a while, if you weren't careful."

"No," Amber said.

"What about the third world?" Jane asked. "Deirdre."

The counselor touched the console on her desk and another landscape appeared behind her. The colors were bright, almost electric: a thick tangled jungle of red-leaved plants, brown vines, grey-trunked trees, silver flowers, all beneath a lemon yellow sky. A sun blazed in the heavens, huge, fiercely white.

"This is Deirdre," the counselor said. "It's a newly colonized world and our colony there is small, only one settlement and not much more than a hundred people. The entire world is jungle, as far as we've been able to determine, and the colonists have to engage in a constant struggle to keep the jungle from reclaiming their settlement. We don't know if there are any seasons there; in the two years (our time, the rate's a bit faster there) since the colony was founded conditions have stayed pretty nearly constant, but of course it's still too early to tell anything for sure.

"Though some of the insects are dangerous—very dangerous, so that the colonists have to stay in their huts at night to avoid them— none of the other animals yet discovered seems to be any sort of threat and no colonist has yet caught any sort of disease. But though the jungle produces far more edible fruits, seeds, and the like than an equivalent Terrestrial jungle would, all the colonists' attempts at cultivating edible plants and domesticating the native animals have been complete failures. But wild food is plentiful and they've been able to make some technological progress in other areas. The production of metal implements, for example.

"But one can only support a limited population on a hunting and gathering economy, even if food is as plentiful as it is on Deirdre. And that population has to devote most of its time to the basics of survival. So the colony will never be able to make any real progress toward a more civilized mode of life until they learn to domesticate the native plants and animals—which may, for all we know, be impossible for some reason. So the future development of the colony's still very uncertain, and that in turn has meant that it hasn't achieved any great popularity. But it sounds as if it might be right for the two of you, if you can live with the idea of having to spend every night locked up inside where you'll be safe from the insects."

"They're not like spiders?" Jane asked.

"Not overly. And Deirdre's beautiful too, in a rather strident way. And the Deirdrans themselves are rather handsome. Here, let me show you. . . ." She played around with the desk console; the junglescape winked out and a pair of tall green figures looking as though they were wearing purple gauntlets and boots took its place.

On second glance the figures were less human than they seemed at first. They were completely hairless and what had appeared to be gauntlets and boots were actually smooth coverings of tiny purple scales. The eyes were lidless, yellow, with black pupils. The nose was large and wrinkled, with three nostrils. The lips were thin and bluish, the teeth a darker blue. The ears were large, rounded and set close to the head. Though both figures were about the same size, one had the external genitalia of a male and the other had small, squarish breasts.

"After hearing about life on Veldte's Paradise, you may be curious about the Deirdran's sex life. Well, Deirdrans don't *have* any sex life. They seem to be well enough equipped for reproduction and their secondary sexual characteristics are surprisingly analogous to ours, but something's missing. Perhaps there's a mating season in the offing, perhaps something else is needed, but whatever the case, the colonists there have found themselves completely sexless for all practical purposes since transfer. That's another reason the colony's not too popular.

"As for the society they've set up, it's one of our standard models. It's based on a system of labor credits, with everyone required to earn the same number of labor credits in a given ten-day period. Once every ten days all the colonists get together and rank the tasks that need to be done in order of preference. The more undesirable the task, the more credit you get for doing it. And so forth."

"Will they take us?" Amber asked.

"Quite possibly. They need people who, like yourselves, are willing to work hard for very few creature comforts. So far they haven't been able to find the people they need just to do the work the colony needs done to survive on a day-to-day basis, much less enough workers to free the people they need to work full time on basic reasearch. So I think you'd be quite welcome there."

"We'll apply," Amber said.

"And on Veldte's Paradise," Jane said. "It couldn't help but be better than here. Even if we do have to be conditioned for it. But you said there was another place—"

"Yes. Oneness. The colonists call themselves 'only people'— *not* 'The Only People', but just 'only people' to signify that they aren't any better than anybody else—at least as far as their *innate* worth is concerned. They called their world Oneness to express their commitment to the idea of perfect community, rather than to express any transcendental or mystical concept. As a matter of fact, they repudiate all revealed religions. Their world. . . ."

It was harsh, dark, cold-looking: the sun a pinpoint of intolerable white; beneath, plains choked with tangles of brittle-dry black spikes; in the distance, jagged blue mountains rising. A world all forbidding grandeur, without gentleness or comfort.

"The emphasis in their society is on the perfectibility of man as a member of their society—and on the totally corrupt state of all men and women in present-day Terran societies. No matter what skills or talents an immigrant may have had on Earth, he or she starts at the bottom of their social hierarchy, doing the chores that carry with them the lowest status—which are not, incidentally, always the most menial tasks. After a set period—about three months, as near as we can estimate the equivalency—the newcomer has a chance to begin working his way up the ladder of their society, primarily through participation in the communal encounter sessions—especially what they call their war games during which the members attack the imperfections they perceive in each other's behavior in a verbal and emotional battle. There is no status or ranking during the war games; anyone can attack anyone else and anybody may find him or herself attacked. . . ."

Jane had decided against Oneness even before Vittoria Johnson showed her what the colonists there looked like: tall, gauntly white, with moist, glistening skins, dark solemn eyes, and features as jagged and forbidding as their landscape.

"Despite some of the more negative-sounding things I've just been telling you about life on Oneness, you'd do well to consider life there. Though their chosen way of life places little emphasis on comfort, and though they've chosen to make the transition from life in our society to theirs very hard—to make it an ordeal—they've nonetheless managed to build a society in which self-knowledge, openness, honesty, trust and understanding pervade every aspect of life. A society in which the members are genuinely close to and intimately involved with each other. And that is something that many people would gladly undergo any sort of ordeal to attain."

No, Jane thought. *Deirdre or Veldte's Paradise.*

"One thing that you in particular should think about, Mr. Mallory, is the fact that since everyone on Oneness starts at the bottom, your lack of skills and advanced training wouldn't put you at any sort of disadvantage at fitting into their society. You'd have a chance to learn to use your new strength and—hopefully—your new intelligence before taking any sort of permanent place in the society. Think about it."

"Yes," Amber said.

CHAPTER TWELVE

MANUEL CANDAMO and Delia Slater, the two Deirdre Communicators lay floating in the clear oily fluid of their life-support systems. Brown plastic respirators hid their faces; shiny metal crustaceans inched their ways up and down the limp bodies, massaging them, taking samples of their blood, injecting them with things.

"Will we look like that?" Amber asked.

"After transfer, you mean?" Vittoria Johnson asked.

Amber nodded.

"No. Neither of you has the abilities needed to be a Communicator or an Explorer. And unless you've got those abilities—unless you can maintain two mutually incompatible models of reality on the cellular level and maintain them simultaneously—your body here will die when you transfer."

"Why?"

"Your new set of reality perceptions contaminates your old perceptual system. This is on the cellular level, remember, and what that means is that your cells lose the ability to maintain themselves and reproduce. The result is sort of like an instant total cancer."

"Grandmother died of cancer," Amber said.

"I know. But she didn't transmit the susceptibility to either of you."

"Does it hurt?"

"No. It happens very quickly and we give you drugs to block what little pain is involved.

"You see, the whole process goes somewhat like this. You

transfer and your consciousness creates itself a new physical body consonant with its new modes of perception. But the shock's too much and you snap back to your old body in its old familiar perceptual matrix. Only your old body's cells have already run amuck, and when it dies *that* shock provides the impetus to complete your transfer.''

Amber nodded but Jane recognized the look on his face: he was confused but too embarrassed to ask any more questions. She would explain things to him later.

''Why doesn't the new body die when you snap back?'' she asked the counselor.

''We don't let it. We keep you from losing contact with it, just as we make sure that you do lose contact with your old body during the first part of the process.

''Unless the people involved are Communicators, of course. But in a way they're worse off than you are. After their training they need to maintain both reality models to maintain either: if a Communicator loses *either* body, he dies.''

A bank of lights came alive over Delia Slater's tank. ''He's made cross over,'' a technician said. ''He'll be conscious in a few minutes.''

They waited, watched the figure in the tank. The metal crustaceans slowed, stopped. Minutes passed. Amber felt dizzy with the waiting.

And then Delia Slater was getting to his feet, picking the crustaceans from his body, removing his respirator. He climbed from the tank, wrapped himself in a robe the technician provided.

''Hello, Delia,'' the counselor said. ''Are you feeling all right?''

''Hello, Vittoria. Fine,'' the Communicator said, wiping his face with a cloth the technician'd handed him. He studied Amber and Jane for a moment. ''You're the new applicants?'' he asked.

''Yes,'' Amber replied.

''Manuel'll be here soon. He's the Membership Manager. I'm Assistant Membership Manager, but only because I'm the only other member of the colony who can get back here to take a look at you and ask questions. But I've got some routine business with the computers to take care of first. So if you'll excuse me a few minutes—''

"Go ahead, Delia," the counselor told him. He left the room, his walk slightly unsteady.

"He has to get used to a whole new way of balancing whenever he transfers," Vittoria Johnson told them. "But give him another five minutes and he'll be walking perfectly."

"What's he doing?" Jane asked.

"Using the computers. He's got a photographic memory where numbers are concerned and the research staff on Deirdre just programs him to program the computers here."

They waited.

Lights began to flash over Manuel Candamo's tank. "Manuel's over," another technician said.

Within moments the second communicator was standing up and stripping off his respirator. He was a small man, very thin, with honey-dark skin and deep-set eyes. "It's much easier on Manuel that it is on Delia," Vittoria Johnson explained as the communicator finished wiping the oil from his skin and shrugged himself into a green robe.

"Much," the communicator agreed, seating himself in a chair facing the three of them. "Is Delia still busy with his computer?"

"I'm afraid so."

"Let me know when he's finished." To Amber and Jane he said, "We can't really start without him but while we're waiting I'll give you a little information. First of all, Delia and I have already transmitted your resumes back to the colony and the vote was to accept you. *But* that doesn't mean you're all the way accepted: both Delia and I have the power to veto that decision and reject you. And whether or not we choose to exercise our veto power will be dependent on how the two of you strike us today.

"On the other hand, there are a number of things you shouldn't be worrying about. One is your general qualifications: you seem quite acceptable, Jane, and we've decided to take a chance on your intelligence and physical strength, Amber. The real question that concerns us here today is, are the two of you going to be able to adjust to the kind of life we lead on Deirdre?"

"The tests show—" Vittoria Johnson began.

"They don't show *enough*, Vittoria. Remember Jack Ryerson? Your tests proved he was our ideal colonist. And he might have been a valuable addition to our little society *if* he hadn't decided to go for a walk the first night he could walk. Which of course meant that the insects got him. And *if* he'd bothered to seal the doorflap behind him to keep the insects from killing his roommate. Which, unfortunately, they did.''

''You don't know why—''

''No. And neither do you, despite your tests. But we lost two of our people when we shouldn't have lost any.''

''Right,'' Delia Slater said, entering. Jane noticed his walk was more confident than it had been when he'd left the room. ''Let's get started.''

''All right,'' Manuel Candamo said. ''Let's start with you, Jane. How do you feel about insects? Scared?''

''If they're dangerous.''

''They're worse than that. Deadly, all but one or two types.''

''Then I'm scared of them.''

''No special fears? Nothing that would make them worse than other things you're afraid of, that gives you nightmares about them, for example?''

''Not insects,'' Jane said. ''I'm afraid of spiders, but not so afraid that I can't stand to be in the same room with one or anything. And these insects aren't all that much like spiders, are they?''

''Not much. A little, some of them.''

''The resemblance isn't close enough to be a problem,'' Vittoria Johnson said.

''That's what your report says,'' Manuel Candamo said, ''but I'm asking Jane.''

''I've never been scared of bees or ants or anything like that,'' Jane said. ''And I've been stung a few times.'' She thought for a moment, then added, ''And I like fireflies.''

''All right. What about you, Amber?''

''I like fireflies too. And—I had a butterfly collection. For a while. I don't like bees but—I'm not really scared of them.''

''You will be,'' Delia Slater promised.

''Which is all for the best, as long as you remain rational about it,'' Manuel Candamo said. ''I think that's enough on the subject. Now—''

''You're never going to learn anything useful with questions like those," Vittoria Johnson said. "They're too superficial."

"No new facts," Candamo agreed. "But I'm not looking for facts. And you know it."

"Manuel used to work for Baja Continental Life," Delia Slater told Amber and Jane. "The insurance company that hates computers. He still thinks he's better than a computer."

"Different."

"No, better."

"More flexible, anyway. But, to continue with what we're here for—How do you feel about working? Amber?"

"We want to work hard."

"That's how we were raised," Jane added.

"Have you ever tried it, either of you? Real physical labor?"

"No," Jane admitted. "Just being a waitress."

"What about you, Amber?"

"No. My body—I can't do very hard work. Work that's hard for other people. But I want to do hard work. I want to have a good body so I can work hard."

Candamo studied him a moment, gave a little nod. "All right. Perhaps you'll get that chance on Deirdre. But you realize it'll be your only chance? Once you're there you're there for the rest of your life."

"Period," the other communicator said. "No friendly Institute of Dimensional Transfer to provide you with a way out for a trifling sum." He made a face at Vittoria Johnson, then turned back to them. "Some of us can be pretty hard to live with. Me for example. But Manuel's worse. And the rest of them—"

"Which brings me to my next point," Manuel Candamo said. "The Deirdre Colony's an attempt at a Utopian Society. And for it to survive as something any of us would like to be a part of, its members have to be willing to commit themselves to it, not to it just as a, what you could call a material-comfort machine that provides help when someone needs a hut built or food cooked, but—"

"Not just as an economic unit," Slater said.

"Right. The colony is not just an economic arrangement. It's a community. Which means a group of people who stick together, help each other and, above all, care for each other. A community of people who are willing to give and share, not just materially, but emotionally and spiritually as well.''

"That's what we want," Jane said and Amber nodded.

"But you've never seen any of the rest of us," Delia Slater said. "Can you make a total commitment—that's what it is—to a bunch of people you've never met?"

"What choice do we have?" Jane demanded.

"None," Slater admitted.

"Then that's what we want to do."

"What about you, Amber?" Manuel Candamo asked. "Do you understand what's involved?"

"It's like the Fellowship. Everybody tries to help everybody else.''

"I guess that's a fair enough description. Do either of you gamble?''

"Well—Just the Sweepstakes," Jane said.

"Both of you?"

"Yes."

"Good. Delia, time for your gambling lecture."

"If you come to Deirdre you're taking a big risk," the other communicator said, his voice absolutely serious. "A bigger risk than you'd be taking in most other colonies.

"Take a place like Alter. All you'd have to worry about is getting along with the other colonists. That's the lowest level of risk. Then take a place like Nacre, where you'd have to get used to life as a sort of overgrown clam. That's another level of risk. You might not be able to adjust to life as a clam. Then take Thorntree, with its bluebarb bushes, or any other alternate world where the local life wants to eat you. That's yet another level of risk. And you've got to face all three levels on Deirdre, though it's probably a lot easier to get used to being one of us than it is to get used to being a clam.

"*But*—there's a fourth level of risk on Deirdre. Everything I've mentioned so far is a danger to you as an individual; on Deirdre the colony itself is in danger. We may not survive. And if we don't there'll be no society to protect you and nourish you.

"If we can't figure out how to grow crops and how we're supposed to reproduce ourselves we'll never be able to develop a more comfortable, more sophisticated way of life. The Institute never exactly abandons its colonies but think what things would be like on Deirdre if we go thirty or forty years without getting any new colonists. Think about it: no crops to depend on, no youngsters to help with the work, and everybody old and feeble—*but* you still have to work just as hard to survive. How would you like that, growing old and feeble knowing that every day until you die's going to be spent in back-breaking labor? And that it's all for nothing—that nobody's going to come after you to benefit from the way you've spent your life? Don't try to come up with any quick answers now. Just think about it.''

"Listen," the communicator from Oneness said, "We're not going to lie to you. None of us, ever. And the first thing you've got to learn if you're going to try to join us is that we don't want you. Not the you you are now. Not the corrupt, lying, cheating, selfish you that you've got to be to survive in this society. And if you're not willing to help us kill off that old you, then we'll do it to you.''

"You're not making things sound very inviting, Charlie," Vittoria Johnson said.

"Inviting? You mean, fun? Like a party? It isn't. Look," he said, turning to Amber, "growing up in this society means you've got part of the society inside you. Like a cancer that's going to kill you if nobody operates. Right?

"And we can cut it out of you and save your life. But we don't use any anesthetics. It'll hurt. It'll hurt worse than anything you can imagine. But you'll be glad you did it. Afterwards.''

"We've got to tell them where we want to go tomorrow," Jane said. "Have you decided yet?"

"I—need help. Like with the Sweepstakes, Jane. A Question Session."

"You never won the Sweepstakes."

"No. I guess not, but—I'm here. Just like I won.''

"All right. We'll do a Question Session if you want. After dinner?''

Amber nodded.

•   •   •

Jane stated the question for both of them: "Should we transfer to Deirdre, Veldte's Paradise, or"—she hesitated, then conscientiously added—"Oneness, or should we stay here?"

They had no Inductor but sitting facing each other on the blue-carpeted floor of their suite's living room they felt the Latihan peace welling up within them. . . .

Amber was hacking his way through the dense Deirdrean undergrowth with a crude machete. His muscles moved smoothly, rhythmically beneath his skin; he felt quick, alert, confident in his strength. Harsh, white sunlight filtered through the red-leaved branches overhead, struck brilliant colors from the tangle surrounding him, flashed bright from his blade.

A purple frond fell away before the knife, revealing a cluster of small purple globes: fruit. He plucked a globe and ate it.

Nothing he had ever eaten had tasted as good.

. . . and Jane was on Deirdre, looking up at Amber: his handsome green face alive with intelligence, his muscles powerful beneath his skin. So relaxed, so confident, so happy.

"That's wonderful!" he was telling her. "Wonderful! Now that you're pregnant we know the colony'll survive—"

. . . and Jane was on Oneness:

"Stupid, stupid, stupid! Stupid like your brother!" They were dancing in a circle around her, pale skins repellent with slime.

At a motion from the dance-leader the others froze balanced in midstep. "Now Jane," he said, "this is your last chance. If you don't get the steps right this time we'll have to hit you again. But we know you're perfectible, Jane, just like the rest of us. Perfectible, Jane: you can do it if you try.

"All you have to do is imitate me." And his feet were suddenly moving in complex ugly patterns that Jane knew she could never imitate—

. . . and Jane was on Veldte's Paradise, listening as Amber said, "I can't take it any more!" His red scales flashed as he tossed his head in a gesture that had become characteristic. "It's not that

I don't care for you anymore, I do, but—You can't discuss philosophy! You can't make love right! You can't even make up interesting stories! You can't do *anything* right!''

"I try," Jane said.

"I know you try. And that's the worst part of it all, maybe, watching you trying and trying and trying and never coming up with anything that isn't boring. So boring I feel like killing myself.

"Anyway, I give up. I'm leaving. I made myself a boat this morning and I'm leaving. Now. Maybe we'll run into each other someday. . . ."

She watched him walking down to the beach . . .

. . . but no, she had never left Earth after all.

Jane stepped into the elevator, pressed the button for the floor where she and Amber had rented a temporary apartment. The cosmetic reconstruction of her face was finished and she was more beautiful than she'd dreamed possible. *She* was more beautiful than she'd ever dreamed possible.

Amber burst into tears when he saw her. "You're beautiful," he told her and she wept with joy.

The next morning she found the note on the kitchen table: "Dear Jane," it read, "I have transferred to Diamond. You're so pretty now I'm a weight around your neck like father said. I'm going away so you can be happy. Goodbye. Love, Amber."

She called the Institute but the people there would tell her nothing. She never did find out if he had really transferred to Diamond.

"What did you get?" Jane asked.

"I was on Deirdre. Everything was beautiful. I was really happy and I ate a piece of fruit and it tasted better than anything. What happened to you?"

"Deirdre." She did not feel like elaborating.

"We'll go there?"

"Yes."

Manuel Candamo caught Amber as he was coming out of the simulation booth where he'd been experiencing the closest analogue to existence as a Deirdran colonist that the Institute could devise.

"How're things going?" the communicator asked.

"All right." They sat down together at a table, both punched for coffee.

"It's not the same, you know," the communicator said. "It helps a lot but it's not the same."

"I know. They told me already." The communicator's exaggerated efforts at making Amber understand those things which he was capable of understanding on his own always irritated Amber. He resented the fact that, like Joseph, the communicator treated him as if he were even less intelligent than he knew himself to be; he felt degraded by the well meant attempts.

"Listen, Amber," the communicator said. "There's no going back. You'll never see someone who looks like a human being again. You'll never hear a voice made by a human throat again. Never. Think about it. Think about all the big and little things you'll have to miss if you transfer."

"Our father's Alfred Mallory," Jane told the counselor. "Do you know who he is?"

"No."

"He does something electronic here on Espanore, something to do with transfer. I don't know what. Anyway, the thing is he hates us. I'm scared that he'll do something to, to hurt us somehow if he has a chance to. Could you have, well, somebody else do what he usually does during our transfer?"

"You're really afraid of him?"

"Yes."

"Then he probably shouldn't be in a position of responsibility anyway. But let me check up, see what he does." She punched an inquiry into her desk console, read the answer off the screen.

"Nothing for you to worry about," she told Jane. "He quit work here ten days ago."

"Why?" Amber asked.

"He didn't give us a reason."

At first they went there in their dreams. Lying sleeping in plastic wombs, their bodies and brains awash with drugs while machines fed the proper electronic stimuli to their brains, they began to perceive their new world.

In the beginning they were thin hazes permeating air and rock, life and nonlife, without differentiating between them: dimly aware, exulting. Slowly, over the course of dozens, then hundreds of sessions, they began to coalesce, their consciousnesses becoming less diffuse, their joys more pointed. They began to resonate less with the inorganic, more with the organic; soon they were drawn by the magnetism of the colonists' translated beings to the settlement, where they floated like sluggish impalpable mists over the rude, gray buildings. Each session found their impalpable beings closer to taking on material form, each session the dream came closer to waking consciousness.

"It's your last chance to stop," a blue-clad technician told them after their hundred and thirty-seventh session. "Next session you'll take the template from the other colonists and any interruption from then on will kill you."

"Go ahead," Amber said.

"Make sure Brother Ashoka's here for our snapback," Jane added to Vittoria Johnson.

. . . growing inward . . . a collapsing that was at the same time an explosive expansion . . . two bodies sucking suchness from the air around them, from the ground suddenly there beneath them, exploding into material existence—

Amber lay on the ground, staring up at the tree above him and at the sky beyond. The leaves on the tree were red, but no red he had ever seen before, ever imagined possible. . . . The sky was such a clear, soft, singing yellow; the sun such a fierce blazing white. . . . Nothing he had ever seen had been so brilliant, so beautiful, so overwhelming.

It was so strange to perceive the world with an unstunted brain.

"There he is! He made it across!" The slurred words sounded strange but he could understand them easily enough.

He struggled to get to his feet, felt a moment of panic when his muscles refused to obey him.

"Don't try to move. You'll have to learn to use your body all over again." Green faces, strange but not frightening, firm hands lifting him and carrying him into a wooden hut where he was laid on a bed of dry purple leaves.

"Inn—nuuhh. . . ." He could not shape the words with his new vocal apparatus.

"Don't try to talk yet," someone said. "It's all right. She came through fine. You're going to snap back in a few minutes but when you return you'll be here in this hut with us."

Amber felt warm and comfortable and very tired. He slept.

Brother Ashoka stared down at the mindless bodies of the two who had been his friends.

"They'll be asleep when they return," the technician told him. "You'll know they're back when the lights start blinking, but it'll take them a few minutes to regain consciousness."

The minutes lengthened into hours. Suddenly the lights were blinking, and the technician said, "They're back," but Brother Ashoka could detect no change in the limp bodies floating in their tanks of fluid.

The technician drained the fluid, removed their respirators. They remained limp.

"Are you sure they're OK?" Brother Ashoka asked.

"Pretty sure. It'll just take them a while to recover consciousness."

Brother Ashoka waited. At last Jane stirred, opened her eyes.

"Brother Ashoka!" she said. "It's wonderful there. So beautiful! So incredibly beautiful—"

"Yes," Amber agreed, sitting up. "Like I never saw anything real before—"

"You're glad you did it, then?" Brother Ashoka asked.

"Yes," Amber said. "It's so— It feels bad here. You should do it too."

Brother Ashoka smiled. "Perhaps I will. You'll keep me informed about life over there, won't you?"

"Of course," Jane said. "You're our contact person."

"I brought you something for your last moments on Earth. I asked the children in my class to bake you a cake for a going-away present. . . ." He handed each of them a plate with a small square of cake on it.

"You won't be able to get any cake there, from what I hear," he said.

"It's good," Amber said. He took another bite.

"Very good," Jane agreed. "Will you thank them for us?"

"Of course," Brother Ashoka agreed.

They continued talking until first Jane, then Amber, closed their eyes, slid into sleep.

"They're dead," the technician said. "Transfer's complete." He stared at Brother Ashoka. "You look calm enough. It doesn't bother you, seeing them like this?"

"No."

"It does me. Every time. I can't get used to it." He gestured at the bodies. "Sure, they tell me that they're alive somewhere else but I never get to see that part of it. All I ever see is the meat that's left behind."

Without sense of transition Amber found himself back in the darkened hut on Deirdre.

"Don't worry," he was reassured. "Everything's all right. You're both fine and you're here with us for good now. But it's a shock getting used to a new nervous system: nothing to worry about, but you're going to need a lot of sleep tonight. We'll have a party for the two of you tomorrow morning when you're feeling more awake. But right now you should try to sleep."

Amber slept.

CHAPTER THIRTEEN

THE FOREST MIND SLEPT. A crisis would awaken it, but there was no crisis: the colonists from Earth had as yet created little real disruption, less than an earthquake, volcano or windstorm, and the Forest Mind was not yet aware of them.

A buzzbomb exploded into a cloud of spores. Of the millions of fertile spores in the cloud, two came to rest on land cleared by the colony, while another came to rest in an unrelated spot where a new buzzbomb was needed. Those three spores were allowed to live and germinate. The others died.

Sleeping, the Forest Mind's body reached out for the light of the sun, sent questing tendrils ever deeper into the rock in search of the minerals it needed. It required meat: nine fruitbears made their way into the cavern where the Forest Mind housed its body and gave themselves to it while other fruitbears mated so as to produce nine young. The Forest Mind slept.

A tree cracked in the wind, fell. Night came; insects, no longer kept from the tree's edible interior by the protection of its thick bark, settled on it, burrowed into it, devoured what there was for them to devour. By dawn they were gone, leaving what was left for the fungi and microorganisms: the only living things, other than the insects themselves, which the Forest Mind had not incorporated into itself after it had defeated the other minded forests and taken all Deirdre for its own. And even the insects had a place in the Forest Mind's ecology.

The day waned; a rankorchid opened its dark bloom; the evening breeze caught the odor of carrion it exuded, spread it wide. Attracted by the stench, insects gathered, crawling one at a time through the narrow throat that gave entry to the blossom's center.

Inside the blossom insects fought, devouring each other only to be devoured in turn by the orchid. A new rankorchid was needed to replace the one that had been killed by the falling tree; without awakening, the Forest Mind weighed and judged, selecting imperatives, stimulating and inhibiting: rather than allowing an insect to escape the blossom to pollinate another orchid the flower closed itself at dawn and began the process of self-fertilization. The seed, when it formed, would be entrusted to a fruitbear, which would thrust its long yellow tongue into the cooperative flower, obtain the seed, then carry it some hundreds of paces to deposit it where it was needed.

Sleeping the Forest Mind did not dream. It did not know what it was to dream.

Awakening in darkness, the close air of the hut smelling of something that was not quite vanilla, Amber felt the wrongness. The leaves on which he was lying were soft but their softness was unlike any softness he had ever before known; his breathing, slow when he'd awakened—far too slow—was now inhumanly fast, and it was *wrong*: a continuous flutter of tiny muscles in his chest drew the air in through his central nostril to flow in a single, uninterrupted motion down through his chest and then out again through the two flanking nostrils, inhalation and exhalation not alternating but simultaneous.

He felt his body defined by strange muscular tensions and unfamiliar visceral sensations and, what was worse, by the absence of not only the familiar human rhythm of his breathing but of tensions and sensations that had been so much a part of him that he had never before realized his awareness of them. It was as if his body had been pulled and stretched and bent and twisted on some inquisitor's rack and yet there was no pain. Somehow that was the worst thing of all, that he should feel an alien wellbeing instead of a multitude of mortal agonies, for that estranged him from all he had been on some level so basic that nothing he could tell himself had any effect on his panic.

I'm not hurt, he told himself futilely. *Nothing's wrong. This is a new body, a healthy body. I'll get used to it.*

I have to get used to it.

But nothing had prepared him for the terrifying wrongness.

Jane had materialized on the far side of the colony and Amber was already asleep by the time they brought her to the hut. One of the colonists who had carried her from the other side of the settlement, a man—*No,* she thought, *not a man. A Deirdran. We'll never go back to being human again*—who told her his name was Will, held her up in a sitting position and cradled her lolling head in his hands so she could see Amber. "That's your cousin," Will told her. "He's sleeping now—you sleep a lot right after transfer, in little cat naps—but he came through fine."

The figure stretched out on the bed of purple leaves had been hard to see in the dim light. What Jane could see of it was alien, at first totally strange, and yet the longer she looked the more the sleeping form reminded her of the Amber she had known on Earth. But he was so big, so powerful looking here! Taller than any other colonist she had yet seen, broad shouldered, his body corded with unfamiliar configurations of muscle—

He'll be so happy here, Jane thought as gentle hands stretched her out on a leaf bed of her own.

"We're going to seal the hut for the night to keep out insects," one of the unfamiliar slurred voices explained. "They get pretty nasty here at night. The two of you won't be alone, though; Will sleeps here and we've got another newcomer who came through a few weeks before you did. Morning we'll come for you and have a party where you can meet everybody."

Lying in the sweet-smelling darkness, too excited for the moment to sleep, Jane heard Amber's breathing suddenly quicken to a rasping whistle, heard the sounds he made thrashing around in his bed of leaves, his low formless moans. He's terrified, she realized, wanting to reach out to him, to hold him and comfort him, but knowing she could do nothing. So she waited, listening, unable to do anything but will him to share the joy she felt.

In time his breathing calmed. She hoped he was asleep.

Suddenly she herself was very tired. She slept.

•   •   •

Awakening once again to darkness and wrongness, Amber struggled for calm. *I'll do a Latihan,* he told himself, *a Question Session. I'll ask God how to get rid of the wrongness.*

In the context of the Latihan, relaxation was suddenly easy. He surrendered his will and posed his question: *What can I do to make this body right?*

But there was no answer, no vision, no sense of God's presence. Only a terrifying void.

Maybe I need Jane, he told himself, clutching at the only hope that presented itself. *It's harder alone.*

He tried to force his strange throat and vocal apparatus to form the word "Latihan" but succeeded in producing only a few agonized croakings. After a while he gave up.

He lay on his bed of soft, soft leaves, unable to move, unable to speak, helpless. Abandoned by God.

The party was held in what the colonists called the plaza, the cleared space at the settlement's center where they ate together and held meetings. It was early morning. Will and a colonist introducing himself as Tom propped Amber and Jane up against the trunks of two trees that the colonists had left standing when they cleared the area. Then one by one the colonists came forward, embraced the two and kissed them on the forehead, then introduced themselves and described the parts they played in the life of the colony. Amber felt himself almost smothered by the near-vanilla scent, flinching from the touch of so many strangers.

There were John Abercromie, Karl Archard, and Robert Cortona, all Planners (the colonists, as they themselves explained to Amber and Jane, in charge of long-range planning and over-all coordination), Ray Jarvis, the Research Coordinator and Ecologist, Mircea Van Horn, the Health Manager—which Amber took to mean Doctor—and numerous others with titles such as The Spy, Santa Claus (a woman named Catherine Cypers, who was in charge of "rewards and negative sanctions"), The Wooden Leg (in charge of the timber supply), The Fly in the Ointment (a woman named Jo Anne Rittner, whose function was to veto any decision anyone else made which she disliked, at which time she would cease to be the

Fly and the community as a whole would vote to decide whether or not her veto would be upheld), The Charity Case, The Parking Lot Attendant, The Voice in the Wilderness. . . . There were too many people and positions for Amber to remember. And after John Wosky, The Cruise Director—which meant he was in charge of entertainment and community festivities—told Amber that part of a Cruise Director's job was to change the titles which designated every position whenever it struck his or her fancy to do so, he quit even trying. And soon afterwards he fell asleep to the sound of crude wooden flutes, to awaken once more in the Newcomers' Hut.

In the tendays that followed (the colonists having decided to abandon the seven-day week) Amber's outrage at God for having abandoned him slowly faded from the forefront of his mind, though sometimes during the brightly lit days and often during the long nights it would rise up to choke him. Then he would again attempt the Latihan, again fail to achieve it.

But he and Jane had other things to occupy their minds, for as the days passed they began a rapidly accelerating slide back into childhood. Soon they were infants again—strange infants, with the knowledge and comprehension of adults yet with the newly born's inability to speak or coordinate their bodies. And with this physical reversion came a corresponding mental reversion, a quick rebirth of infantile attitudes. Though they could understand adult speech perfectly and were lectured every evening on the things they needed to know if they were to become functioning members of the community, they both took an infantile joy in babbling, thrilled by the sounds of their own voices. Like infants they crept around on the ground, taking pleasure in their ability to move and undisturbed by their inability to walk; like infants they learned hand and eye coordination by playing simple games and using the simple toys the other colonists had made for them, doing everything over and over again for the pure joy of doing; like infants they were fed by hand and dressed by Will and his assistants in loose fitting clothes made from the softened bark of trees. But unlike human infants, they had no problems with bowel and bladder control: the Deirdran eliminated his or her wastes in the form of a sweet-smelling gas.

But as weeks became months and they went from mashed blackish fruit (no matter what its original color, all Deirdran fruit turned black as soon as its skin was broken, though that made it no less edible) to fresh fruit, vegetables, seeds, tubers, and occasional pieces of meat, from creeping to crawling to walking, from meaningless babble to hesitant speech, Amber's childish joy in accomplishing the simplest actions faded and died.

And at last, after months of babble, Amber managed to articulate the word "Latihan" in a form comprehensible to Jane.

"Yemf," Jane said, nodding her head. They sat down facing each other and closed their eyes, willing themselves to relax.

"No," Jane said presently. "No."

"Laftihan!" Amber said, angry. He pushed her. "Laftihan!"

"No," Jane said, undisturbed. She got up and wandered off to watch some of her new friends at their work.

Jane never lost that early sense of joy. She was excited by her new sense of belonging, by the novelty and beauty of the world around her. But Amber still felt an overpowering sense of wrongness, of estrangement from his clumsy body despite its newfound size and strength, and though he searched himself daily for sign of increasing intelligence he seemed to himself no less stupid than he had ever been.

And though his fellow colonists had accepted him, he knew that God had cast him out.

CHAPTER FOURTEEN

A WIND WAS RISING. The propellor tree felt its sensitive pink leaves fluttering, felt its four-bladed seeds twisting on the ends of their long stems, felt its seeds' longing to spin drunkenly through the air.

An imperative. But sleeping, the Forest Mind balanced the tree's imperative with an inhibition: the wind was blowing in the right direction but it was the wrong wind: the seeds would not live to germinate.

The tree clutched its seeds tightly, refusing to set them free.

"Tell Amber I've been able to think of two reasons why he hasn't been able to experience the Latihan which still leave him some hope," Brother Ashoka told Manuel Candamo over the phone. "The first is that possibly he's still too young—in Deirdran terms: remind him that the Fellowship doesn't open anyone until they're sixteen years old."

"And the second reason?" the communicator asked.

"Possibly neither he nor Jane is radiating a strong enough signal to trigger the Latihan and that if someone who'd been doing it without the Inductor long enough were there with them it would be possible. That's assuming that your neural structures are compatible with the Latihan in the first place, of course."

"Of course. Any other news you want me to pass on to them?"

"Just one thing. Tell them that their father's become a publisher. He's started his own book company, specializing in erotic manuscripts. Onan Books. He's having a lot of trouble with the authorities on Drummond Island."

"All right. I'll tell them. I'm sorry I don't have any more time to spend talking to you, but I've got a lot of other calls to make."

The lemon sky had congealed, not clouding over but seeming rather to thicken, like pudding solidifying, and now the rain came down, barrages of heavy black drops slanting from the west. Puddles began to form. Amber dropped the heavy copper flowers he'd been bringing back to the settlement and ran for his hut.

It would have been fatal to step in a puddle. In the spreading blackwater pools microscopic eggs were hatching. Millions of wormlike insect larvae were writhing free and beginning to grow, attacking anything living, devouring each other when they could find no other victims, but growing, growing with fantastic speed. Had Amber stepped in even a tiny puddle he would have been dead within seconds, consumed in minutes, the larvae growing ever larger as they flashed from his feet up through his veins and arteries, devouring everything in their path. But his barkcloth sandals kept him safe from the moist ground—as long as he did not step in a puddle.

The little tan armor frogs squatted by the puddles, spearing larvae with their spiked forelegs and gulping them down while they waited for their true prey, the adults the larvae would become. The frogs almost covered the ground near where Amber had dropped his flowers but they grew less numerous as he approached the settlement, vanishing entirely when he reached cleared ground.

Though the puddles were spreading rapidly, there was still high ground enough—some of it natural ridges and rock outcroppings, some of it man-heaped earth—for Amber to make his way in safety to the hut he shared with Jane. Since the larvae had no taste for wood, the hut was built, as were all the settlement's buildings, on short wooden stilts.

"Thank God you made it," Jane said as Amber pushed his way past the doorflap into the dark interior of their hut. She began lacing the flat back into place. Outside the normally reddish ground was almost completely covered with viscous black fluid.

Jane had the flap nearly laced when the rain stopped and the wind died. The sky shimmered, seemed to run; the white sun began to pulsate, flashing three, four, even five times its normal size. Wave after wave of heat struck them. The blackwater was giving off thick oily steam, making breathing difficult.

"Hurry," Amber said.

"We wouldn't be in a hurry if you'd been more careful," Jane said. She finished lacing the flap into place, checked to make sure it was secure. The darkness was thick in the hut, tense and stifling, the air heavy with the almost vanilla scent of their bodies.

"I wish, just once, I could see Lake Huron again," Jane said. "Or even a glass of real water. I'd give anything to be able to drink a glass of real water again."

"We don't get thirsty here," Amber said.

"It's not the same. Drinking was nice. And I miss going swimming."

"There was more rain this time," Amber said. "It never covered all the ground before."

"No. It never did. What happened to you? If you'd been any later—"

"I was out collecting flower metal. Copper. Ali told me where to find it. Anyway, I didn't see the sky change so I didn't have time to dig myself into a tree. So I ran."

He froze, listening. A buzzing, thrumming sound filled the air as the surviving insects, adult now and thousands strong, took flight.

"I hope the glidetoads get them all," Jane said. "But I guess that's too much to hope for."

"Yes."

Something tapped on the wall: an insect, as yet unsure of itself in the air, colliding with the bark wall of the hut. They waited, tense, but the sound was not repeated.

"If we could only have a light in here," Jane said. "Some way to see things, so we could know that none of them's found its way in. I wait here in the darkness, I just wait, and I never know if—I thought maybe one of them had stung you and was laying its eggs in you and that maybe after it finished with you it would come after me . . . ."

"Nothing got in," Amber said. Outside the sound of wings was beginning to die away. "We're safe this time. And they'd smell it if we had anything burning in here: you *know* what the smell of smoke does to them."

"Yes." She paused a moment, then went on, "I think there were more of them this time. The buzzing was louder."

"It lasted longer too."

"John—John the Meteorologist, not John Abercromie—told me the rains have been getting worse. When he and Cassie first got here the puddles were really tiny and you could stay out in the rain if you avoided low ground and got inside as soon as the sun came out again. And that was just a little over a year ago."

"There were too many insects for the glidetoads," Amber said. "Most of them'll be back tonight." He could feel the darkness inside the hut smothering him like an oiled shroud.

"I'm glad you tried to make it back here," Jane said. "If you'd stayed in the forest some of the adults might have gotten to you. Like the one that got John Abercromie."

"How's he doing today?" Amber asked.

"He still can't really walk but he says his leg doesn't hurt as much. Mircea says he should be walking in another two or three days."

"They didn't tell us about the insects," Amber said. "Nobody told us. If they had—"

"Yes they did. But there just wasn't any way they could tell us what it really felt like. They tried—"

"Not hard enough. They would have tried harder if they hadn't needed us. Needed anyone they could get." He knew the futility of his bitterness, felt bitter nonetheless.

"We'd have come anyway. We couldn't have stayed *there*. You know that—"

"We could have gone to Veldte's Paradise."

"Maybe, but we're better off here than where we were, aren't we? Even with the insects. Life's real here."

"For you, maybe."

"Anyway it only rains every couple of months."

"What if the rains keep on getting worse?" Amber could see it, his mental image almost as vivid as a Latihan vision: *blackwater rising around the hut while he and Jane crouched inside listening to the heavy thudding of the rain on the roof, rain going on and on while the blackwater seeps up through the floor, comes flowing sluggishly in through the walls, a deadly syrup swarming with*

*insatiable armored worms growing with incredible speed as they
feed on each other and on the contents of the hut . . . The two of
them clinging to the walls and roof, perhaps losing their grips on the
wooden supports, falling: short choked screams from throats no
longer human, the sounds the larva make as they feed, all over in
instants . . . or waiting clinging in the moist oily darkness, waiting
for the worms' maturation, the fatal thrumming of horny wings
within the hut. . . .*

A voice from outside the hut: Jo Anne, Community Rooster for
this tenday. "You two all right?"

"Fine," Jane called. "Is everybody else OK?"

"As far as I know. You can come out now if you want. They
won't be back till tonight."

Amber fumbled with the doorlaces in the darkness, felt relief
flooding through him at the first glimpse of the light outside.

"There's a preference request meeting tonight," Jane said.

"I'm not going," Amber said. "I've got to get my copper
flowers and work them into shape."

"That won't take all evening," Jane said.

"It might."

"But you never come to meetings. Why? You've got opinions—
you want people back on Earth told more about the insects, don't
you—and your vote's as good as anyone's. And you'll never get to
choose your own work if you don't come to preference meetings."

"I don't care what I'm doing as long as I'm helpful," Amber
said. "And I help: I work hard, don't I? But it's not my world,
here."

"But you're so much stronger and smarter here—"

"So what? I'm still stupid and clumsy. And this body—it's
wrong, it's not me—God must hate it; he's angry with me for trying
to cheat the destiny He had planned for me. Or something, I don't
know what, but—I should be humble, stupid. . . . Every night after
you go to sleep I try to do the Latihan but all I feel is emptiness. . . ."

Jane took his hand, squeezed it. "You're not alone here,
Amber."

"Yes, I am."

"No. Everyone here likes you. And I love you. I'm here with
you. I'll always be here with you."

"But—The darkness, the blackwater rising, the insects—what can you do? What can any of us do? We're going to die all alone here and there's nothing any of us can do about it. Nothing!"

"Amber, please—"

He squeezed her hand back, pulled away. "I've got to get the flowers I dropped. I'll see you tonight after you get back from the meeting."

He stooped and stepped out of the hut, then paused and turned back to Jane. He forced a smile. "I'm sorry, Jane. Sometimes I get so sad. . . . I hate the darkness, just waiting in there. . . . But I feel better now. Honest I do. I'll be all right."

"Will you come to the meeting? Please?"

"No."

"Manuel's going to transmit messages back afterwards and it's our turn. Please?"

"No. I've got too much work to do. That's the only time I feel happy, when I'm working. I need to work. If you get a chance, have Manuel tell Brother Ashoka that I'm doing fine but I miss the Latihan a lot. OK?"

He's smarter and stronger now, Jane thought. *A lot smarter than he realizes.* She watched him until he disappeared into the forest. *But it's only made him miserable.*

"Any luck with your crops, Lyn?"

"Hi, Eric. You Spy this tenday?"

"Afraid so."

"Well, they're not crops. They won't grow."

"The jungle seems to grow fast enough. I had to chop off about twenty new runners today and they found a buzzbomb growing over by Mircea's hut. Plus the usual assortment of unidentified shoots."

"The problem's not that plants won't grow here. The problem is that they won't grow here for us. If I uproot a plant and transplant it to a spot two feet away from its original location it dies. Same climate, same soil, same amount of sunlight, same everything—but it dies. Even if I transfer the soil it was originally growing in it still dies. And that's not just for adult plants: seeds, spores, runners, you name it and it refuses to grow for me. For any of us."

"Why?"

"I don't know. Ask Jarvis, maybe he knows—even though he told me this morning he doesn't have any idea either. But it's like each plant had one place where it was supposed to grow and that's it. Period, as Manuel likes to say."

Amber made his way through the forest. There were no paths—the undergrowth grew back too fast to make cutting them practical—but he had learned to guide himself by familiar landmarks: an outcropping of greenish stone that resembled a turtle, a small hill with three young propellor trees on its crest, a hollow choked with greenberry bushes. The greenberries were almost ripe, he saw. Somebody would have to pick them before they got all the way ripe or the fruitbears would get them. That is, if the insects didn't beat them all to them.

The flowers were where he'd dropped them, six heavy disks of wood and metal—they called the metal copper because it was reddish and soft, though he'd been assured that it wasn't the same as earthly copper. Amber had eaten the succulent blue center fruits when he'd first found the flowers shining in the sun—that was a collector's privilege, little enough compensation for lugging the heavy flowers back through the forest to the settlement—and each of the disks had a small round hole in the center where the fruit had been.

He put the flowers in the heavy barkcloth sack he'd brought, slung the sack over his right shoulder, and began making his way back through the thick undergrowth to the settlement. Once back he'd burn away the wood and hammer the hot metal into crude sheets which someone with greater metal working ability—probably Josephus Cypers, the Blacksmith, though it might be one of his forge assistants—could use to make knives, tools, shovel heads, arrow heads or cooking utensils.

"Jane, why doesn't Amber ever come to preference request meetings?"

"I'm not sure, exactly. He just, well, prefers to do whatever work he gets assigned."

"But that's—What if you brought him one of the slates? He could make out his preferences even if he didn't come to the meeting. It'd be a bit of extra trouble for me, but nothing I couldn't handle, and if you could make sure that he gets his slate to Delia before the writing fades—''

"It's not that, Laurent," Jane said, tense with the knowledge that despite the Labor Manager's genuine desire to be helpful she had to guard her words. For Amber's sake: Laurent Eliade was being groomed to replace Karl Archard, the outgoing Planner, and he was already beginning to act like a man in authority. If she gave him the wrong impression he might decide it was his responsibility to report Amber's behavior to Sandra Moss, the psychological adaptation specialist whom John Wosky had christened, in what Jane was coming to find a most unfunny attempt at humor, The Thought Police. Perhaps it wasn't supposed to be funny: maybe John had meant it to be a constant reminder to Sandra (whom Jane had found both charming and warm the few times she'd spoken with her) that her function was not the suppression of deviation, but the fostering of as wide a spectrum as possible of compatible adaptations. Still—

She doesn't love him, Jane thought. *How can I trust her to understand what he needs when she doesn't love him?*

"It's not that Amber's trying to avoid meetings," she continued. "What I mean is, he's not trying to cut himself off from the community or avoid people or anything like that. It's more like, well, you've got to remember he's had special treatment all his life, he's never been able to do much of anything except special jobs that people made up for him just so he'd feel good, and, now, well, I think it's sort of the idea that no matter what it is somebody needs to have done, he can do it. I don't know, for sure, but—well, do you see what I mean? Why he doesn't want to fill out his Labor Preference Slates?''

"The way you put it, yes, but—shouldn't he still be helping to elect people and establish new positions? Surely that kind of participation wouldn't, well, interefere with the pleasure he's getting out of being a jack-of-all-trades?''

"No, but—'' Jane paused, amazed at her self-confidence, at the way she was able to marshal arguments. *It's like Earth kept me stupid too,* she thought. *Like I never had a chance to learn I could be anything but gawky and tongue-tied. They told me I was stupid and I believed them. But here—*

"You're right, of course," she said. "But look at the situation from Amber's point of view. I think that right now it would just make him feel more alienated from the rest of us to come to your meetings. Here we all are, writing out our work preferences on our slates and giving our lists to Delia so he can transmit them back to Earth for computer processing, and what's Amber doing? He's just sitting there, feeling embarrassed, not making out a list, not saying anything to Delia—Don't you see how *that* would make him feel like even more of an outsider? You've got to remember how self-conscious he is; he spent sixteen years being mocked and jeered at for being mentally retarded and now, now he's just a little shy still. Give him a while to fit in. That's all he needs: just a little while to get used to being a member of the community."

"It's not as if he doesn't do his share of the work, but—perhaps he does just need a little longer to adjust. I hope so."

"I'm sure that's what it is." But mixed with Jane's relief at having protected Amber from unwanted scrutiny was worry for him:

He's changed since we came here, she thought. *He used to be open and trusting when we were alone together, but now he's all closed up, he's made himself a little room inside his head and locked me out of it.*

And when he locked me out, he locked himself inside.

She had to help him; she loved him; it was her responsibility. But it was too big a responsibility to bear alone; she needed help. If John had christened Sandra differently. . . . But he hadn't, and Jane was afraid to seek her out and ask her for help.

Brother Ashoka could have helped her, of that she was sure, but the only way to convey the true state of affairs to him was to relay the information through Manuel Candamo. Manuel was a kind, trustworthy, and very discreet man, not at all given to gossip—but part of his responsibilities, as Jane had been informed even before she transferred, was the duty to inform the community of anything he learned from the messages which he transmitted which in his judgment affected community welfare.

I'm thinking crazy, Jane realized. *Like it's a police state here, everyone spying on me all the time, waiting for me to give myself away.*

•   •   •

The metal hammered into sheets, Amber returned to his hut. Jane
had not yet returned and he could hear the sound of voices from the
center of the settlement: the meeting must still be going on. For a
moment he was tempted to join them, but he realized the temptation
for what it was and rejected it.

He walked around his hut, feeling with his fingers the seams
where the sheets of bark had been stitched together into walls which
insects were unable to penetrate. Whoever Jo Anne chose to replace
herself as building inspector at tonight's meeting would be around
presently to check the hut's security, as he or she would check the
security of every building in the settlement before nightfall, but
Amber preferred the security of having made his own inspection as
well.

He entered the building, checked the lacing on the skylight—
tight—laced the doorflap closed. Sitting, he surrendered his will,
triggered the Latihan.

Nothing.

"There's nothing more for me to do here tonight," Laurent
declared. "So unless anyone's got any objection I'll close my part
of the meeting. Manuel doesn't have any important community
business to transmit back tonight, so those of you whose turn it is
can make use of his services."

Jane was the eighth. Manuel Candamo, looking like everyone
else, was sitting on a stump.

*If he guesses how badly Amber feels cut off from everything he'll
tell Sandra,* she thought. *And if they find out how depressed he is
they may decide he's gone insane.*

*Maybe he is insane. Maybe they can help him; maybe he needs
their help, needs it really badly.*

*But I'm the only one he trusts with his secrets. If he finds out that
he can't even trust me—*

"Do you have a message tonight, Jane?" Manuel asked.

"Yes, but I'm afraid it's pretty much the same as it was last time.
Tell Brother Ashoka that it's very important to both Amber and me
to find a way to do the Latihan here. Ask him to do a Question
Session."

"There's not much he can do, Jane. He's there; you're here. But you really miss the Latihan that badly?"

"Very badly. We both miss it."

"You have to give up a lot here. We all do. Myself, I had one of the world's best collections of American black jazz. Records as well as tapes and holopyramids. I thought I'd be able to listen to my records while I was back in my body on Earth; nobody told me that it wouldn't be safe to go back for any longer than was absolutely necessary. And drums and wooden flutes just aren't the same."

"No," Jane agreed.

"You miss a lot of things here. Sex, for example. Still, all in all it's worth it. Or at least I hope it is."

He stood up and walked over to a bed of leaves on a raised mound of earth. He lay down, folded his hands on his chest, and went limp. A while later he stretched and sat up.

"Brother Ashoka says he'll see what he can do, but he's afraid you'll just have to hope the ability'll come back to you with time," he said.

"Thanks," Jane said.

CHAPTER FIFTEEN

"MORNING, AMBER, JANE!" Tom called through the doorflap. "Are you two all right?"

"Yes!" Amber shouted, groping for his sandals in the dark.

"Didn't you hear the gong?"

"No, but we're up," Jane said. "We never hear the gong unless the wind's just right. We've been waiting for someone to tell us it was safe to go out." Amber slipped the sandals onto his feet, hastily belted his barkcloth robe closed.

"Breakfast's probably ready. You two are the last on my wake-up list."

Amber unlaced the doorflap but held it in place, keeping the light from penetrating until Jane said, "I'm dressed now, Amber." He pushed the flap aside. The harsh morning light showed Jane smiling, her green skin mottled with darker healthspots.

She looked at him, felt her smile fading: *He always looks so sad.* His face was too creamy a green, creased with deep-grown lines. The lines followed a different pattern than they would have on a human face, but Jane had learned to read Deirdran expressions.

"I'm ready," she said aloud. "Let's go."

They walked toward the center of the settlement, passing clusters of huts similar to their own, came eventually to the plaza.

A dozen men had gone out hunting the day before, returning with a number of fruitbears, some wood pigs and a few near squirrels: the animals were not particularly common but they had so little fear of the colonists that they were easily bagged once sighted. So there was meat today, cooked on an open fire far from the colonists' huts so that the smoke residue would not prove too inviting to the insects that would awaken with nightfall, and served on stiff barkhusk platters alongside the more usual fruit and vegetables.

"Good morning, Amber, Jane!" a short, unusually stocky Deirdran called. "Come sit with us."

"Good morning, Josephus," Amber said as he and Jane put their platters down at his table.

"Jane, do you know my wife, Catherine? She plays Santa Claus."

"I'm afraid I haven't come up for any rewards yet," Jane said.

"Nor any negative sanctions. Not that I've ever had to apply many of them to anyone here, which makes it a welcome change from what I used to do. Policework. Hello, Amber."

"Hi, Catherine."

"You know we've only got a half day's work today?" Josephus asked. "Manuel says it's Christmas on Earth and we've got to celebrate. Have some more meat, Amber; I got two of the pigs myself and they're unusually good."

"But tough," his wife said.

"No tougher than usual," Josephus said.

"How are things going, Amber?" Catherine said presently.

"All right. Nothing special."

"Do you feel yourself getting any smarter?"

"No. Well, I can remember things better, and I can see and hear things more clearly but I—I still think just about the same. Like I always did."

"That's not true," Jane said. "You're learning a lot of new stuff. Like what Josephus's teaching you at the forge."

"You're a good worker," Josephus said. "And you're not stupid. You learn things; I've watched you. You don't need to be any smarter than you are."

"Why are you here? On Deirdre, I mean, Josephus?" Jane asked. She felt uncomfortable at the turn the conversation was taking.

"Because we're in love with each other and there's no sex here. That's the short answer; the explanation of what it means takes a little longer. Do you want to hear it?"

"Yes," Amber said.

"Well, when Catherine and I decided to get married we opted for the FullMarriage—"

"I don't know what that is," Jane said.

"It's Swiss," Josephus said. "I don't think they have it anywhere else yet—"

"It's illegal everywhere else," Catherine said.

"Yes. Anyway, in a FullMarriage both partners undergo conditioning to ensure that neither of them will ever again be able to have sexual relations with anyone else.

"Some friends and I were in a, I guess you could call it a dueling society, though that's not exactly what it was—just entertainment, you understand, but we used real broadswords. And since the government wouldn't give its approval to anything that dangerous—"

"The Dutch government," Catherine said. "We're from the Netherlands."

"We had to meet in the Peking Extralegal Preserve. Anyway, a friend and I were hacking away with broadswords, not trying to do each other any great harm, you understand—we were both wearing plastic armor—but if there's no chance of getting hurt where's the sport?"

"There isn't any," Catherine said. "Whether or not you can get hurt at it: it's a stupid thing to do."

"Mikhail caught me in a seam in my headgear and the plastic split. There aren't any doctors in the Preserve and by the time Mikhail got me to one on the outside I had permanent brain damage. Nothing like yours, Amber: it didn't affect my intelligence. What it did do was make me permanently and hopelessly impotent.

"Catherine and I were still sealed to each other and we still loved each other but it was an impossible situation, she with a full spectrum of sexual desires I was unable to fulfill and me, well, my libido hadn't changed but I was totally incapable of finding fulfillment. So we decided to transfer."

"We got the money by suing the company that made Josephus's headgear," Catherine said.

"We were originally going to transfer to a world where we could have sex again—Alter or Veldte's Paradise or someplace else; there were a lot of worlds that looked promising—but the Institute's psychologists told us that the conditioning we'd undergone would prevent either us from every having sex with any *body* other than the one we'd been conditioned to, even if the proper personality was inside. So we decided that a world without sex of any sort would be the next best thing. And here we are.''

"State your question," Brother Percival told Brother Ashoka.

"What can I do to help Amber and Jane?" Brother Ashoka asked.

There was a baby lying crying in a crib. Brother Ashoka knew its mother would be back in a few minutes to comfort it but the crib was air conditioned, covered by a heavy glass dome through which the sounds of Brother Ashoka's reassurances could not penetrate, and the cover was locked.

He could hear the mother in the next room but she seemed in no hurry to return and for some reason he knew it would be impossible for him to speak with her and ask her to hurry.

Beneath the glass lid the baby was choking, its eyes bulging, its wrinkled face swollen with helpless anger.

"You done cleaning up?" Tom asked.

"I think so. Let me ask Ned—Hey, Ned, do you need me for anything else?"

"Not right now. After dinner."

Tom led the way out into the forest. "There." He pointed at four delicate, crystalline-looking spheres on tall grey stalks. "Ever seen those before?"

"No. What are they?"

"Insect traps. Here, bend closer but don't touch them. See the insect in that one? The globes open up at night and they've got some sort of perfume that the insects can't resist."

The insect was still alive. It was twice the length of Amber's longest finger, with beautiful purple and gold wings like those of a butterfly.

"It's beautiful," Amber said unwillingly. "Like a butterfly. I thought they were more like, well, wasps or, not spiders, but—"

"Some are. And don't let this one fool you. Watch."

Tom held his hand close to the globe. The insect suddenly arched its back and a barbed black sting almost half as long as Amber's thumb extended from its abdomen. The insect jabbed at the transparent wall separating it from Tom's hand again and again.

"Not really much like a butterfly," Tom said.

"What do the plants do with them after they catch them?" Amber asked.

"They digest them. It takes a couple of days. Come back tomorrow and you'll see this one dead; three or four days later and the body'll be gone.

"I often come out here to watch the damn things die," he added. "It cheers me up."

Though Amber had only been assigned to help with the cleaning, he volunteered to help serve dinner as well. He was given the task of pushing the cart that was used to transport meat from the out-of-the-way-place where it was cooked to the Plaza.

When the colonists had finished eating they brought out drums and wood flutes and the odd other instruments people had devised and were trying to learn to play. The music was crude but everybody seemed to enjoy it, even Manuel Candamo.

Even Amber. But when he had finished his assigned tasks he forced himself to return to the solitude of his hut.

CHAPTER SIXTEEN

"AMBER? JANE? YOU AWAKE?"

"That you, Tom?" Jane called from the darkness to Amber's left.

"Still doing Rooster duty. Good morning."

"Morning. We'll be out in a minute."

"Take your time: I decided to start at the end of the list and wake the two of you first. I don't suppose either of you heard the gong?"

"No," Amber said, beginning to unlace the doorflap.

"The new gong?" Jane asked.

"We tried it for the first time this morning. It almost deafened Jo Anne when she hit it. She said she wants to resign as Timeclock and go back to being Rooster."

"Maybe we would have heard it if we'd been awake," Amber offered. He pushed the doorflap aside and stepped out of the hut, followed closely by Jane.

"Not good enough. It's supposed to wake you up."

"But it would still be good to know it was safe to go outside."

"True. If you didn't sleep through the gong."

"How about a series of gongs?" Jane asked. "Somebody hits the first one and when the other people hear it, they hit theirs."

"It would take a lot of metal," Tom said. "And a lot of people."

"Not that much metal. And it wouldn't take more than a few minutes before breakfast when nobody's doing much of anything, anyway."

"Yes, but—Look, we invest all that work in, oh, say four more gongs, right? And then we just use them to wake people up, when there're all sorts of other activities scheduled for other parts of the day that we're having trouble getting people to on time? So pretty soon there'd be four more people whiling away their time outside their huts waiting for the signal to hit *their* gongs.''

''Why not put one in the forge?'' Amber asked. ''And put them other places where people'd be working anyway?''

''Fine, but then they wouldn't be much good for waking people up in the morning. You'd need a whole different set of gongs, and we're already up to eight gongs. What if—''

''You're going to be late,'' Jane reminded him.

''Right. I'll talk to you later today.''

There were only about a dozen people eating when Amber and Jane arrived at the Plaza, most of them members of the kitchen and serving staffs. They sat down at a table where three servers were finishing their meals, but before they had had a chance to get beyond the exchange of good mornings and hellos other colonists began trickling in and sitting down, forcing their companions to gulp their remaining food and get to work. A few minutes later they were joined by Bill Simmons.

''How do you like it here, Amber?'' he asked.

''All right, I guess.''

''You don't seem too grateful for the wonderous opportunity vouchsafed you.''

''Vouchsafed me?''

''That's right, it wouldn't be part of the vocabulary you came here with. How about, for the second chance the Institute granted you?''

''I'm doing all right.''

''Sure. Like the rest of us: you're discovering that living on Deirdre isn't quite what you'd been led to hope it would be. Remember what they said? 'A new life—new in EVERY respect. . . . Perhaps in one of these worlds or in one as yet undiscovered you can find the life for which you've always yearned, your fantasy come true—' Jesus!''

''You didn't have to believe it,'' Jane said.

''Believe it? A good friend of mine *wrote* it. And I illustrated it. Of course I believed it! You remember that picture, the one with all the scarlet log cabins?''

"Yes," Amber said.

"That was here. Deirdre. I got it all wrong because nobody bothered to give me the right details in the first place and they used it anyway. It was a nice picture even if it didn't look like anywhere real, so they used it. And you remember, how you never used to see pictures of any of the colonists in those brochures? A lot of nice scenery, some pretty plants and animals, but no people? Except the pretty jewels on Diamond, of course, but everywhere else. . . . The Institute was afraid pictures of the colonists would scare people off. Damned right, too. Wish they'd scared me off."

"Why are you here?" Amber asked.

"If you knew better," Jane added.

"Glamour. I was blinded by the glamour of the whole thing. I even took the job with the Institute to get the employee's rate on transfer."

"But why here?" Jane asked.

"I got to talking to Manuel Candamo one day and he told me how wonderful it was here, how all you had to do if you wanted something to eat was wander out into the forest and pluck the fruit from the trees. He made it sound like Every Boy's Tropical Paradise, so here I am. When I could have gone to Veldte's Paradise—"

"Wrong again, Bill," Manuel said, joining them. "I don't like telling tales as a rule, but since you've already brought my name into this discussion. . . ." His nostrils quivered with amusement. "Actually," he said, addressing his remarks to Jane, "Bill's got a pathological fear of snakes. It's something to do with the fact that they slither. And he's got a criminal record. So he couldn't have gone to Veldte's Paradise."

"Some criminal record," Bill said. "One conviction. A misdemeanor: disturbing the peace."

"Enough to render you ineligible for transfer to Veldte's Paradise. Especially considering the fact that an assault charge was lodged against you."

"If you really wanted to be fair, Manuel, you'd mention the fact that the charge was dropped before the case ever came to trail. *And* that the man I ended up getting in the fight with was the local mayor's son.

"Look," he said, appealing to both Amber and Jane with unconvincing camaraderie, "It was a barroom fight and if I'd had any sense I would never have gotten mixed up in it. Fair enough: I made a stupid mistake. But I was drunk, it wasn't my fault, and I ended up getting thrown through the mirror by a redneck half again as big as me. It was a small town in Texas: I was just passing through but the guy I got into the fight with was a local with relatives. You *know* how they feel about people from big cities in those little towns. So I got charged."

"Yes," Jane said, realizing that she knew exactly how small town people felt about people who made a point of the fact that they were from the big city.

"Manuel," she demanded, "how come you made such a point of the fact that we'd have to be able to get along with all the people here, and then we get here and find people like *him* here? Was it because he worked for the Institute?"

"No," Bill Simmons said. "Because I'm extraordinarily valuable here. *I'm* one of the people you've got to be able to get along with, because the colony needs me."

"Which, unfortunately, is the truth," Manuel said. "Though we would never have accepted him if there'd been any danger of violent behavior on his part here."

"I got myself conditioned first," Bill said. "Before even applying. As a sign of good faith. And *that's* why I think they might have accepted me for Veldte's Paradise."

"What do you do that makes you so valuable?" Amber asked.

"My unique artistic genius and my incredible mathematical talents. Put them together and you've got a camera capable of taking a picture here and transmitting it back to Earth. By which I mean, that all I have to do is see something and I can devise a program, in my head, which will enable a computer to reproduce what I see."

"So you're transmitting pictures of the landscape back to the Institute so they can make their brochures more accurate?" Jane asked.

"No," Manuel said. "He's making observations for the scientific community and conveying them back to Earth."

"A picture's worth a thousand words, as the saying goes," Bill remarked.

"And there's the gong," Manuel said. "Time for the meeting."

They made their way over to the cleared part of the Plaza where meetings were held, Amber and Jane drawing away from Bill Simmons as they walked.

John Abercromie, dressed like everyone else in a sleeveless cloak of gray barkcloth, his purple-scaled arms shining in the harsh white morning sun, was making his slow way up onto the Leadership Mound. Since his bad leg made most types of physical labor impossible for him, the colony had voted to temporarily relax the regulation stipulating that Planners had to earn the rest of their mandatory labor credits as members of the general labor pool, doing whatever work was required of them by anyone who needed assistance. Hence, he was serving as Task Manager.

"We're all here," he said presently.

"Where's the other John?" Jo Anne asked.

"Paralyzed. A pseudowasp got to him last night. They must not like people named John." He waited for the murmuring to die down, then said, "Somebody's got to cut the egg cases out of him before the wrigglers hatch. That's your job for today, Mircea."

"How many egg cases?" Mircea asked.

"Five, maybe six. One of the lumps is awfully big."

"I'll need help," Mircea said. "Krishna?"

"Of course,"

"Wait a second," John said. "Judy had some nursing experience back on Earth. I know she's still a Newcomer, so you can't expect her to be any help, but I'd like to have her watch so she can start getting some idea of what you do. In case she ever has to take over for Krishna."

"All right, but if she gets in the way—"

"Will'll get one of his babysitters over there to make sure she doesn't. As soon as she starts to bother you, out she goes. All right?"

"Sure. You've got John over in the medical hut?"

"Yes. Will, do you have anyone you'd recommend to keep a watch on Judy?"

"How about Pat?"

"It's fine with me," Pat said, and hurried off after the Health Manager and his assistant.

"Delia transmitted all your preference requests back to Earth for computer processing," John continued. "The results were pretty much the same as last tenday, except that foraging and hunting are a bit more popular, and so won't be worth quite as much, while being the Spy has lost a bit of its attraction and moved up—"

"Who's the Charity Case this time?" Bill Simmons demanded.

"Rosabeth." John went on to detail the two hundred and twenty-three tasks the colonists had judged worthy of receiving labor credit, and gave the rankings the computers had determined for them, ranging from a half hour of credit per hour of labor for the tasks judged most preferable to two hours of credit for every hour of work for the tasks judged least desirable.

Since Amber had not turned in a preference list of any sort, the computers had assigned him to the labor pool. Rosabeth was being replaced in her capacity as Parking Lot Attendant (which she did in addition to her work as an ecologist) by Justine, but when Amber volunteered to help her she turned him down.

"Rosabeth says you've been uprooting stuff and chopping off runners too often. It's hard work; you shouldn't have to do it all the time."

"I don't mind," Amber said.

"I'd still rather get somebody else. Let me check—Hey, any of you want to dig up flowers and hack off roots? We've got over thirty runners this morning."

"Sure," Catherine said.

"All right, but we need someone else."

"I'll do it," Ray Jarvis volunteered.

"But what about your own work?" Justine asked.

"I haven't had any luck with studying the ecology here; what I need is inspiration. And I'm as likely to get inspired uprooting weeds as I am doing anything else."

"That lets you out, Amber," Justine said. "Why don't you see if Dan needs any help." She smiled. "You don't want to get too specialized."

Her teeth are so dark they're almost black, Amber thought. *Like they're rotten. We're all ugly when we smile here.*

"Why don't you pick somebody and go out in the forest and strip those greenberry bushes you were telling me about yesterday—no, day before yesterday, wasn't it?'' Dan asked.

''Sure,'' Amber said. He looked around. Though he knew everyone's name, most of the other colonists remained strangers to him after six months among them. ''Tom?'' he asked uncertainly.

''Certainly. Glad to oblige. I like the forest, anyway.''

They got barkcloth sacks from a storeroom and made their way into the forest. Amber had no difficulty in relocating the hollow where he'd seen the berries.

''Another couple of days and the fruit bears would have gotten them,'' Tom said when he saw the patch.

''Yes,'' Amber agreed.

The berries turned black as soon as they were picked, the dark stain spreading from the severed stem to blot out all of the berry's original green.

Like rot, Amber thought. They were excellent eating nonetheless, with a taste vaguely reminiscent of limburger cheese and honey—not a combination that would have appealed to Amber on Earth, but one that he found quite satisfying here. Tom ate continuously while working; Amber ate an occasional berry, but no more than he needed to compensate for the lunch he was missing.

''We've got a lot of food back at the settlement,'' he said after a while. ''Too much. It doesn't seem right to keep on taking more than we need.''

''Fruit doesn't keep,'' Tom reminded him.

''Yes, but—what about barkpulp? It'll keep forever and Ned told me we had enough to last us nine months.''

''Do you like barkpulp?''

''Of course not. Nobody does. I just eat what I need to keep healthy. But then why are we wasting so much time—and killing so many trees—if we don't want to eat it?''

''Because it'll keep forever. And because we're afraid of winter.''

''There isn't any winter here.''

''You're sure of that?''

''Of course not. But there hasn't been one yet.''

''No. Not in two and a half years. And there isn't any sign that there'll ever be one. Or, rather, there isn't any sign that any of us can recognize that there'll ever be one. But what if winter or something like winter's just around the corner? What if it starts tomorrow and lasts three years? Or ten years? Deirdre's still a strange world and we've got to be prepared to deal with any surprises it comes up with.

"Though I don't much like the idea of eating barkpulp for ten years," he added.

"The testing fee will be five thousand dollars," Curtis Adamaski told Brother Ashoka, "refundable if you should turn out to have the talents that will enable you to become either a communicator or an explorer."

"The Fellowship has offered to pay for my examinations," Brother Ashoka said.

"Good. But that brings me to something else: I'm afraid that even if you do do well in the examinations we won't be able to accept you for immediate transfer. It's because you're a member of the Fellowship of Prismatic Light. Not that we've got any sort of prejudice against your religion as a religion you understand, but until we see whether or not the Mallorys manage to adapt successfully to life as colonists we'd rather not translate anyone else who's been exposed to your Inductor."

"And if they don't adapt successfully?"

"Then we'll have to determine whether or not that's a result of their membership in your Fellowship. The situation's complicated in Mr. Mallory's case, of course. . . ."

"Of course. How much longer will you need to make your decision?"

"To be absolutely sure? Years. But we should know enough to make a decision regarding you much sooner. That is, to be sure, if the examinations show you an appropriate subject for translation."

"But you'll give me the tests now?"

"As soon as you'd like."

First Cliff, who was serving as Wooden Leg, had selected a tree. Then his assistants had cut it down, made a preliminary slit in the bark, then peeled its bark from it in great spirals, leaving the barkpulpcoated core behind for Dan Webster.

Some pulp, however, adhered to the bark. Had a blackwater rain been imminent, the tast of disposing of the remaining pulp would have been left to insects; as it was, Jane found herself scraping the bark clean with a sharpened stone. The work could have been boring and monotonous, but she found she enjoyed its unhurried simplicity.

"We can't really get much further without some sort of microscopes," Ray Jarvis told John Dolland. "You're the instrumentalist. Figure out a way to make us some lenses."

"With what? You can't even make pottery from the soil here, much less glass."

"What about organic materials?"

"For example?"

"Oh—Take that pseudowasp that got John Frye. It had some sort of transparent shell protecting its compound eyes. And the armor toads must have some sort of protection for their eyes, otherwise the insects would get *them*. Use your imagination."

"Thanks. Do you know what happened to the John's wasp?"

"Brian's studying it. As best he can without a microscope with which to examine it."

"I'll go check with him, see if there's anything useful for me in it."

"Thanks."

After the bark was scraped it was necessary to pound it with stone hammers to ensure that when the horny outer husk was peeled off, the inner layers would be flexible enough for use as cloth. Jane had found herself enjoying the unhurried monotony of scraping but she found that the extra effort involved in the use of the hammer destroyed the pleasure for her.

Perhaps when I'm stronger, she told herself.

"You don't seem to be enjoying your work as much as you were earlier," Grace Benson, the Textile Manager, told her.

"I suppose not," Jane agreed. "Scraping's more fun. But I'll get used to pounding."

"You're from a small town, aren't you?"

"From a township, actually. Drummond Island Township."

"Do you know anything about spinning or weaving?"

"I'm afraid not. We bought our clothes in stores and made our money renting boats to big city tourists."

"Actually, the only people I've ever met who *did* have any experience with spinning and weaving were the idle rich," the Textile Production Manager said, then paused significantly.

She's giving me time to realize that she must have been one of the idle rich, Jane realized. *So what? It doesn't make any difference here.*

"I guess you must know quite a bit about spinning and weaving," she said.

"Quite a bit," Grace Benson agreed. "And I'd like to start teaching what I know to other people so we can get started producing some *real* textiles."

"What's wrong with barkcloth?" Jane asked.

"A lot of things. It's scratchy, for one thing, and it's too heavy for this climate, for another. It's more like leather than anything else. Tree leather. I'd like to see us producing something more like cotton, or perhaps a light wool. Would you be interested in learning?"

"I'd like to try it, but I'm supposed to be pounding bark today."

"I already told John I needed someone else and asked him who he could spare."

"Me?"

"You. Actually, it's just a formality, me asking him, since you're already working for me. Barkcloth's my responsibility. But since you'd made up a preference list without spinning or weaving on it I thought I'd better check with him. You don't really *enjoy* pounding bark, do you?"

"Not too much," Jane admitted. "But I'm not trying to get out of my responsibilities."

"You won't be." Mrs. Benson smiled. "There's no lack of work."

"That's all the berries and the sacks are only about two thirds full," Tom said. "Do you think you could get them both back to the settlement on your own?"

"I guess so. Why?"

"This patch wasn't all that big. I'd like to go out looking for another one. OK?"

"OK," Amber said, hoisting the sacks.

"You don't seem to have the necessary coordination," Grace Benson told Jane. "You've been doing the exercise routine Krishna taught you?"

"Every day," Jane said.

"Well, let's hope that it's just a matter of time. It just takes some of us a little longer to adapt than others. Perhaps you'd better go back to pounding bark today. Maybe you'll develop the necessary coordination in a couple of weeks. If you do, we can try again."

Not a chance, Jane thought.

Tom stared gleefully at the insect trapped in the crystal globe. It was vermillion, with jaws, fangs, and pinchers of olive green, and night-black wings. Not a pseudowasp: had it been free its interest in Tom would have been limited to killing and eating him. None of that complicated business with ovipositors and egg cases.

The insect crawled relentlessly up and down, covering the inside surface of the globe. Seeking a way out that wasn't there.

Feeling greatly daring, Tom tapped the globe with a stick. The insect buzzed angrily, wings vibrating, snapping and unsnapping its pinchers. The tips of its fangs glistened with drops of some brown fluid: undoubtedly some sort of poison.

You're in there and I'm out here, Tom thought. *You're the one getting eaten this time.*

He hadn't really hated the things—feared them, yes, but not hated them—until the night when a number of them had gotten into one of the huts and eaten David, the first communicator the colony had had and his closest friend.

Careful to keep the tip of the stick from coming into contact with any part of his body, he lifted it so that the part with which he'd touched the globe was just below the olfactory opening on his right cheek. The perfume was there, just as he'd remembered it: sweet and subtle, fresh like the air after an Earthly thunderstorm. Not at all like the stench of a rankorchid.

He made his way out of the trapglobe patch, using the stick when necessary to keep the globes from brushing against him: one drop of the volatile oil on him and he'd awaken in the middle of the night to find himself being eaten. And even if they were unable to breach the walls of his hut, the perfume's powerful effect would keep them from lapsing back into hibernation with daybreak: they'd get him as soon as he left his hut.

But he was always careful, and it was worth the risk to see them trapped and being eaten. He walked away laughing.

The bags of greenberries were bulky but quite light and Amber had no difficulty in carrying them; the route back to the settlement was familiar enough to require little attention.

The Latihan doesn't work for me, he told himself, returning as he always did when free of distractions to the matters that most concerned him. *But God wouldn't just cut me off from Himself, no matter how mistaken I was to think he wanted me to come here. He's not vindictive, not like the Christians think. This is a test of some sort. It must be a test. But what does he want from me?*

He was briefly aware of the complicatedness of his thought structures, but he pushed the awareness out of his consciousness: self-examination was necessary but too much self-consciousness was arrogance.

When he saw the turtle-shaped outcropping he turned to the right, aiming for two tall trees that grew from a single trunk.

This world, he thought. *Everything in it's a distraction.* He looked up at the glowing crimson leaves of the trees. To his left he could see some bronze flowers too small to be worth collecting gleaming in the dappled forest light. *It's beautiful here but I'm not ready for beauty yet. I don't deserve it; it distracts me, keeps my thoughts from God. I've got to devote myself to you, Lord, turn my back on this world and concentrate on You alone.*

Then maybe God would fix the wrongness inside him. Then maybe God would take him back.

The settlement was coming into view, but Amber wasn't ready to face his fellow colonists. He put the bags of greenberries down, seated himself on the ground beside them. He had to think.

●   ●   ●

Ray Jarvis hacked away at the runner. This section of root was long enough to make a good shovel handle, if they could get it straight enough in the fire.

His machete was dull again. He went back to the forge to get Josephus to put a new edge on it.

Amber's course of action was suddenly clear to him. He would have to build himself a hut of his own, move out of the hut he shared with Jane.

It was wrong for the two of them to sleep naked in the same hut. Even here, where there was no sex. It would be difficult to explain his decision to Jane without hurting her feelings, but he had no choice. He had to do what was right.

He got to his feet, shouldered the bags. Began walking the rest of the way back to the settlement.

CHAPTER SEVENTEEN

JOSEPHUS HAD bagged two fruitbears and Bill Simmons had come up with something that John Wosky immediately labeled a dire mouse: a mild-looking animal with pink fur and a long pointed nose, about twice the size of a fruit bear, which Robert Elgin pronounced an insectivore on the basis of its teeth. So there was meat on the table for dinner.

But Amber refused to touch it, despite Jane's pleading.

"Remember what happened to you on Earth when your mother didn't give you any meat to eat," she said finally. "You don't want to hurt yourself."

"Things are different here, Jane," Tom said in an attempt to keep the peace. He was the only other one at the table. "It's a lot easier to keep healthy on a vegetarian diet here. Krishna says you can do fine with just fruit and a little barkpulp."

"He should eat meat," Jane insisted.

"No," Amber said. "Not any more."

"Why not?" Tom asked.

"I need to—" Amber paused, searching for the words. "I need to purify myself," he said finally.

"By not eating meat?"

"Yes. Not having any part in killing things. That seems like a good place to start."

"You don't object to the rest of us eating meat, do you?" Tom asked.

"No. I just— It just doesn't seem right for me. That's all." He took a final bite from the melon he was eating. "I've got to go work on my hut," he said, standing. "I'll see you later."

"You didn't get enough to eat," Jane said. "You'll get sick. Please. Eat something else."

"No. Thank you, but—I don't need any more." He picked up his platter and left.

"He won't listen to me any more," Jane said.

"He's an adult now," Tom reminded her gently. "He's got a right to think what he wants as long as he does his share for the community. And there are quite a few of the rest of us who don't eat meat: Krishna, Catherine, Ed, probably a lot of other people I don't know about. Meat really isn't necessary to stay healthy here."

"That's not it," Jane said. "He's—he's not really part of the community any more. He's cut himself off."

"I don't know," Tom said. "He's got a right to his privacy. And it's not as if he didn't contribute. He does more than his share of the work, as a matter of fact. Like that hut he's building himself. If he'd put in a request I'm sure he could have gotten at least some labor-credits for his time, but he didn't want any. And when I offered to help him with it, he said he'd rather do it completely on his own in whatever time he had left over after doing his share for the community."

"But that's just it," Jane said. "Don't you see—he's just going through the motions, pretending to be one of us, when really he's locked himself up inside his head where he can hide from all of us—"

"From you, you mean?"

"Yes. I can't touch him anymore. He's—distant, polite, but—I don't know! I'm *worried* about him, Tom."

"Have you mentioned anything to Sandra?"

"No. I didn't like the idea of, well, reporting him, like he was a criminal."

"You're being stupid, Jane. If you think he needs help, talk to Sandra and get him some help. And maybe she'll tell you that things aren't as bad as you think they are."

"But," voicing her fear for the first time, "what if he's going insane, Tom? What if he's already gone insane?"

"Then he needs help more than ever."

• • •

"He says he still loves me and that he still wants to be a part of the community here, but . . . he's so cold now, so distant. Like I'm not even there when he talks to me. He was supposed to get smarter, but—"

"He is smarter," Sandra said. "There's no doubt about it. He's learned to do things he could never have done on Earth."

"Yes, I know, but . . . he was always so much like a child, always trying to learn new things and I'd hoped that, here. . . ."

"That here he'd blossom, take a greater and greater interest in the world around him, find everything new and wonderful and joyous?"

"You make it sound so foolish."

"He's starting to grow up, Jane. That means he's starting to change. There's nothing you can do about it."

"But he's shutting himself away from everybody, just closing himself in, not telling anyone what he thinks. . . . And that idea of his, that because we aren't married we shouldn't sleep in the same hut. Like he was trying to become some sort of a saint."

"It sounds as though he *is* trying to become some sort of saint. And saints are different, Jane. It's a whole different way of thinking."

"Then you don't think there's anything wrong with him?"

"I didn't say that. To be blunt, the chances are far, far greater that he's going insane than that he's going through any sort of transformation that will leave him sane from our point of view. But what I'm trying to make you see is that he's just as lost to you as a saint as he would be if he was insane. So the question is, do you want to do what you can to help him, whether or not it means you'll end up losing him, or do you just want to hang on to him?"

That night, back in the hut he still shared with Jane, Amber heard the scrape and buzz of horny wings as two huge insects fought or mated on the other side of the doorflap.

They sound worse than that butterfly thing Tom showed me, he thought. *I've got to make sure I build my hut safe. Otherwise I'll end up like John.*

Suddenly he was back at John's funeral: *John Abercromie, the Planner, standing on his gimp leg watching while the four grave*

diggers—Karl Archard and Robert Cortona, the two other Plan-
ners, and the two other Johns in the colony, John Dolland and John
Lanier—dug the shallow grave-hole in the loose-packed, reddish
soil. Naked—the colony could have afforded to waste the barkcloth
for a shroud but as a matter of principle had declined to do so—his
body showing the wounds where Mircea had successfully removed
five out of the six egg cases the pseudowasp had deposited in him
and the black gash in his abdomen where the eggs had been so
deeply buried that Mircea's attempt to remove them had been fatal,
he was lowered into the hole. The colonists filed by, each throwing
a handful of earth onto the body. When everyone had had a turn the
four grave diggers shoveled the rest of the soil onto the corpse and
tramped it down. The ceremony over, everyone stood around a
while in awkward silence, then people began drifting away singly
and in small groups. . . .

But that's just a memory! Amber realized with a start. Yet it had
been so vivid, so convincing, so much like reality.

My new brain, he realized. *I really am smarter now; I can*
remember things so they're just like they're real. So real. . . .

The Latihan, he thought. *My Latihans, back on Earth. If I can*
just remember being with God, remember the times so exactly that I
can feel myself living them, if I can recreate for myself what it is to
be in the Presence of the Lord, to be pure, then maybe, maybe I can
make myself worthy of Him again.

Jane would not return to the hut for some time. She was at a Slash
and Vomit Meeting. As usual, Amber had chosen to stay away: he
had no desire to take part in the verbal battles in which the colonists
vented pent-up angers and attacked what they disliked in each
other—all in the name of perfectibility, but the perfection they were
striving for was not the same as that to which Amber had given his
allegiance.

Before, God made it easy for me to feel His Presence because I
had no strength of my own. But now that He has allowed me to find
the strength of mind and of will that I lacked then He demands more
of me.

My first Latihan, he decided. *When I first realized that God was*
speaking to me. . . .

Memory blotted out the present. And suddenly it was memory no longer, and the sky broke open and God descended on him in flames of fire and ice.

"Were our examinations the only factor under consideration, we'd accept you for transfer," Curtis Adam told Brother Ashoka. "But the Mallorys are our test case for persons who've undergone the alterations in consciousness resulting from exposure to your Inductor, and while Manuel Candamo tells us that Jane Mallory seems to be adjusting quite well to life on Deirdre, her cousin seems to be withdrawing completely from the life of the community. And his reasons for doing so seem to be religious."

"But—"

"Of course we realize that his former mental retardation makes him very much a special case, but Manuel Candamo has reported that he speaks of almost nothing but his efforts to purify himself in order, as I understand it, to make himself worthy of God. His cousin has said very little about him, which is wholly understandable, but she has stated that he's moving out of the hut they've shared up until now because he feels that it's immoral for two unmarried people to sleep in the same hut. Which, you must admit, is a pretty bizarre irrationality on a world where there's neither sex nor sexuality."

"Amber's attitude towards the Latihan was never quite the same as that of the rest of us in the Fellowship," Brother Ashoka said.

"So I understand. But perhaps it's a case of something universally present showing itself most clearly in extreme cases. However, I grant you the Inductor may have had nothing to do with his present mental state. And, for that matter, he may come out of it none the worse. But, since he does seem to be deviating further and further from the Deirdran norm, and since his deviations are assuming a religious direction, we think we should observe him further before allowing anyone else from the Fellowship of Prismatic Light to transfer."

"But Jane's doing all right, isn't she?"

"To the best of our knowledge."

"All right, then. I see your point, but—Listen. I've known Amber since he was a child; he's the closest thing I've got to a son and I was the one who initiated him into the Latihan: if any harm's come to him as a result it's at least partially my responsibility. From what you've told me it sounds as if he's badly in need of spiritual guidance. I can help him.''

"I sympathize with your feelings, of course," Curtis Adamaski said, neither looking nor sounding as though he sympathized with anyone or anything, "but I'm afraid that we can't permit you to transfer."

"But if you decide that Jane's going to be all right—"

"Then perhaps you can transfer."

"Ray's been talking to me about the insect problem," John said. "That's why I called this special meeting. He's got a—well, not a solution, but an idea that might help some. He thinks that if we collect a lot of armor frogs and bring them back to the colony—"

"They'd just wander off," Robert Elgin said. "They stay where the undergrowth's thickest."

"But that's the whole point. They can't climb and they can only hop a few inches. Now, if we were to build a barkhusk fence a foot or so high all around the settlement they couldn't leave and they'd help keep the insect population down. Building the fence would be less than a day's work if everyone who wasn't doing something else essential helped."

"How do we catch them?" Catherine asked.

"Simple. Except when its raining they sleep days. We can just pick them up and pop them into sacks like fruit."

"What about the barbed spears on their forelegs?" Mircea asked. "They could produce pretty nasty wounds. And they've got to be pretty damned strong to spear those worms."

"The frogs don't wake up when you handle them," John said. "Ray and I both tried it."

"What if they die when we bring them here?" Lyn asked. "Like all the plants I try to transplant do?"

"Ray?" John asked.

"I think it's worth the risk. I'd like to put Dan in charge of getting the fence built. Any objections? OK, let's decide who's doing really essential stuff and who can spend today on the fence."

• • •

"Would you like to help with the Newcomers?" Will asked Jane.

"I don't know anything about babies or anything like that," Jane replied doubtfully.

"You don't have to, really. You just have to have patience. These babies understand English. And your experience with your cousin, back on Earth when he was mentally retarded, might be helpful."

"All right," Jane said.

"I've talked to Grace and she says she can spare you today. Come on. I'll show you how to feed them."

The framework was completed and the bark slabs were in place. Amber was punching holes in them so he could lace them tight. It was dull, boring work and when he felt the urge to memory come over him as it had so often of late he surrendered to it gratefully:

God looming sky tall, His body the world itself, His face all created beings, His Smile, the Smile that encompasses all possible expressions, moon-wide. He begins to speak and Amber is transfixed by the majesty of His utterance, by words too awesome for mortal comprehension—

Amber snapped back to the present. It was almost dark. He'd have to hurry if he hoped to get back to the hut he still shared with Jane before the insects awakened from their daytime hibernation.

He picked his way carefully back to the hut. The armor frogs were awake and hopping around; it was hard to avoid stepping on them.

Back in the hut, lying on his back on his bed of leaves, he suddenly realized, *It wasn't like that the first time. That was new.*

Had he at last found the way back to God that he was intended to find? Or was this a delusion, a temptation perhaps that he was intended to overcome?

I can't be sure, he told himself, resisting the voice within him which told him success was within his grasp. *I've got to be stricter with myself from now on, keep a closer watch on myself. That way maybe I can find out the truth.*

In a part of Deirdre far from the settlement a long dormant volcano suddenly erupted. It belched forth great clouds of smoke and cinders and poisonous gases, sent streams of red-molten magma flowing over the countryside, burying hundreds of thousands of plants and animals beneath the liquid rock, killing untold others in the fires it caused. Two species of a mosslike plant that had grown on the volcano's slopes and nowhere else were completely destroyed.

The disaster was serious: the Forest Mind roused itself from its centuries-long slumber. The shape of the event was perceived: an imperative took form. Similar events were recalled; the pattern of response which had proved most appropriate was selected. A sequence of recolonization was determined.

Plants that ordinarily reproduced asexually began to develop flowers: cross fertilization would be required to produce offspring appropriate to the new conditions. Plants able to break down rock for the formation of soil began to produce spores. Everything around the periphery of the dead area began to grow at an accelerated rate, roots creeping out to grip the once-molten rock almost before it was cool.

The sequence of recolonization established, the Forest Mind found its attention drawn to the human settlement: the colonists were an obvious threat to the Forest Mind's dominance.

The shape of that threat refused to conform to any previously perceived pattern: the imperative that formed was unclear. But there was a partial correspondence with the pattern that signified the competition of another minded forest. An attempt would be made to respond with the sequence of actions that had rendered the Forest Mind victorious over all its competitors.

Around the colony's perimeter fruit began to wither. Edible roots and tubers began to die. An insect-trapping globe opened, releasing a white-winged moth capable of killing and devouring a colonist within minutes; around the opening globe the other globes increased their secretion of volatile oils a hundredfold. Insects swarmed to them, departed maddened and unconsumed.

Fruit bears, near squirrels, wood pigs, and dire mice sought each other out and mated.

Tom kept an armor frog in his hut in the hope that it would take care of any insect that managed to make its way into the hut. He was in the habit of petting it before he went to sleep. The armor frog had never responded with anything approaching affection, but it had never seemed to mind the attention.

This time it stabbed him in the hand with both of its spiked forelegs.

It was dark in the hut; he couldn't see the thing to catch it. It stabbed him again in the foot and he caught it.

It struggled in his hand, trying to stab him again. Outside the night was full of insects; he didn't dare open the doorflap and throw the frog outside, but if he released it in the hut it would stab him again.

In the end he crushed it underfoot.

CHAPTER EIGHTEEN

"RAY JARVIS asked us to call this meeting," John Abercromie said. He was standing with the Research Coordinator on the mound; Laurent Eliade and Robert Cortona, the two other Planners, were off to one side. "The armor frog he keeps in his hut stabbed him in the neck while he was sleeping last night. It didn't kill him, of course, and Mircea says the wound isn't serious, but it hurt. What we need to know is, has anyone else had trouble with their frogs? Raise your hands if you have."

Four hands went up.

"You first, Brian," John said. "You keep a frog in your hut too, don't you?"

"I did. Anyway, as soon as I stepped inside last night the damn thing tried to stab me. My scales protected me pretty well—it aimed for my foot—but it hurt like hell. Then it tried it again and I had to kill it."

"What about you, Tom?"

"Same story, only it got me in the hand and *then* in the foot."

"Sarah?"

"My frog stabbed me in the side when I lay down. I couldn't catch it in the dark and it kept trying to get me so I wrapped myself up in barkcloth to keep the insects away and ran over to Justine's."

"That's crazy stupid, Sarah," Brian said. "You're lucky you weren't eaten."

"What about making some sort of protective clothing people could wear when they had to go out at night?" Bill Simmons asked. "Out of frogskin or something?"

"We'll go into that later. It doesn't sound like a bad idea. But you had your hand raised, Will."

"I heard some noise last night but didn't think anything of it; a lot of the newcomers have trouble sleeping regular hours. But when I opened up the roof this morning to let in some light I saw that both Ellen and Mike were hurt. Not seriously, luckily, but Ellen was pretty much helpless and if one of the frogs had gotten her in the eye—"

"It didn't happen," Catherine said. "Let's worry about what did."

"Right," John said. "Who else keeps frogs in their huts? Nobody? That's what I thought. So that means that *all* the armor frogs that could get at people attacked people last night. What does that suggest to the rest of you?"

"That they don't like to be kept in huts?" Bill Simmons suggested.

"This is serious, Bill," John said.

"So am I," Bill said. "Why couldn't it be a reaction to being kept caged up?"

"Anyway," Ray Jarvis said, "the point is that if they're attacking people now it's not safe to have them around. We've got to get rid of them."

"That's what I was leading up to," John said. "We need two people to gather up all the frogs inside the fence and put them outside the fence. There's no danger involved; they're sleeping today."

"I'll do it myself," Jarvis volunteered.

"So will I," Sally added.

"Good. That takes care of that. Now—"

"John, I'm afraid that doesn't take care of it," Jarvis said.

"What do you mean?"

"Look what happened last night. An animal we thought we had pegged changed its behavior and changed it completely. And not just a single individual, but every specimen of the species that we could observe. *And* the change was such that, for the first time on Deirdre, we were attacked by something other than an insect. This is important; we can't ignore it. What if everything else starts changing? What if, say, the insects start coming out during the day? It's vital that we discover why the armor frogs all started attacking us."

"I agree," Rosabeth said.

"So do I," Robert Elgin said.

"And speaking in my capacity as The Department of Defense, I feel I should warn you all to be very careful whenever you're around any type of animal now," Josephus said. "The others might get violent too."

"How?" Bill Simmons demanded. "They're too little and they don't have any fangs or claws. Are you scared of being nuzzled to death?"

"You're out of order, Bill," John said. "Ray, I want you and Bob, and I guess you too, Josephus, to make a study of what's going on with the frogs and the other animals. Meanwhile, let's the rest of us get back to our normal routines."

"Last night the forest sent out almost ninety runners and plants are sprouting up all over inside the fence," Rosabeth said. "Including some types I haven't seen before. I'm going to need at least five people to help me today, three to chop off runners and two to uproot stuff."

"What about repairing the fence?" Ted asked. "Some of the runners went right through it."

"Dan's taking care of it. Besides, we don't *want* to keep the frogs in anymore."

"I'll help pull weeds," Jane said.

"OK, but we need four more people. How about you, Amber?"
Amber did not reply. He stood absolutely still, staring into nothingness.

Tom passed a hand in front of his eyes. Jane grabbed him by the arm. He did not react.

"Paralyzed!" the colonist on the other side of Amber yelled, backing away from him. "A day wasp—"

"No!" Brian cut him off before he could panic the group. "There aren't any day wasps. And look at him. He doesn't have any of the signs: he's not rigid; his face isn't contorted; there aren't any lumps on him. He's just in some kind of trance."

"Is he doing that spiritual exercise you and he used to do before you came here?" Rosabeth asked Jane.

"The Latihan? I don't think so. No, I'm sure he's not doing a Latihan—I'd be able to feel it, inside me, if he was. Our brains are wrong for the Latihan here. Neither of us can do it anymore."

"Then what's he doing?" Brain asked.

"I don't know," Jane said. "He's been—different lately. All he thinks about is God. Sometimes he acts like he doesn't hear me. But I've never seen him like this."

"Brian," Rosabeth said, "you and that idiot who started yelling about day wasps take him and put him with the Newcomers. Will can keep watch over him until we can get Mircea and Sandra to take a look at him.

"And somebody go find John," she said as the two colonists carried him off.

"I thought Tom said these fig apples wouldn't be ready for another week."

"They must have been ripe or the fruitbears wouldn't have eaten them."

"Let's move on to the next patch. I found that one myself; I *know* the fruit there's not ripe yet."

Three cream and beige fruit bears scampered away into the underbrush at their approach.

"Well, Jarvis was wrong. They didn't attack us."

"Maybe so, but you usually have to shoo them away. These bears were scared of us."

"And look at the fig apples they were eating. They *aren't* ripe enough."

"The fruitbears were eating them, weren't they?"

"They shouldn't have been."

"We'll report it when we get back. But as long as we're here let's get what they left."

But there wasn't much fruit left on the bushes.

Amber came out of his reverie to find himself lying on a bed of leaves in the Newcomers' hut. He sat up.

"You OK now?" Will asked. Amber noticed Mircea standing by Will's side, watching him.

"Sure. What am I doing here?"

"You went into some sort of trance. We couldn't wake you up. What happened?"

"I was thinking."

"Pretty deep thoughts. Anyway, John told me to tell you he wants to see you. Sandra'll want to see you too, as soon as we find her, but we haven't had a chance to tell her about you yet."

"John's over talking with Manuel," Mircea said. "Would you like me to take you over to see him?"

"I don't need any help. I'm fine."

"I'm sure you are. I checked you out while you were unconscious and as far as I can tell you're in perfect health. But if you don't mind, I'd like to accompany you."

"I guess I don't mind."

I came so close, he thought as they made their way across the settlement. *But I'm not ready yet. Not quite.*

He ignored the stares the other colonists directed at him. What did God want of him?

The rankorchid obeyed new imperatives. Mottled yellow patterns had appeared on its blossom; the perfume it exuded was sweeter, subtler, less like the odor of carrion. Insects which usually never visited rankorchids were drawn to it, crawled in through its narrow throat, brushing against the new organs that had formed there, were allowed to escape uneaten but smeared with reproductive substances to visit other plants. Rankorchid to propellor tree to bronze-flower vine to flowering redmoss: a long chain of plants contributing genetic materials usually kept separate.

Seeds formed, germinated, grew into plants not seen on Deirdre since the last of the Forest Mind's rivals had been destroyed. Fruitbears, near squirrels, wood pigs and dire mice ate the hybrid plants. Most of them died.

The survivors mated. Most of the offspring were stillborn and the majority of those that were not were useless to the Forest Mind. They died.

A few, a very few, were allowed to survive.

● ● ●

"What happened to you?" John asked.

"I was thinking," Amber said. "Sorry. What do you want me to do now?"

"Now? I want you to tell me some things. Then I'm going to want you to talk to Sandra, if we can ever find her. What were you thinking about? God?"

"Yes."

"Care to tell me about it?"

"I'd rather not."

"You don't have any real choice, Amber. And I'm not all that unsympathetic. My uncle was a priest. Try me."

"I used to talk to God in the Latihan, but—I can't do the Latihan here."

"I understand. So—"

"This new brain, its memory's much better than my old one's was . . . I can remember the times I spoke with God, I—"

"That's all you were doing?" Manuel asked. "Just remembering?"

"No. Lately—" Should he admit it? Yes: he had nothing to hide. From anybody. "Lately the memories have been—changing."

"You know the day's three-quarters gone," John said. "You weren't just thinking or remembering, you were in a trance. Like Manuel here when his mind's back on Earth."

"The memories. . . . My new brain makes them so real for me, like they're really happening to me again—"

"Do you go into these trances often?" John asked.

"Sometimes," Amber admitted. "But they never last very long. And I always get all my work done."

"Nobody's ever said you didn't. But do these—trances—just happen to you? And can you come out of them when you want to?"

"I never want to come out of them," Amber said. "They're the only way I can bring myself closer to God right now."

"Isn't that arrogant on your part?" John asked. "To think that *you* can bring yourself closer to God? Isn't that up to God?"

"It's not like that, it's—I can't explain. It's not like that."

"Can you keep these trances from happening to you?" Manuel asked.

"I don't know, but . . . I don't want to keep them from happening, they're—"

"But can you?" John asked.

"But I don't—why should I try to stop them? They're. . . ."

"Look," Manuel said, "I know something about trances. I go into trances every day. And I've always got two people to watch over me to make sure nothing happens to me. Otherwise it wouldn't be safe."

"Say you were out in the forest collecting fruit or something," John said. "And it was late afternoon. And then say you went into one of your trances. You might still be in it when night came. Or you might get caught in a rainstorm. Either way you'd be dead. The insects would get you for sure. See?"

"Yes." He knew that he could never convince them that God would not let anything like that happen.

"There's another thing," John said. "I've been hearing a lot about animals acting strangely in the last few days. And I'm afraid that this behavior on your part's just another aspect of the same thing."

"No. I'm—" He stopped, unable to put words to his thoughts.

"Yes, I know. *You* think you're just doing what you need to do to become a saint. And you may be right. But *I* don't know that. So I want you to put yourself under Mircea and Sandra's care and do whatever they tell you. All right?"

"I guess."

"I'm not finished. Even if Mircea doesn't find anything wrong with you physically—"

"Which, considering the state of the medical arts here, I'm not likely to do," the Health Manager said.

"And even if Sandra and Catherine decide that your—let's term it your belief-system—doesn't make you an active danger to the community—"

"I'm not," Amber said. "I wouldn't hurt anybody. Ever."

"Nonetheless, I don't want you leaving the settlement until I give you permission to do so. And whenever you feel a trance coming on I want you to fight it off. OK?"

"No. I can't do what you're asking me to. I do my work, you can't say I don't do what I should to help the colony, but this is too important, God used to speak to me in the Latihan and now He—But if I can bring myself closer—I can't not—No.''

"At least you're being honest," John said. "But I can't let you out of the settlement until I'm sure you can keep yourself from going into a trance whenever you're somewhere it might not be safe. And until I'm sure that you *will* keep yourself from going into trances whenever you're outside the settlement.''

"I can't stop them," Amber said. "I—won't. It would be—you used that word, arrogant. . . .''

"Listen, Amber, you're shirking your duties by going into trances when you should be working. Aren't you? You say you do your work but you wasted almost the whole day today, didn't you? And not only your day but Rosabeth's day, Will's day, Mircea's day, my day, and part of Sandra's day as soon as we find her. Well?''

"I—'' Amber stopped, thought. "I've got to do my work. And it's not right for me to keep other people from doing what they're supposed to do. I'll try not to think too much about God when I'm working but—I can't make you any promises, I don't want to lie to you about anything, I—''

"That's all right, Amber. Just do your best.''

"What do you want me to do now?''

John thought a moment. "Why don't you go look for Jane? She's been pulling up weeds all day and worrying about you. Go tell her what's been happening with you and take over for her. Then send her back here to talk with me. I'll send someone to get you as soon as we find Sandra.''

Amber left.

"Manuel, cross over to Earth and see what they can tell us about Amber's condition," John said. "If it's something like what happened with the armor frogs—I'd hate to think what would happen if we all found ourselves going into trances whether we wanted to or not.

"Mircea, take care of Manuel. I'm going to go look for Sandra.''

He limped off.

The Forest Mind was aware of the colonists, not only as a cancerous disturbance in its ecological body, but as a cacophony of discordant imperatives which it could integrate into none of the patterns which were the essence of its being. The imperatives pulled at it, demanding satisfaction, but it was powerless, unable to stimulate and inhibit them, to guide or control them. Yet it groped tirelessly for contact, itself stimulated to full awareness by the resemblance of the present threat to that once posed by the rivals from which it had wrested control of all Deirdre. The imperatives of all the lesser plants and beasts were subsumed to its own, overpowering imperative.

"The situation's too complicated," Manuel said. "If the only factor was the new brain capacity he gained when he was translated, or if the only factor was his former exposure to the Latihan and that damned Inductor—But as it is, we can't be sure of anything."

"What about the frogs?" Catherine asked. "If everybody's going to go insane and start attacking each other we'd better figure out what to do about it, and fast."

"There's a chance that whatever affected the frogs is affecting Amber," Manuel said. "But it may not affect anyone else. Maybe his augmented brain capacity renders him vulnerable where none of the rest of us would be. Or maybe the time he spent with the Fellowship of Prismatic Light's responsible."

"Jane seems perfectly normal," Sandra said. "And Amber doesn't seem dangerous in any way."

"But he's not rational," John said. "And we don't know *why* he isn't or what's likely to happen to him next. He might grab a knife and start killing people."

"You're assuming he's insane," Sandra said. "Worse than that: to listen to you talk, we've got a homicidal maniac on our hands. I'm not convinced he's insane, and if he's insane I don't think he's dangerous."

"What about the frogs?" Catherine said. "This isn't Earth: the important thing isn't that his actions appear harmless, but that *we don't understand them,* and what we don't understand on an alien world may very well turn out to be dangerous."

"I said they told me they couldn't be sure of anything," Manuel said. "But they did have a theory that would explain the facts, even if they couldn't be sure just how likely it was to be true."

"You might have mentioned this a little earlier," John said.

"I wanted to get some of the objections out of the way first."

"I'm not at all sure I want my objections 'out of the way,' as you put it," Catherine said.

"But you haven't even heard what he has to say," Sandra said.

"Sorry, Catherine," Manuel said. "I expressed myself poorly. What I should have said was that I wanted to have some of the objections stated before I continued so they would serve to qualify what I said. Is that more satisfactory?"

"Much."

"Good. Then, to continue—the Institute's psychologists think that what's happening to Amber may very well be analogous to what happens to a person in a sensory deprivation tank."

"Sorry," Catherine said. "You've lost me."

"And me," John said.

"Do you want to explain it, Sandra?" Manuel asked. "You can probably do it better than I can."

"All right. To begin with, sensory deprivation's only one term for it; it's also known as profound isolation, which has a lot less negative sound to it."

"It still doesn't mean anything to me," John said.

"Well, a classical sensory deprivation tank was filled with fluid at about body temperature and so designed that the person in it floated free of all sense of gravity, seeing, hearing, and feeling next to nothing of the outside world. Thus a lot of the subject's brain's computer capacity, which would otherwise have been taken up with relating to the world outside the subject's body, was freed for other uses, often with quite interesting results. Some people were—and are—able to use the additional computer capacity to modify parts of their personality and to actually change the way their brains functioned.

"But for the ordinary person in a sensory deprivation tank all that happens is that he or she begins to hallucinate. Sometimes the hallucinations are bizarre and seemingly meaningless—for example, one person saw an endless procession of scissors of all kinds—but often the brain produces whole scenes and conversations which the person in the tank is unable to distinguish from reality."

She stopped and looked at Manuel, who continued: "Now in

Amber's case, something similar could well be taking place. He suddenly has all this new brain capacity which has no assigned function, no designated part to play in his normal personality, and no one to train him to integrate his new capacities successfully into the rest of his personality."

"Which is partially my fault and partially the Institute's," Sandra said.

"Yes. So he's had to achieve the integration on his own and his need for unreality—his need to perceive God—has resulted in the integration of all this new brain capacity as a sort of internal holovision set with which he can watch religious dramas and see God."

"Which still doesn't prove he's going to remain harmless," Catherine said.

"Why didn't you keep this from happening to him?" Jane demanded fiercely. "You seem to have known all about it; you must have been able to do *something* to keep it from happening."

"On Earth we would have been able to keep a closer watch on him," Sandra said. "And maybe somebody would have realized what was happening and been able to help him. But here? Jane, there's never been a case like Amber's before. And—Jane, it's easy enough to come up with theories to explain things after they happen but it's a lot harder to predict what's going to happen. And he seemed to be doing fine. *You* knew he wasn't, but you were too scared to tell anybody, so. . . . Did you ever hear about the boy who was raised by the wolves?"

"No."

"It happened in India, I think it was, a long time ago. When the boy was discovered—I don't remember how old he was, maybe a teenager, maybe an adult—it was too late for him to learn to be a normal human being. Do you understand what I'm saying? He'd been raised as a wolf and no matter how hard people tried to educate him he stayed pretty much a wolf. Well, we thought Amber would stay pretty much like he'd always been, just getting a little smarter as time went on. But the point is, we didn't know what was going to happen to him—and even if we'd known exactly what I know today we still might not have been able to do anything to help him."

"But you could have done *something!*"

"Maybe. If you hadn't pretended that everything was all right."

"I was afraid. And I thought that, you know, he was just taking a long time to get used to being here. It's so beautiful here, I knew he'd learn to love it if he just had a chance—"

"You must have suspected something was wrong."

"I knew he wasn't, wasn't . . . but I was afraid you'd think he was insane. I was afraid you'd think he was insane because he couldn't do the Latihan here and that you'd think I was going to go insane too."

"He may not be insane, Jane. He may just be different."

"No."

"It might be easier on you if he *is* insane, Jane."

"What do you mean?"

"If he's sick he might recover. But if what's happened is that he's changed. . . ."

"Listen, Jane," John said, "he may come out of this, he may not. Catherine thinks he could be dangerous. I don't but I can't afford to take the chance that I'm wrong. So we're going to have to keep a close watch on him from now on. It'll be easiest on him if he doesn't suspect he's being watched, and the easiest way to make sure of that is to have you be the one watching him."

"I don't want to spy on him," Jane said.

"Do you think I like asking you to? Think about the fact that I'm the one asking you, not Catherine. This is supposed to be a utopia, not a police state; the whole idea of people spying on other people and making secret reports makes me sick. I hate it. But I don't know what else I *can* do, except lock him up, and I don't want to do that. Though in a way it would be the more honest thing to do.

"Look, I want you to tell me about anything strange he says or does. Don't tell me anything else. And the only people I'll tell are Sandra, so she can help him, and Manuel, so he can get the advice of people back on Earth. And Catherine—but only if you tell me something that makes me think he's getting dangerous. And I don't think he'll ever get dangerous. I hope he doesn't."

● ● ●

"We've decided to accept your application for transfer to Deirdre," Curtis Adamaski told Brother Ashoka.

"But with the problems Amber's been having adjusting—"

"I'm afraid I was never informed of the details of his difficulties—the psych staff keeps such things confidential—but I've been assured that his behavior conforms so closely to models devised on the assumption that the *only* basis for his problems is his augmented brain capacity that the people in charge of determining such things are no longer worried about the Latihan. And, of course, Ms. Mallory is still doing quite well."

"Good."

"So. Do you want me to submit your resume to the colony now?"

"Not just yet. Frankly, I still haven't convinced the Fellowship to fund my transfer."

"Well, if you do convince them, let me know and I'll set the process in motion. Meanwhile, good afternoon, Brother Ashoka."

"Good afternoon, Mr. Adamaski."

Night came. The armor frogs continued their slow hopping trek away from the settlement; the glidetoads were already long gone. But the insects remained, fighting among themselves over the food that remained.

And the offspring of the animals that had eaten the hybrid plants had mated and were about to produce offspring of their own.

CHAPTER NINETEEN

DINNER WAS barkpulp again: bitter, stringy and boring. What little fruit was still good had been set aside for the Newcomers.

Jane was sitting with John. Tom sat down next to them.

"Where's Amber?" he asked Jane.

"He's not eating tonight. He told me he didn't need any food, that he'd already had all he needed to eat for one day. He's out finishing his hut so he can sleep in it tonight."

"We may all have to cut down on our eating if things keep going the way they seem to be," John said.

"Another virtuous act," Tom said.

"He's not coming to the general meeting tonight, is he?" John asked.

"No. He's working on his hut. He'd come if it would mean breaking a rule to stay away, but unless some rule was involved he wouldn't come even if he wasn't working on that damn hut. He works and he works and he never complains about it—"

"I know he works," John said.

"—but he doesn't seem to care at all about what happens to the colony."

"Maybe he'll find God," Tom offered. "Would you care for some more pulp, Jane? I can't finish mine."

"No thanks. I'm not hungry."

Amber sat cross-legged on the rough floor of his completed hut. He felt hungry but he was getting used to the hunger, even coming to welcome it. As long as he remained fit enough to fulfill his worldly obligations he would continue to reduce his food consumption. Already he was down to a single small meal in the morning.

All the fruit and vegetables are gone, he thought. *All eaten by insects and nothing new growing in their place. It must be a sign: God must want me to learn something from it. But what?*

He sat alone in the darkness of his hut, feeling the air glide in through his central nostril, swirl around the interior of his chest without losing momentum, and then flow from his flanking nostrils. He knew Yogis on Earth concentrated on their breathing as a way of achieving inner peace but the more he focussed his attention on his breathing the more alien the rhythm became.

Yet despite the alien stink of his body, the wrongness of the breath flowing through him, he knew the time was approaching when he would grasp the purpose God had for him.

But still it eluded him, still he found himself unable to comprehend it.

I must have the patience to wait until the time comes which He has chosen, he told himself. *I must rise above my hatred for this unclean body. I must free myself, so God will deem me worthy of His Grace.*

It was Robert Cortona's turn as speaker. He mounted the mound and held up his arms for silence.

"Make yourselves comfortable," he said. "This is going to be a long meeting. It's probably going to be too long a meeting. So sit down.

"Now, before we get on to the real business—by which I mean, the matters which made us decide to call this meeting—we've got somebody here applying to us for his franchise. Emile, declare yourself."

One of the few colonists who had remained standing said haltingly, "My name is Emile Fontanas. I am a botanist and I ask to be included in this assembly."

"You've learned how to talk again, Emile, and that's the main requirement," Robert Cortona said. "Do any of the rest of you know any reason—moral turpitude, enemies in powerful places, perhaps a loathsome disease—why Emile shouldn't be enfranchised?'' The speaker looked around. "Nobody? OK, Emile, you're one of us. Sit down.

"The next order of business is food. There's no new fruit growing and what fruit and vegetables were to be found have been eaten by insects. Does anybody have any idea what's behind all this?"

"Why not ask Ray?" someone said.

"I already have—you'll get his opinions a little later. Right now I'm looking for other opinions."

"I've got an idea," Bill Simmons said.

"Stand up and tell us about it."

"I think we're in for a seasonal change. Look what's happened so far. First the armor frogs get vicious, then they disappear altogether. Because of the longer rains the insects have been getting worse and just in time to avoid getting eaten by them the fruit and vegetables cease to grow. Then there's the fact that the animals seem suddenly scared of us—and the wood pig I shot yesterday was pregnant. That's the first pregnant animal we've ever seen here. Plus, the forest sent out eighty-some runners last night—correct me if I'm wrong, Rosabeth."

"Eighty-three. And there seems to be a lot more stuff sprouting inside the settlement than there used to be."

"Do you remember when we used to get twenty or twenty-five runners a night at the most, and none of them as big as the monsters we're getting now? All these changes coming at the same time makes it pretty obvious that we've got a seasonal change on our hands."

"What do you suggest we do about it, Bill?" Robert Cortona asked.

"What anybody does about winter. Stock up on supplies and wait for spring. That's all we can do."

"Does anyone else have any different ideas? What about you, Ray?"

"I think—"

"Stand up and yell, Jarvis," somebody shouted. "We can't hear you over here."

The Ecologist and Research Coordinator stood up, looking tired. "I don't think it's seasonal," he said. "Or even cyclic. The cycle wouldn't make sense. Why would the armor frogs disappear now, at the very moment when there are more insects than ever before for them to eat? And they haven't all metamorphosed into glidetoads, either—Bob Elgin tells me the glidetoads are gone too. And Tom tells me that the trapglobes aren't trapping insects anymore. Now, that pregnant wood pig that Bill shot yesterday—and Mike killed two pregnant near squirrels too—what kind of cycle would involve animals bearing young only at the one time when there isn't any food to feed them with and when the danger from insects is so much worse than usual? And, why would the forest be sending out so many more runners at the very same time that the fruit and vegetables are all dying? It doesn't make sense." He sat down.

"What do you think's happening, then?" Bill Simmons demanded. "Maybe what we've seen is just the beginning of the change, maybe when real winter—or whatever—hits we'll all see a perfectly good reason for everything that's happening now."

"Maybe, but I doubt it."

"Robert—"

"You've got something to add, Lyn?"

"I think so. You all know how nothing'll grow for me if I transplant it or if I do anything to interfere with the way stuff grows wild? Well, I've pretty much come to the conclusion that this whole planet's ecology is regulated in some way. Everything's tied together. *Everything.* Or else how would every plant know *exactly* where it's supposed to grow."

"What's your point?" Robert Cortona asked.

"Just this. I think the whole ecology's acting against us. This world's never cooperated with us—you *know* how the plants and animals ignore us—and now I think Deirdre's at war with us."

"How do the pregnant animals tie in?" John Abercromie asked.

"Replacements for the ones we killed hunting, maybe. I don't know. But I'm positive that what we're up against is no normal seasonal change."

"It sounds as though you're saying that you believe there's some sort of intelligence directing everything against us," Sandra said. "Do you?"

"Seven Mystic Tibetan Masters up on a mountain thinking evil thoughts at us," Bill Simmons said.

"Shut up, Bill," Ray Jarvis said. "*Do* you think there's some intelligence directing things against us, Lyn?''

"No. Not exactly. I just think that the ecology here's unified in some way and that it's reacting against us as a unit."

"It's a possibility," Jarvis said. "Rosabeth?"

"It's a possibility but it's pretty unlikely."

"What do you think we should do if it isn't some sort of seasonal change?" Robert Cortona asked the Research Coordinator.

"I don't know. Lay in a good supply of bark pulp, maybe. It's our only remaining food supply and it might be the next thing to go. But you'd do better to ask somebody else."

"Meat," Grace Benson suggested.

"There's never been enough meat to feed us all," Ned said.

"So let's not waste our time on hunting," the speaker said. "It seems to me that if either Lyn or Bill's right we'd be smart to collect as much bark pulp as we can as soon as we can. Does everyone agree? Good.

"Now, does anyone want to venture any other ideas about what's behind the problem? No? Then how about ideas about what we should do about it? Manuel?"

Manuel Candamo stood up. "I'm speaking in my capacity as Membership Manager," he said. "I'm not a scientist; I don't know what's causing this; I don't know how long it's going to last. But what I do know is that until it's over we're going to have hard times. We may have trouble feeding ourselves—and we certainly don't need any more new mouths to feed. And if we find we're struggling for survival—really struggling—then we won't be able to spare anybody to take care of Newcomers. So I submit that you authorize me to tell the people back at the Institute that we don't want any more new people—at least new people who don't have special talents that we need desperately—until the crisis is over." He sat down.

"That sounds good to me," Robert Cortona said. "Does anyone have anything to add before we put it to a vote?"

"Are you saying that this is the end and the colony's doomed?" Grace Benson demanded.

"No! Maybe we are doomed if Lyn's right, but even if all we've got to deal with is some version of winter we'll have a much better chance of surviving it if we don't burden ourselves with a lot of people who are helplessly dependent on the rest of us."

"If it is winter, and it lasts a long time, we may need people with special skills we don't have," Will said.

"You mean, Eskimos, Siberians, people like that?"

"Yes."

"Quite possibly—if winter here means it gets cold. If it gets dry we'd be better off with Australians. So let's say that the vote is on whether or not we want to cut off immigration of all people who don't have *specific* special survival skills that we need. Raise your hands if—What is it, Josephus?"

"I think we need as many generalists as we can get. Ray and Rosabeth are good ecologists, sure, but maybe another ecologist would be able to see some sort of pattern that the two of them have missed. *We* don't know what's wrong but maybe somebody with a broader grasp of things would be able to find an explanation in ten minutes."

"I can answer that," Delia Slater said. "I transmit all the scientific data back to Earth and they've got all the generalists *and* the specialists you could want working on it from that end."

"I'm with Josephus," Ray Jarvis said. "Somebody new might notice something none of the rest of us've seen. The data's here, not on Earth, and nobody back there's going to make sense out of information we don't give them. I don't care how competent they are. Or even how good Bill is at translating visuals into computer language: a thousand perfect pictures of the wrong things won't help."

"So you think we should accept more Newcomers?" Robert Cortona asked.

"Not unless they've got skills we need for survival, no. I think you're right about not wanting too many people helplessly dependent on the rest of us. But I think Josephus is right, too: some of the people we may need most are scientists, not wilderness survival experts."

"All right," Robert Cortona said. "Let's make the wording vague enough to cover both possibilities: no Newcomers unless the people have skills which the colony decides are vital in some way to its survival. Now, raise your hands if you want to cut off immigration. . . . Twenty-four, twenty-six. OK, twenty-nine against cutting off immigration. How many *for* cutting it off? I won't bother to make a count unless somebody insists.''

"Manuel, do you mind crossing over to Earth and telling them about our decision?''

"Not at all. Now?''

"You might as well wait until we finish the rest of the meeting. Catherine, you had something to say?''

"Yes. It's about Amber. You all saw him go into that religious trance three days ago. Some of us talked to him after he came out of it and he says he goes into them all the time. John and Sandra've talked to him and neither of them thinks he's likely to be dangerous to anyone; I'm not as sure as they are but I'm willing to accept their word for the moment.''

"What's your point?'' Josephus asked.

"My point is that John asked Amber to stay in the settlement for his own good—it could be dangerous for him to go into a trance out in the woods; he might not wake up until the insects were nibbling on him—but John doesn't have any real authority to give him orders like that. And neither do I, really; I just have the authority to see that community orders are carried out. So I'd like a vote.''

"You'd like a vote on whether or not the community should restrict Amber to the settlement?'' Robert Cortona asked. "What's Amber got to say about that?''

"He's not here,'' Tom said. "He's working on his hut.''

"Somebody go get him. He should have a right to say something for himself.''

"He wouldn't come,'' Jane said. "Not to a meeting like this. But he'll go along with whatever you vote.''

Even Jane voted in favor of restricting Amber to the settlement.

"You were in that religion too, weren't you?'' Rosabeth asked after the meeting broke up.

"You mean the Fellowship of Prismatic Light?''

"Yes.''

"Yes.''

"Did you ever—well, have ideas like Amber's?''

''No. Amber saw the Fellowship very differently than I did. And he needed a faith a lot more than I did.''

Amber scraped himself clean with sand, then entered the hut. He laced the doorflap in place. There was no bed of leaves to lie on, only the rough wooden floor, but he had built the hut secure. He was safe inside it.

Safe. He rolled the word around in his mind. There was something about it that wasn't right.

CHAPTER TWENTY

JANE FINISHED grinding the stringy barkpulp into a form her charges could eat. She carried the platter over to the Newcomers' Hut.

"Sorry, Ellen, Jim," she apologized, beginning to spoon the bitter stuff into Ellen's mouth. "I know it's awful." On the other side of the hut Will was feeding Virgil. "I know it's not as good as the fruit mash you were getting. And it's hard to get used to eating dryish food without any saliva. Try to get a more circular motion out of your jaws, Ellen. Think of it as if you were grinding instead of chewing."

"How's Amber doing?" Will asked.

"I don't know. He sleeps by himself in his new hut and never talks to me anymore." She began feeding Jim.

"He's getting awfully thin," Will said.

"I know."

"I tried to talk to him yesterday. I told him he should eat more but he wouldn't listen to me, though he was polite enough."

"He doesn't really listen to anybody anymore," Jane said.

When she'd finished feeding Jim she encouraged her charges to creep out of the hut into the morning sunlight. The two sat babbling happily to each other while Virgil played with a little wooden pull-cart John Dolland had made.

Why can't Amber be more like he used to be? Jane wondered. *More childlike. Not helpless or incompetent or anything like that but more. . . . He used to be so happy. Like Ellen and Jim.*

It was a joy to be with the Newcomers, help them as they

discovered the world around them. She was happy. It didn't seem fair that she was happy so much of the time when Amber was going insane and the colony was on the verge of going under, but she was.

In a burrow near the colony a creature descended from a near squirrel gave birth to thirty-nine offspring. Twelve were stillborn; another nine were born crippled, malformed or in some other way defective: these she devoured. The other eighteen she allowed to nourish themselves from the layers of excess tissue beneath the loose skin of her belly.

In another burrow an infant was born to a creature of her kind which, though an inappropriate response to the imperative which had called it into being, was yet viable and part of no pattern which the Forest Mind had learned to inhibit. The unique infant was allowed to live.

Judy Conterreal, former Health Assistant and newly elected Colony Pathfinder, and Lyn Garcia, Agriculturalist, were ready to go. Their backpacks held enough barkpulp to feed them for the three to five days they expected to be gone; should they need more they could obtain it easily enough. Knives of hard flower bronze were tucked into their belts and Judy, who was the better shot, had a bow and twenty gold-tipped arrows for hunting.

"You're sure you want to go?" Manuel Candamo asked. "We could ill afford to lose either of you."

"Me you can afford to lose," Lyn said. "I haven't grown one plant successfully in almost two years. And if we really are heading into winter I'll be even less useful than before."

"Mircea and Krishna don't need my help," Judy said. "And if they did need help, Sandra could do it. Besides, I'm looking forward to this."

"And if *I'm* right," Lyn said, "and what looks like a winter's just a local response to the colony's disturbing influence, it's vital we find out."

"Why?" Manuel asked. "Wouldn't the same thing happen to us anywhere we go?"

"Maybe—unless there was some mistake we made we could

learn not to make again. But even if it does happen all over again—it took over three years this time, remember.''

''That's not long enough,'' Manuel said.

''No?'' Judy asked. ''Why not? A semi-nomadic way of life. . . . It could be a good thing. A nomadic society in which women weren't burdened with taking care of children. . . . It could be a good thing. I think I'd like to try it.''

Though a few colonists were out looking for flower metal, most of the other settlers had been diverted from their normal tasks to stripping bark and pulp from the trees immediately surrounding the settlement. Since any pentration of a tree's protective bark during the day opened the way for an invariably fatal invasion by insects of the tree's vital tissues during the coming night, no attempt was made to do anything but strip trees bare and leave them to die.

Back at the settlement, Jane helped scrape the pulp from the outer husk. The husk itself was discarded; the pulp was stored in newly constructed storage huts. The need for food had been judged more pressing than the need for either cloth or hut-building materials.

Amber hacked at the tough wooden runner with his axe of flower bronze. The machetes were no longer adequate to cut the larger runners: Emile Fontanas said that the trees seemed to be incorporating metals into their roots. Whatever the cause, the runners were getting both larger and tougher.

Though the axe Amber was using was newly forged, it was getting dull: he would have to take it back to Josephus and get a new edge put on it soon.

Not too soon, he told himself. *Not until it really won't cut right.* Though he was tired, weary with a fluttering exhaustion like nothing he had ever before experienced, he knew his weakness gave him no excuse to shirk his responsibilities.

Perhaps I should eat more, he thought. *If I'm not strong enough to do my work. . . .* But the weariness felt strangely good to him, as though it were a sign of his coming triumph over his alien body.

"How's it coming, Amber?" a colonist using a bronze machete to hack off the smaller runners asked him.

"All right, I guess. The axe is getting a bit dull."

"Why don't you take it over to the smithy? I'll spell you while you're gone."

"No thanks. I can still get some good use out of it."

"No, I mean it," the colonist—was his name Ted?—insisted. "I'd like to take over your job for a while."

"All right. I'll let you know when the time comes."

Ted nodded, moved away. *We're all too proud here,* Amber thought. *I'm too proud of how big and strong I am. Jane's so proud of the way she's been able to find a place for herself here. And all of us . . . we've all been so proud of conquering this world and making it over in our image. The rest of them, they're proud it's fighting back now, that'll make them real heroes if they win. We shouldn't be here. Everything around us is dying and we still keep on acting like we've got the right to act like we were still on Earth.*

Is that our sin? he asked himself. *Trying to force ourselves on a world that doesn't want us?*

He stared down at the axe in his hand. *The jungle's only trying to get back what we stole from it. I can't keep on fighting it. I'll tell Rosabeth I can't work for her anymore.*

"Where are you going, Amber?" Ted asked.

"I've got to go talk to Rosabeth and John. Here, you can have my axe."

"Something wrong?"

"No."

Is that my sin? he asked himself. *To think I'm right and they're wrong? To think that I'm different, better? To think that I know?*

In a burrow near the colony a unique creature whose grandparents had been near squirrels began devouring the other creatures with which it shared the burrow. The Forest Mind tried to inhibit its behavior, but without success: the unique ignored its commands.

But the unique was one among many; there were dozens of other creatures in the burrow with it and acting in concert they killed it easily.

● ● ●

Jane watched Ellen digging clumsily in the loose red soil.

"Thaa?" Ellen asked. "Thaa—urrumph?" She unearthed a rounded greenish pebble, played with it a moment, then threw it away.

Jane smiled at her.

Late in the afternoon of the third day Judy said, "Look!" and pointed. There, in the distance, a bush gleamed yellow with fig apples.

The fruit tasted exquisite after the bitter bark pulp. They ate their fill, rested, and continued on. Soon they came across a greenberry bush. Beneath it, sleeping, they discovered an armor frog.

"The forest's back to normal," Judy said. "You were right."

"It looks normal but I'd like to look around a bit more. And even if it is normal here, that still doesn't prove I was right. There might be some other explanation."

"But it would prove Bill Simmons was wrong."

"Yes."

"That's good enough for me. Let's do some more exploring."

Bush after bush was laden with fruit; melon vines were everywhere; potatoweeds poked their mauve crowns up through the soil. They found a cluster of trapglobes in the process of digesting some insects.

"Pretty," Lyn commented. "I don't think it was *ever* this luxurious near the colony."

"Not that I remember," Judy agreed. "Let's get rid of the pulp."

"Right. Wouldn't it be nice if we never had to eat the stuff again?"

They filled their backpacks with fruit, adding a sleeping armor frog for additional proof, then started back to the colony.

"Nomadic life isn't so bad, is it?" Judy asked.

"It's better than barkpulp," Lyn agreed.

Amber bent down and picked the spirals of foil-thin silver from the still-warm ashes.

"Amber," he heard Jane's voice say.

He straightened up, unsurprised, and smiled down at her. "How are you doing, Jane?" he asked.

"All right. I guess. I mean, I'm happy here, but. . . . You don't talk to me anymore, Amber! You never tell me anything! We were going to be so happy here, the two of us, together—remember? The two of us, Amber! Why've you gone off and. . . . I haven't deserted you, Amber, I still love you but you. . . . Why?"

He touched her lightly on the face, smiled at her. "I haven't deserted you, Jane. I'm sorry if it feels like I have. I don't want to hurt you, but I've just got to be by myself for a while. And you—you've got friends here now. You've found your place in life. But me—I had the Latihan and I threw it away, Jane. And now I've got to find some other way back to God. Once I find my way back, once He's taken me back, then I'll be free to show you how much I care for you. But now I've got to shut out everything, everything but God. Even you, Jane: everything. I've got to strip myself of all my sins, all my greed, everything but my love of God."

"You never spoke with God in the Latihan, Amber. You were just talking to yourself. You can't turn away from me for a—it was just you talking to yourself!"

"I'm sorry you feel that way, Jane. But I know you're wrong: I spoke with God in the Latihan and finding Him again is the only thing that'll make my life worth living. The only thing."

Judy and Lyn were almost back to the settlement when they saw a multitude of reddish animals swarming like furry maggots over the body of a wood pig.

"Judy," Lyn whispered. "You see those?"

"Yes."

"They're new. We've got to get specimens for Bob and Jarvis. Do you think you can shoot one?"

"I'll try." Judy nocked an arrow, sent it speeding into the close-packed mass of reddish bodies. Her arrow transfixed one animal; the others scattered before she had a chance at a second shot.

"A lucky shot," she commented. "Very."

Lyn pulled the arrow carefully out of the dead animal's body and picked up the carcass. The thing was about twice the length of her hand, lean and muscular, its jaws filled with razor-sharp green teeth.

"Drop it!" Judy said suddenly. Lyn let the body fall from her hands. "Why?" she demanded.

"Look at the claws. They're hollow, like rattlesnake fangs. These things must be poisonous."

"Then it's a good thing we discovered them," Lyn said. She stowed the dead animal in her pack. "If these things start showing up wherever we build settlements I'm in favor of adopting a nomadic style of life."

"I'm afraid it's too late for that," Judy said quietly. "Look."

Around them the circle of skirmishers moved inwards in utter silence, yellow eyes gleaming.

Sitting cross-legged in the darkness of his hut, Amber allowed the vision to wash over him.

The colonists, green faces contorted with insane rage, blue-black teeth bared in snarls, were hacking at the forest with silver axes, uprooting defenceless plants, leaping upon animals and tearing them apart, ripping them open with their teeth. Jane tried to stop them. They turned on her and hacked her to pieces with a gleaming silver axe, threw the bloody meat that had been Amber's sister into the fire where they were burning the corpses of all the beings they had slaughtered. The stench of burning flesh hung greasy and exciting in the air.

The colonists linked blood-slippery hands, danced counterclockwise around the flames, naked, singing and exulting. Slowly the evil within them began oozing from their pores, covering them like vile sap, glistening. Thicker and thicker grew the glistening coating. They were moving slower now and as they slowed the evil coating them lost its luster, dulled, solidified, imprisoning them.

A mighty humming filled the air: an iridescent storm cloud of beautiful insects with delicate lacy wings. The insects settled on the motionless colonists and devoured their dulldark shells of imprisoning evil, releasing the beings inside.

Free, the beautiful figures began a stately dance. Wherever their feet trod new plants and animals sprang to life.

Amber shook his head, trying to make sense of his vision. It was no Latihan vision, no direct revelation, but he knew that God had had a hand in its shaping and that there was a message for him in it that he could not escape.

The insects. The insects were not his enemies. They would purify him. He should not be huddling afraid in the shelter of this hut, he should be outside in the open air, trusting to God for his preservation.

But he was afraid. Desperately afraid.

CHAPTER TWENTY-ONE

JOSEPHUS CYPERS was out hunting wood pigs. As Blacksmith he had assigned himself the task of searching for new flower metal and he *was* conscientiously looking for the gleaming flowers, but until he ran across any he was free to spend his time doing what he enjoyed most: hunting. If he found metal, he'd have to give up the idea of bagging a pig, but if he ran across the pig first—Well, he was sure nobody would have any objections if he brought back some fresh meat.

A flicker of movement caught his eye and he saw the pig, its gray body swollen with its pregnancy. *All the more meat,* he thought as he fitted an arrow to his bow, *and maybe the scientists'll be able to learn something useful from it, but it'll be Hell to carry back.*

The wood pig ambled behind a tree. Josephus waited silently, arrow nocked, for it to show itself again. . . .

A sudden pain flaring in his right calf. He twisted, stared: a small reddish animal, something like a ferret but nothing like anything he'd ever seen on Deirdre, was scurrying away.

The damn thing bit me, he thought. With skill born of long practice he brought the bow around, aimed, shot it.

I'm the best shot in the colony, he thought just before the dizziness hit him and he fell.

The skirmishers swarmed over his body.

"Lyn and Judy haven't come back yet. It's been six days," Ray Jarvis said.

"Josephus's missing too," Catherine said. "He was looking for flower metal."

"He still might make it back tonight," John Abercrombie said. "And if something keeps him from making it back he's got as good a chance as anyone here of surviving the night."

"Better," Catherine said. "He's spent nights alone in the forest before—but never without letting me know what he was planning to do beforehand. If he's not back here by tomorrow morning I'm going after him."

"We'll send out a search party," John said.

"Then I'm going with it."

"No, you're not. You're staying here—if he doesn't come back."

"You don't have the authority to keep me from going."

"No, but I can get it. If I have to I'll call a colony meeting tonight. Look, Catherine, anything dangerous enough to threaten Josephus could well be dangerous to anyone who goes after him. And if he's gone—"

"If he's dead."

"If he's dead, you're the only one of us left with the skills and knowledge needed to do much of what he did for the colony. If he's dead, you're irreplaceable."

"Then you think Lyn and Judy have run into something dangerous?" Jarvis asked.

"I don't know, Ray. It's possible, but maybe they just decided to spend a few extra days exploring."

The search party that went out looking for Josephus the next day found nothing. But none of the colonists who went unaccompanied into the forest that day returned.

"We've lost thirteen people," John announced. "Fifteen, if Judy and Lyn aren't just late getting back."

"And how likely do you think that is?" Jo Anne asked.

"Not likely at all," John replied. "Which is one of the reasons I'm turning the meeting over to Catherine now. With Josephus gone she's the nearest thing we have to a Department of Defense. And I think we need one right now. So, Catherine?" He made his way from the mound.

"There's something in the forest that's picking us off," Catherine began. "It's getting us one at a time—"

"What about Judy and Lyn?"

"Or two at a time, then. But the point is, that whatever it is is acting like, oh, say a wolf or a tiger. Not like some sort of new natural phenomenon, like quicksand. And whatever it is is more than a match for any two of us, now that Judy and Josephus are gone. So from now on I don't want any of us leaving the settlement in groups of less than three. And that means three *armed* people."

"But what's out there?" Mary asked. "Insects?"

"I don't know," Catherine said. "Bill the Butterfly Collector's one of the people missing, so we can't ask *him,* but it doesn't sound like insects to me. More like some sort of animal. Or one of us."

"You're kidding, aren't you?" Bill Simmons asked. "I don't think that's very funny."

"It wasn't meant to be," Catherine said.

"If you're implying that one of us is a homicidal maniac, you're wrong," Sandra said. "Nobody like that could have gotten through the selection procedures. And I think you're doing a lot more harm than good by even mentioning the possibility."

"What about Amber?" Grace Benson asked.

"Impossible," Sandra said.

"Sandra's right," Catherine said. "He was under observation here in the settlement all day yesterday. He's one of the few people I know couldn't be responsible. But even though he couldn't have been personally responsible for what's been happening—"

"What other kind of responsibility are you implying?" Sandra asked. "Perhaps you think he's morally responsible?"

"No. All I'm trying to say is that he's living proof that we can't trust the selection procedures the way we'd like to be able to trust them."

"Amber—was an experiment," Jane said. "You all know that. Nobody pretended they knew that . . . what he'd end up like here."

"Jane," Catherine said, "No one's accusing Amber of anything. But you said he was an experiment: well, how do we know that some of the rest of us aren't 'experiments' the Institute didn't bother telling us about?"

"I'd know," Sandra said. "And we aren't."

"You're probably right," Catherine said. "Look, I'm just trying to make sure we investigate *every* possibility. I don't think *anyone* here's at all likely to have done whatever's been done, but I don't want to take *any* chances on anything. Any chances at all."

Krishna led a party of twenty-seven colonists out into the forest to cut barkpulp. Two smaller groups, one of five colonists led by Jo Anne, the other consisting of Tom, Mischa, and John Dolland, also left the settlement. Jo Anne's party was looking for flower metal; Tom's for roots and branches suitable for the making of spears and arrows.

The Forest Mind had too few skirmishers to split its forces. It ignored the party cutting barkpulp, chose not to attack Jo Anne's party.

Only three skirmishers were lost killing Tom, Mischa, and John Dolland, less than the patterns derived from the Forest Mind's struggles against its long-dead rivals would have predicted.

"Dan told me there was a clump of bronze flowers growing somewhere near here," Ted said. "He was going to bring as many back as he could carry."

"Over there," Sally said. "Shining. Isn't that them?" She pointed.

They found the clean-picked bones by the base of the tree around which the bronze flower vine twined. The bones were blue.

"Dan?" Ted asked.

"I think so," Mircea said.

"But those aren't human bones!" Sally said. She had been close to Dan.

"None of us are human anymore, Sally," Ted said. "Those are Dan's bones."

"Something ate him," Jo Anne said.

"Insects?" Alexis suggested.

"Look!" Jo Anne said, pointing. A few yards away from Dan's skeleton lay a small skeleton. Reddish fur still covered its lower legs but the rest of the body was bare green bone.

"Whatever it is, its back's broken," Bob Elgin said. "Maybe Dan killed it."

"It's too small to have killed him," Sally said.

"Look at those teeth," Jo Anne said. "Maybe there were a lot of these things, like piranhas or army ants. . . . Dan killed this one before the rest of them could kill him and then they ate it just like they ate him."

"Why'd they leave the legs?" Ted asked.

"Look at the claws," Bob Elgin said. "Don't touch them, just look. They're hollow, see? Probably poison glands in the legs."

"Let's bring it back to the settlement," Ted said.

"We'd better wrap it in something before we try carrying it," Alexis suggested. "If there's still any poison on those claws they could end up scratching somebody."

"They're strange animals," Ray Jarvis told the meeting. "Everything else we've met on Deirdre—the fruitbears, the near squirrels, the wood pigs, dire mice, even ourselves—*everything* has blue bones. These things have green bones."

"Which means what?" John asked.

"I don't know. None of us know. Except that it means that these things are *different*. Maybe we'll find out what that difference means if we can catch one alive."

"Anyway, the claws aren't very long. If we all wear thigh boots of four or more layers of barkcloth when we're out in the woods we should be pretty safe. And Bill's frogskin trousers should keep him pretty safe, but he only had the chance to put together the one pair before the frogs disappeared."

"What if they jump?" Catherine asked. "Or drop on us from trees?"

"Well, the leg bones don't look like the things're built for jumping," Robert Elgin said. "As for dropping on us from trees—that's possible too, of course, but those claws don't look like they'd be good for climbing. So I think we'll be safe with boots."

"What's to keep them from attacking us here?" Karl Archard wanted to know.

"Nothing that we know of, but so far they've avoided us when we're in large groups," the zoologist said.

"But that's no proof they're going to keep on avoiding the settlement," Catherine said. "Before yesterday they were only attacking solitary individuals; today they got Tom, Mischa, and John Dolland—and all three of them were armed. I think it's suicidal to just assume that they'll keep on letting the settlement alone. And that means we've got to devise some way to keep them out if they do decide to attack the settlement. I'll let Ted give you the details.''

Ted stood up and faced the group. ''Most of the ideas that sounded best from the point of view of defense weren't possible with the materials we've got to work with here. Try building a castle without proper stone for the walls and with nothing to fill the moat with. So what Catherine and I eventually came up with is a barricade of pointed stakes, facing outwards. That way the things can't climb it and if Bob's wrong and they can jump there's a chance they'll spit themselves on it. But we don't know how old the one we found was: it might have been just a baby. So we'd better make the barricade as high as we can.''

''What makes you so sure they can't climb, Bob?'' someone asked.

''The things—I call them snake weasels but if anybody's got a better name for them, feel free to offer it—don't have climbing claws. Those claws would be useless for anything but injecting poison.''

''What if they have, oh, suction pads?'' Krishna asked.

''Then we're in trouble. But I don't think they will; suction pads wouldn't be very efficient for anything but a very small animal. But I think Ted's barricade'll keep them out during the day and I doubt if they'll risk the insects at night.''

''The settlement's too big,'' Sally said.

''Right. We've got to abandon the outlying huts. All of you living in them will have to move in with people more centrally located,'' John said. ''Besides, we need the wood.''

While the snake weasels continued to multiply, the offspring of the fruitbears which had eaten the mutagenic fruit were beginning to give birth to young of their own. The third generation bore little resemblance to either their parents or their grandparents, but that was as it should be; they were born as triplets and their birth was invariably fatal to the mothers that bore them.

Those not in proper accord with the imperative that had called them forth were inhibited and died, but the majority survived: they were a more stable type than the snake weasels.

The dead were eaten; the living grew. Soon they would be mature enough to reproduce.

"You're going to have to give up your hut, Amber," Jane said. "Ted's going to have to leave his hut too, but he's moving into Tom's old hut and he said he's willing to share it with you."

"What about you?"

"I'm giving up my hut too."

"You're not going to be moving in with Ted?"

"No. I'm moving into the Newcomers' Hut. Will's strong and they need him to help build the barricade so I'm going to take over as Head Nursemaid."

"I don't have to move tonight?"

"No. Tomorrow, when they start work on the barricade."

"I think that's going to be good, taking care of the Newcomers. For you, I mean."

"I think so too."

"Are you scared, Jane?"

"Yes. Of course. Aren't you?"

"I'm not sure."

"Then you're stupid." She turned, left.

Alone, Amber laced his hut secure. *Are they dying because of me?* he asked himself. *Is this God's way of showing me how impatient he is with me?*

But he was not yet ready. He was not a coward, but he was not yet ready.

Tomorrow night, he told himself. *I'll fast all day tomorrow and do the Latihan tomorrow night.*

CHAPTER TWENTY-TWO

IN THE morning the colonists sorted themselves out into groups of twenty and began felling the trees previously stripped of bark, splitting them, and dragging the wood back to the settlement for use in the construction of the barricade.

David Heaton, serving his first term as Axe Murderer this tenday and very conscientious about his responsibilities (unless, of course, his conscientiousness was a pose hiding innate sadism—as Ned, Sally, and Bill Simmons claimed, and as Sandra and Manuel denied) had protested the cancellation of his Slash and Vomit Meeting and forced it to a community vote. He had been overruled: Laurent Eliade had argued that it was impossible for dead Utopians to build any sort of Utopia and had managed to convince the meeting that the colonists' best hope of remaining live Utopians was to build the barricade as quickly as possible.

So even David Heaton, who had argued that Laurent's position was merely another variant of the argument that the end justified the means, had wrapped his legs with strips of stiff barkcloth and waddled clumsily out into the forest to help. Bill Simmons was reasonably comfortable in his frogskin trousers, but Jane and everyone else found the rough barkcloth chafed their skin unmercifully; the awkward, undignified waddle with which they were forced to get around soon eroded most people's tolerance for additional irritations, with the result that a lot of ordinarily quiet people found themselves yelling at a lot of other people who were just as unused to being yelled at. Jane, more experienced than most at dealing with hyperirritable people, managed to avoid most people's hostility, but enough gratuitous criticism came her way to make her miserable.

The work proceeded slowly but without unexpected delays. Ted and Catherine were everywhere, supervising and helping with the physical labor when their help was needed. The barricade began to take shape.

The snake weasels continued to multiply. The second variety of skirmish beasts had reached maturity and were beginning to reproduce. They were much larger than the snake weasels, lightly armored, and equipped with fangs and talons against which barkcloth would have been no protection at all.

And the time was fast approaching when the woodpigs would begin producing their own very different young.

Amber was assigned to work digging trenches into which the stakes for the barricade were to be set. In its natural state Deirdran soil was only loosely packed and the holes were easy to dig even with the improvised wooden shovel he'd been given, but because the soil packed so poorly the stakes had to be buried quite deeply to stay in place: the trench Amber was digging was chest-deep on him and he was tall for a colonist.

A short distance from Amber, Alexis and a lot of other colonists were aleady setting stakes into place and shoveling dirt in around them, then tramping the dirt down firm. Their work went quickly and they spent a good deal of their time either lounging around waiting for new stakes or waiting for Amber and his fellow ditchdiggers to dig them holes into which they could put their stakes.

Men armed with bows, knives, spears and axes stood around looking bored but nervous.

The work was difficult and Amber's every muscle ached—and they were the wrong muscles, not the muscles a man should have had. Though his weeks of fasting had not resulted in the visible gauntness a similar regime would have brought out in a Terran body he was weak with hunger, but he forced himself to work on, not stopping to rest when those around him did. He tried to work through the lunch period but the guards wanted to eat and would not allow him to continue working alone and unprotected—and, he assumed, unsupervised—so he sat with the others in the plaza until they finished their meal. Then he resumed work.

Jane was alone with the Newcomers now. Will was splitting logs.

"I'm sorry," she told her charges as she spooned them bitter mush, "but you can't go outside the hut today."

"Whaa?" Mike asked. He would be talking soon.

"Why?"

He nodded, got it right: "Why?"

"There are dangerous animals out there, things like poisonous rats. They're new. Nobody ever saw anything like them before. You've got to stay inside until we finish the barricade to keep them out, then you'll be able to go back outside again."

Mike looked worried, but though Ellen, Jim and Virgil had listened attentively to what she'd said they went back to gurgling placidly to each other as soon as she finished. They'd understood her words but the threat to the colony which she'd described was too abstract to catch their interest, not nearly as interesting as the sounds they could make with their new vocal equipment or the faces they could make at each other.

Delia Slater was an important man to the colony, too important to be risked out in the forest or even on the settlement's perimeter. Wherever he went now, he found himself accompanied by two rather embarrassed guards. But of course he had to work, everybody had to work, even the guards. All three of them were in the forge hammering cooking utensils into knives and arrowheads and axe-blades.

The colonists took their evening meal in silence, then went back to work in the twilight. But only a small portion of the settlement's perimeter had been enclosed by the time Jo Anne's gong announced quitting time.

"But surely news of their mother . . ." Brother Ashoka said. "It's not a long message: just tell them she's doing better at the Sahara Camp and she's been given a position of some trust."

"No. I'm sorry, but we're not accepting *any* personal messages for anyone on Deirdre right now. If you want to leave us a cassette, we can save it until a time comes when we can give it to Manuel Candamo, but it's utterly impossible for you to talk to him now."

Amber lay on the bed of leaves that had once been Tom's and pretended sleep. He waited until long after he was sure Ted was asleep, then stood up cautiously. Though he tried to make as little noise as possible getting out of bed, the dry leaves rustled and crackled when he moved, but Ted remained asleep.

Amber unlaced the doorflap with quick, practiced movements. He paused a moment, summoning up his courage, then slipped outside and laced the flap closed behind him: he and he alone had chosen to trust in God's mercy for protection against the night.

He and he alone had been chosen.

The night was choked with the sound of rasping wings. Amber forced himself to take no notice of them, sat down in the dirt in front of the hut and waited. He would trigger the Latihan in himself at daybreak.

Ted was awakened by a scream. It had sounded like Amber's voice.

"Amber?" he called tentatively. There was no reply. "Amber?" he repeated, louder.

He reached over, explored Amber's bed with his hand. Empty. The scream had come from outside the hut.

Had seemed to come from outside the hut? No. He hesitated a moment, his mind full of wings and mandibles, then unlaced the doorflap. In the dim light of Deirdre's two tiny satellites he could make out Amber lying naked and still on the ground in front of the hut. Dead? But if he wasn't—Ted scuttled out the door, reached down and pulled Amber's heavy, rigid body up onto the platform, then dragged it into the safety of the house. He held the doorflap shut while he laced it tight, then gave Amber his full attention.

"Amber?" he asked again. He felt Amber's chest. Both hearts were beating, though slowly. Alive, then.

Paralyzed, Tom decided. *A pseudowasp. At least it wasn't something that'd make a meal of him immediately.* He ran his fingers over Amber's body and limbs. There was a rapidly swelling lump on his right inner thigh.

Just one egg case, then, Tom realized. He was relieved: Mircea would be able to cut it out of Amber the next morning and he would be all right in a few weeks.

I wonder what he's thinking? Lying there, paralyzed but completely conscious. . . .

"You're all right, Amber," he said aloud. "You've just got one egg case in you; Mircea or Krishna will cut it out of you tomorrow morning and you'll be fine."

He could have been killed out there! Why? What was he doing?

"You know, Amber," he said, "you almost killed yourself out there. And I could have been killed when I went out after you. I don't have any idea why you decided to sneak out, and I'm not sure I really care at this point, but I'd like you to think about one thing: you almost got two people killed."

Can he even hear me? he wondered. *John said that most of the time he's completely lucid but that there are times when he loses touch—Damn him! He could have gotten both of us killed!*

He remembered his struggle to unlace the doorflap: Amber would have had to pause outside unprotected and lace it shut. So he could leave without endangering Ted. Maybe that was what he had been doing when the wasp got him.

"Sorry, Amber," he said, arranging the stiff form as best he could on its bed of leaves. "I know you tried to shut the door after yourself. Mircea will cut the egg case out of you in the morning and you'll be just fine. Just fine."

Lying there in the floating darkness Amber wondered how he would recognize daybreak when it came. It did not feel bad, this paralysis, despite the momentary agony he had experienced when the wasp had sunk its ovipositor into him. A cool, soothing lassitude separated him from the wrongness of his alien body as effectively as the lake waters separated Drummond Island from the mainland.

When they open the doorflap and I see the light, he decided. *That's when I'll trigger my Latihan.*

CHAPTER TWENTY-THREE

THE SOUND of the morning gong being struck. Ted jerking awake, ripping at the doorlaces, shoving the flap aside and sprinting for Mircea's hut, while Amber—

As soon as the light flooded in he triggered his Latihan: a dazzle of strange fleshfeelings, fountains of piercing cacophony, rivers of cool brass and soft silky heat, all coming together, flowing into infinite counterpoint, becoming the Presence of the Lord.

The Forest Mind sensed the change. It thrust itself through the suddenly permeable membrane, found itself drifting confused through strange labyrinths, feeling and perceiving in ways it could assimilate to none of its patterns. It had never known abstract thought, language, conceptualization: the incomprehensible grandeur of Amber's mind terrified it.

It attempted to take refuge in the immutable patterning of its personal imperatives, found the attempt impossible: the structures it needed could not be forged from the alien's imperatives. So it was left without choice and had to flee back into itself.

Yet not without attempting to force a single compulsion as it fled. Often, in the ages when it had struggled for dominion with its now extinct brethren, it had invaded and been invaded, and on many occasions it had achieved mastery by the subversion of a single imperative in an otherwise resistant pattern. And it had achieved mastery: there was only one Forest Mind.

But the enemy had been so alien that the Forest Mind did not know whether its attempt at compulsion had been successful, so incomprehensible that the Forest Mind was unable to distinguish between the individual that it had contacted and those that it had not.

The pattern governing its strategies demanded it preserve the life of the enemy it had seeded with its compulsion, so the active attack on the colony ceased.

The skylight and window flaps of the medical hut were open and the hut was flooded with light. Mircea stood looking down at Amber's naked body where it lay on the rough wooden table. Behind him Jane was heating the flower silver knife over a small fire. She had volunteered to assist him now that Krishna and Judy were gone.

"We'll start in a few minutes, Amber," Mircea said. "Just as soon as the knives are sterilized. You won't feel a thing when I operate—John can testify to the fact that wasp venom kills all pain—but two or three days after the egg case is out of you the venom will wear off and your leg's going to hurt like hell. Which is what you deserve for your stupidity, if you ask me.

"But it won't be as bad for you as it was for John; you've only got one egg case in you and it's just beneath the surface of the skin. You'll survive. You're lucky, did you know that? Very lucky: you must have been attacked by a very young wasp. Almost a baby. You'll be walking in a week or two.

"Jane, do you have the knives ready?"

"Yes."

"Hand me that first one, the one with the black handle."

Amber felt nothing as Mircea made the first incision. His mind was still filled with memories of God's incomprehensible symphony, of the music of the Divine Presence from which he had been able to take only a simple melody for his own.

He did not know where it was that he was to go, but that hardly mattered. The music within him would guide his footsteps.

God had taken him back. And from his shoulders God had taken the stern weight of judgment, and in its place given him beauty and certainty.

●   ●   ●

Jane watched Mircea making the first incision, parting the green skin to reveal yellow-gray muscle tissue. She swabbed the wound with absorbent compresses, but there was almost no blood.

Is that what we're really like inside? she thought. *Dry, like insects?* Somehow she had still expected to find the body beneath the green skin the same as that she was familiar with from textbook pictures of human anatomy.

Mircea cut deeper, parting the muscle tissue further to reveal a hard round object about a finger joint in diameter, purplish brown and shiny: the egg case. Jane felt sick.

"Deeper than I thought," Mircea said. He carefully cut the case loose from the surrounding tissue and lifted it gently from Amber's leg, then dropped it in the fire. It shriveled and burst, gushing thick brown fluid, then the husk caught fire and burned with a dull green flame. An acrid odor filled the hut.

"Someday we'll be able to use egg venom for an anesthetic," Mircea predicted as he sewed up the wound with barkfiber. "And if we can get enough eggcases to burn we can have fires whenever we want them; the smell seems to keep insects away."

The operation was over.

"You did a good job, Jane," Mircea said. "It's unsettling, the first time you see that we're different inside as well as out. And Amber's got nothing to worry about. This time."

"Did you hear that?" Jane asked, bending over and kissing Amber on the forehead. "You're going to be fine."

Amber was taken to the hut where Jane took care of the Newcomers. For two days his paralysis and analgesia remained complete; on the third his leg began to pain him and he grew hungry.

"Do you want me to feed you something?" Jane asked when she realized he was attempting to speak.

With difficulty he nodded.

"It's not as tasty as the last time we were here together," she said as she spooned mashed barkpulp into his mouth. He was able to swallow a little of it. "But we haven't lost anyone to those animals since the night you got yourself hurt. And the barricade's almost finished."

God isn't angry anymore, Amber thought. He felt at peace, comfortable for the first time in his Deirdran body.

Three days later he was able to sit up. Mircea stopped in to see him that afternoon as he had every afternoon since the operation. He checked the wound and changed the dressing.

"You're healing nicely," he said. "How do you feel?"

"Tired," Amber whispered. It was the first word he had spoken since the wasp had deposited its eggs in him.

"I'll take your stitches out tomorrow. We heal very fast here by Terran standards; you'll be up and walking around in another two or three days if you're careful."

"Can you talk well enough to talk to me yet?" Jane asked the next morning. Mircea was due by a little later.

"Yes," Amber whispered. "I'm so tired but I feel. . . ."

"Feel what, Amber?"

"Happy."

"Good, but . . . why'd you do it? Why'd you go out there like that? You could have been killed. You almost *were* killed. If Ted hadn't pulled you inside or if some other kind of insect had gotten to you—"

"I know." He paused, then said, "I wanted to show God that I trusted Him completely."

"Why?" Jane asked.

"He came to me, Jane. God came to me."

"You won't risk your life again? Promise me you won't. Amber?"

But Amber was asleep.

He's like a child again, Jane thought. *Sweet, trusting.*

She loved him more than ever. But he was insane and she would have to tell Sandra about what he had said to her. For his own good. To keep him safe.

"He spent the night outside the hut he was living in and got attacked by a pseudowasp," Manuel Candamo told Brother Ashoka.

"What was he doing out there?" Brother Ashoka asked.

"Trying to commune with God. Mircea cut the egg case out of him and he'll survive, but if he persists in these self-destructive acts. . . . Jane told Sandra that he told her that God came to him while he was paralyzed but what exactly that means. . . . I hope it means he's going to get back to normal now because with things going the way they are we can't afford to waste people protecting him from himself."

"What will you do with him, then?" Brother Ashoka asked. "If he does persist?"

"I don't know and I don't think anyone else does, either. Jane's going to continue to keep watch over him, but if he's bent on destroying himself there's probably nothing we can do to stop him in the long run."

"He trusts me," Brother Ashoka said. "And not just as a friend, but as a religious counselor. If you accept me—"

"You might be able to help him where no one else can," Manuel Candamo said. "Granted. But the consensus is still not to admit anyone who doesn't have the special skills we need to deal with the threat to the colony as a whole. None of which, I'm afraid, you have."

CHAPTER TWENTY-FOUR

THE IMAGE of Christ crowned with thorns haunted Amber awake and asleep. Amber was not a Christian—God was a presence he felt within himself whose correspondence or lack or correspondence to other peoples' gods and creeds had never concerned him—but the crown of thorns would not leave his mind.

And though he did not know its meaning, he did know it signified neither mortification nor humiliation.

During his convalescence the barricade had been completed: a chest-high wall of outward-pointing, sharpened stakes. Though no snake weasels had been seen since the day on which they had presumably accounted for Tom, Mischa and John Dolland, guards still circled within the perimeter. But armed parties were once again going out foraging and the colonists were less afraid.

But for Amber the barricade and guards were traps, not defences. His trances and the nighttime vigil which he had refused to discuss with anyone but Jane had been too bizarre for his fellow colonists; they thought him mad and dangerous; no one wanted the responsibility of watching over him in the forest. He would never be accepted for a barkpulp-cutting party, and that was the only way he could think of to get past the guards at the gate.

Had the insects not controlled the night it would have been simple enough to heap up a pile of barkhusks and vault over the fence to freedom but now that he danced to the music of God's purpose he knew it to be his duty to remain alive to complete the dance. And if he tried to vault the fence during the day he would be seen and stopped.

The crown of thorns.

He was still living in the Newcomers' hut where Jane and Will cared for their three remaining charges, Mike having learned to speak and been accepted as a full member of the community.

But the community no longer accepted Amber. He ate three meals a day in the plaza now; he continued to do the work assigned him; he had even attended a Slash and Vomit Meeting. But there the fact that no one cared to attack him and that he had no criticisms of his own to voice had branded him, as nothing else could, as an outsider. Tolerated, even liked, but set apart.

It seemed hopeless, but he acted the lie of belonging and trusted in God. There had been a time when he would have found such pretense unbearable, impossible, but now—the pain was still there, but it was surface pain only, and beneath it he remained serene and joyous. Yet he still could not bring himself to work at hammering metal into spear points and arrowheads: he would not allow—it was not possible for him to allow—his pretenses to defile his principles. So he had been put to work scraping and pounding bark, cleaning up after meals, and in general doing the menial jobs around the settlement that no one else particularly wanted to do.

The crown of thorns. . . . As the uneventful days passed and his strength returned to him his sense of urgency began to return to him.

God gave me His music that I might make of myself a dance to His glory, yet I am not dancing, he thought. *And if I refuse Him, others may once again suffer for my sins.*

The tendays passed.

The Forest Mind waited. Its patience was infinite, but the patterns within which it moved called for a response from the enemy in whom it had attempted to plant a compulsion within the duration-span of a rankorchid's germination. If the response did not come the Forest Mind would renew its attack on the colony.

"Why didn't you mention these silver flowers earlier?" Delia demanded.

"I did mention them," Amber said. "To Josephus. But they weren't really all that big at the time," Amber spread his hands to show just how big "and we didn't need metal very badly then, so he wasn't interested. And they were pretty far away. But now we need metal more.''

"True," Delia said.

"And I, all I was thinking about was finding God again. So I forgot about them. But when I found my faith again and was able to think about other things I remembered how badly we need metal—"

"You don't approve of us making weapons, do you?"

"I . . . don't want to use them myself, they're wrong for me, but maybe, for you . . . I don't know. . . . Anyway, you can use knives and axes for other things, like getting barkpulp.''

"You just figured that out?"

"Yes. I've been . . . busy, but now that my mind's clearer. . . .''

"And you can't tell us how to find them without your help?"

"No, they're sort of hidden, but . . . I can take you to them. They're in the same direction as those big copper flowers I found but a lot farther away. There should be a few of the smallest copper flowers left that we could get on the way, but I thought the silver flowers would be more important.''

"And that's your whole reason for telling me this now?"

"Well . . . I'm sick of scraping pulp.''

Delia thought a moment. "OK. I'll check with Sandra and if it's OK with her, I'll arrange to have you accompany a party. I can't go myself; I'm still being kept here for my own good. You'll carry a knife?"

"Yes. But not as a weapon.''

Amber dived into the scarlet tangle, rolled over, squirmed through the springy branches of a whipbush, then he was up and running.

The sounds of pursuit died away behind him. He continued to run, just to make sure, but he knew he was free.

The forest was beautiful.

Which way should he go? The colony was to his right, the colonists who had accompanied him somewhere behind him. (They would be satisfied with the flowers he had found for them, secretly glad to be rid of him. Only Jane would miss him.)

I'm sorry, Jane, he thought, *but I had to do it. I'll try to come back for you. I promise.*

But already such thoughts were beginning to seem strange to him, part of a world of judgment and morality he had left behind. He was an instrument of God's will now, a part in the divine music. Free.

He followed the path of least resistance through the underbrush, now heading right, now left, now straight ahead. As long as he kept moving God would guide his steps.

He was happy. He tried to whistle the melodies in his head but his Deirdran lips wouldn't pucker the right way.

His failure amused him. He had no need to make music; he was become music. The world around him was music.

"I'm sorry, Jane," Catherine said. "He just ran away. We weren't expecting him to try to escape. He obviously planned it; we lost him in the underbrush. Some idiot wanted to shoot him—"

"Who?" Jane demanded.

"It doesn't matter. I stopped him in time. After all, Amber wasn't a criminal or anything like that."

"He wouldn't leave me," Jane said.

"Jane," John Abercomie said. "I think he's crazy now. You're just going to have to accept that. All that new brain capacity—he couldn't handle it. It drove him mad."

"He'll come back," Jane said.

"He's got a knife and he knows how to dig his way into a tree," Catherine said. "And we haven't seen any snake weasels for a while. So maybe he'll come out of this and survive and get back to us. I hope so, for your sake. But I wouldn't count on it."

The animals were suddenly there, one flanking him on each side, one in front of him, another behind. They were bigger than any animals Amber had ever seen on Deirdre, at least four times the size he himself was, and they were covered with plates of thick, gray hide. Yet they looked quick and lithe for all their armor.

Like cats, Amber thought. *Jaguars, maybe, in armor.* The sense of great power held in perfect control, the smooth grace.

Their feet ended in hooked green talons; when the beast to Amber's left yawned Amber could see that its mouth was filled with jagged green fangs. But Amber thought he could see friendship glinting in their sunken yellow eyes; they offered him no harm and after his initial fright he accepted them as his guides.

He had accompanied them only a little way when five wood pigs shambled up to them and dropped dead. The grey beasts each began to devour a pig. After a moment's hesitation Amber took his knife from his belt and began cutting strips of meat from the body of the pig the grey beasts had left for him. He had no way of making a fire and no particular liking for raw meat—even wood pig meat, which tasted something like peaches and almonds and something like barbequed squid—but if God wanted him to eat raw meat he would eat raw meat and thank God for it.

When he had eaten all he could one of the gray beasts devoured the rest of the carcass.

Night came. Amber cut his way into a tree, scraped out the pulp and carried it far enough from the tree so that any insects it attracted would not be attracted in turn to him. He squeezed himself into the narrow space between bark and wood, plugged the opening through which he had entered and prepared himself for an uncomfortable's night's sleep.

In the morning he resumed his journey. The gray beasts led; he followed. Late in the afternoon of the following day he realized that he was again seeing fruit on the bushes, melons on the ground. He picked a melon, stripped it of its rind, and ate it while he walked. From then on only four wood pigs appeared when the gray beasts fed. Amber ate fruit and barkpulp.

In the colony life returned to a semblance of normality. Jo Anne Rittner replaced John Abercromie as a Planner. Felipe Eulojio, who had replaced John Dolland as Instrumentalist, proved much better at the job than John had ever been and managed to devise lenses from the eyes of insects. David Bate, the new Butterfly Collector, managed to devise a means of trapping the insects that Felipe needed. A colony vote removed Judy Damon from the office of Axe Murderer after her first Slash and Vomit Meeting.

The majority of the colonists were of the opinion that they were living through Deirdre's equivalent of winter. Most of them believed the snake weasels to have been migratory animals that had passed through their territory and gone elsewhere. Though they thought it likely that the snake weasels would reappear eventually, perhaps at the onset of the next winter, and though everyone agreed with Catherine that it was a good idea to continue to exercise extreme caution, fewer and fewer people still believed that the colony was faced with extinction.

The colony waited for spring. Jane waited for Amber, but with each passing day a little more hope died until she had none left.

CHAPTER TWENTY-FIVE

THE DAYS passed in silence, clarity. The gray-plated beasts moved at a comfortable pace, seeming neither to lead nor to follow but only to accompany him. Fruit grew in abundance along the way; the landscape rose in low hills and dropped into smooth hollows; and everything was beautiful. At night glidetoads climbed the trees beneath whose bark he concealed himself and kept him safe.

Once it rained. The gray beasts climbed trees of their own and glidetoads completely covered the tree in which Amber slept. His confidence in God was complete; no fear touched him as he slept in the close darkness.

The thrumming of insect wings after the rain was no louder than it would have been on an ordinary night.

"Insects got to one of the storage huts during the last rain," Ted reported to Jo Anne. "The bark inside's swarming with larvae."

"We'll burn the hut," Jo Anne decided. But huge flying insects emerged from the flaming structure and killed seven colonists, Will and Delia among them.

Jane took over the supervision of Newcomers. Will had been an expert in speech therapy back on Earth. Jane began to learn what she could to help her charges use their new vocal apparatus now that Will was no longer there to help them.

She missed him, perhaps more than she missed Amber.

Amber was swept along by God's purpose. He no longer tried to reach out for God with his mind and imagination; there was no need:

his every thought and movement had been integrated into God's transcendent musics. He knew himself to be an instrument, a dancer, a voice, through which God manifested Himself.

A Latihan awaited Amber—the knowledge was certainty, unexamined, unquestioned—but it would have been inappropriate to attempt it before his journey came to an end. His pilgrim's dance through the endless forest—the feel of his muscles, alien no longer, moving with the strength God had endowed him with, the crimsons and scarlets, vermilions and violets, the grays, golds, silvers, and bronzes all around him, the sweet taste of the blue berries from the center of a metal flower, the steady glare of the white sun overhead—all these had become holy to him and he gloried in them.

Bill Simmons led the party out to the skeletons. Hundreds of wood pigs, fruitbears, near squirrels and dire mice, their bare blue bones lying heaped in the clearing.

"They didn't just die," he said. "Not all of them, together like this. Something ate them."

"And I'm afraid that that something was neither insects nor snake weasels," Emile said, examining some bone fragments. "Look at the way these bones have been crushed and splintered. No snake weasel could do that. It would take something really big, with powerful jaws."

"What?" Ted asked.

"Some animal we haven't seen yet. I don't know what it looks like but I know it's big, it's living in this forest, and it's dangerous."

"Are you sure there weren't any human . . . I mean . . . you know what I mean. You're sure there weren't any of our bones there?" Jane asked.

"You're thinking of Amber?"

"Yes."

"So was I. I looked, but I didn't see any bones that looked, well, human. But some of the bones there had been crushed; I might not have recognized them. I'm going to be going back there later today; Catherine wants us to get all the bones we can for tools now that the metal's running so low. So I can check again. But if you want to check for yourself. . . ."

"I've got to stay here and take care of Virgil and Naomi," Jane said.

"They're growing up pretty fast," Ted said. "I think they could do without you for an afternoon if you could get someone to take over for you."

"Sandra might do it."

"If she does, get Mircea to show you a Deirdran skeleton before you go. You want to be sure you know what you're looking for."

But there were no bones that Jane could recognize as colonist's in the pile.

The days passed. Amber ate fruit; the gray beasts ate wood pigs. They had not been fully adult when they had begun accompanying him, Amber realized, for they were growing and developing ridges of sharp spines on their backs. They were reminding him more and more of pictures he had seen of armored dinosaurs in books back on Earth, though they still moved with the quick grace of hunting cats.

Each time the lemon sky congealed Amber climbed a tree and leisurely hollowed himself out a refuge beneath the bark. When the storms came he waited them out, secure in the knowledge of God's protection.

The rain hammered on the roof and walls, gurgled thickly beneath the wooden floor. Jane was sure she could hear the worms writhing through the sluggish fluid.

"Don't worry," she told her charges, touching them reassuringly in the darkness and hoping they couldn't read the despair quivering in her voice.

I hate this world, she thought. *It was so beautiful at first, I thought I was going to be so happy, but it was all lies. Lies. It drove Amber mad and then it killed him and now it's killing the rest of us.*

And yet she couldn't picture Amber dead. *He's got to be dead,* she told herself. *It's over; I can stop worrying about him. He's dead, dead, so why do I keep pretending that if I just wait a little longer he'll come back all strong and sane and happy? Why?*

It would be so easy. No more worrying, waiting . . . just unlace the flap and step outside. All over in instants.

The insects flooding in through the open door to devour Virgil and Naomi. No. She forced herself to think of something else. The Latihan. Amber had loved the Latihan. She could go through the motions for him, do it to remember 'him. Even though nothing would happen here, she could still clear her mind as before, pretend that he and she were doing a Question Session together. If Amber were still alive he would be glad she was trying to do a Latihan for him. . . .

But she couldn't remember any of the questions he had asked. She listened to the soft, inviting gurgle of the blackwater beneath the hut. *What would he ask if he was here with me now?*

A question in memory of Amber, but she could not push the thought of the larvae beneath the hut from her mind. The question took form; she surrendered to it.

Why is this world killing all of us? she asked and triggered the Latihan.

The Forest Mind sensed her mind opening to it and struck, intending to seed this enemy with the same compulsion it had implanted in the other. But this mind was different: it sucked at the Forest Mind, pulled from it images, sensations, memories, then closed again of its own accord.

The pattern had changed: the Forest Mind had no choice but to attack the settlement as soon as the rain was over and the insects were gone.

When she could no longer hear the sound of wings Jane unlaced her doorflap and ran for Catherine's hut. Catherine was just lacing the hut closed behind her when Jane arrived.

"Catherine!" she gasped. "I made contact with something evil. It's got things hiding in the trees outside the walls, snake weasels and armored things and things that aren't full grown yet but—huge things!" She paused, at a loss for words. "Huge things," she repeated. "They're going to attack the settlement."

"How did you learn about this?" Catherine asked.

"I did a Latihan and—" She broke off, seeing the disbelief in Catherine's eyes. "And I contacted an alien mind. But you think I'm crazy like Amber!"

"I don't know yet, but I think it's possible. I'll take you to see Sandra and—"

The sound of the gong at the gate being struck. Catherine running, Jane forgotten.

Gray beasts were rushing the walls from all directions, but their armored hide was easily pierced by the colonists' metal-tipped arrows. Hundreds died trying to cross the cleared space between forest and settlement.

But more made it across the open space before the archers had a chance to take up their positions on the platforms Catherine had had constructed inside the new inner wall.

Most of the beasts that tried to leap the barricade fell short; they were not designed for leaping. Some were impaled on the stakes of the outer wall, others trapped between the two walls; a few, a very few, leaped far enough to impale themselves on the stakes of the inner wall.

Those the colonists killed with axes, spears, arrows and knives.

One beast cleared both walls, landed free inside the settlement. It killed seven people before Bill Simmons shot it in the head with an arrow; it ripped open Bill's leg when, certain that he'd killed it, he tried to pull the arrow from its head. Laurent Eliade finally killed it with an axe.

Not all the beasts attempted to leap the barricade; some tried to break through. Only one made it through both outer and inner walls, and it was killed before it could do any damage to the people inside.

But thirteen colonists died trying to seal the breach it had made and before the gap was sealed hundreds of snake weasels had poured in through it.

None of the other gray skirmishers managed to make it past the barricade. The Forest Mind realized the futility of their mode of attack and called back the survivors.

The archers defending the walls stood on raised platforms; the snake weasels were unable to get at them. But they killed fifty-three other colonists before they themselves were killed.

Virgil, Naomi, and Sandra were among those killed.

• • •

"What about the other things you saw, Jane?" Catherine asked. "The behemoths."

"They're still, still not grown yet," Jane said.

"How long until they are?" Bill Simmons asked.

"I don't know."

"How big are they now?" John Abercromie asked.

"I don't know. It was—just big. But when they're full grown they'll be able to go right through our barricade."

"You're sure about that?" Catherine asked.

"Yes."

"How are you sure?"

"I don't.—I just am."

"We can take care of the gray things as long as our arrows hold out," Bill Simmons said. He seemed happy, as if he had finally found his place in life. "They did as well as they did against us because we weren't ready for them. But we're ready now. And we've got enough barkpulp to last us years."

"And if they're out there for years?" Mircea demanded. "Our arrows won't last forever, as you perhaps unintentionally pointed out. Neither will the barkpulp. Neither will we."

"And as long as they're out there we can't leave the settlement to get new wood," Ted said. "So we can't make the barricade any stronger."

"Which means," John said, "that all we can do is wait for Jane's behemoths to show up."

"At which time they'll kill us all," Manuel said. "We're helpless unless we can learn something we can use against that thing that Jane contacted. And the only way we can learn anything is to contact it again."

"I can't," Jane said. "I—you can't make me."

"Jane, if you don't we'll probably all be dead soon."

"I'd rather be dead. I can't help it, I can't face that thing again. I won't. It was—it was trying to take control of me."

She stared at them, saw they didn't understand her. "Can't you see?" she demanded. "It was—" She paused, searching for an alternate way to explain what she knew and finding none. "It was trying to steal my soul," she said.

Amber plucked a pale yellow fruit from a bush. A black stain spread from the broken stem throughout the fruit but Amber had long since ceased to equate such stains with spoilage.

CHAPTER TWENTY-SIX

"I KNEW that I was inside the bodies of millions and millions of different plants and animals," Jane told the colony meeting that John had insisted upon. "But I was doing a Question Session—I'd focused myself on the question, 'Why is this world killing us all?'— and my question pushed me through all the bodies to the thing that controlled them. It wasn't ready for me and it couldn't keep what it knew hidden but all I could really understand was about how it was trying to kill us. The thing, it was like it knew everything but couldn't think of anything, or . . . I don't know. But once I got the answer to my question I was back out of its mind before it could trap me. It was automatic, you see, my question had been answered, and so the Latihan was over and the thing wasn't prepared for me, but if I try it again I know it'll take control of me or drive me mad like it did Amber."

"But you must be different," Ted said. "It didn't drive you insane."

"I was doing a Question Session. Amber was looking for God."

"Maybe the wasp venom had something to do with it," Krishna suggested. "If it paralyzed Amber's will or made him more susceptible or something."

"But if you asked a question again—" Manuel began.

"No! It'll be waiting for me this time."

"How long until the behemoths you told us about are big enough to be dangerous?" Ray Jarvis asked.

"I don't know. It thought they'd be ready soon but it doesn't think like us. It doesn't really think at all, it . . . I don't know. When they're full grown they'll be bigger than trees but I don't know how big or when or . . . I don't know."

"So 'soon' could mean months?" Alexis asked.

"Or years. Or days. Don't you understand, I was inside *trees,* I could feel them growing and the trees and the snake weasels are the same thing and it's evil. It's evil. You can't make me let it get into my mind again."

"We wouldn't force you to even if we could," Krishna said.

"But we need all the information we can get," Jo Anne said. "We need it desperately if any of us are going to survive, Jane."

"No," Jane said.

"We've got to get our defenses in better shape," Ted said. "If we back the inside wall of stakes with a wall of earth it should be strong enough to keep out the snake weasels and the armored things."

"But not to keep out the behemoths, Jane?" Jo Anne asked.

"No."

"I've got an idea that might work," Catherine said. "Crossbows. You can kill an elephant with a big enough crossbow bolt. I don't know how to make one myself but Manuel can get us plans from Earth easily enough."

"Do you want me to cross over and get them now?" Manuel asked.

"Wait until the end of the meeting." John Abercromie said.

"Do we have the materials?" Felipe asked. "To make crossbows, I mean?"

"I think so," Catherine said. "We can't be sure until we get a better idea of how to make them."

"But that still leaves us trapped in here until the barkpulp runs out," Jo Anne said. "And if that thing controls everything the way Jane says it does we won't be able to defeat it with crossbows."

"I won't—" Jane began.

"I will," Manuel said. "I'll risk making contact with it myself."

"You can't do the Latihan and I can't teach you how," Jane said. "You need a machine for that."

"I can shuttle back to Earth and learn there."

"No," John said. "We can't risk you. You're our last Communicator."

"He's right," Catherine said. "We may need help in a hurry, like with the crossbows. We can't afford to lose you."

"I wouldn't go mad. I've already got two bodies: if anybody can handle this sort of thing I can."

"But what if nobody can?" Catherine asked. "What if Jane's right?"

"They wouldn't just abandon us," Bill Simmons said. "They'd send us a new Communicator. They'd have to."

"But maybe not until it was too late," Jo Anne said. "I agree with John and Catherine."

"And," Laurent added, "if it takes control of you and then shuttles back to your other body. . . . We can't afford to risk it."

"Not with you or with any other Communicator," Catherine said. "If you want I'll put it to a community vote."

"Then let's get someone who isn't a Communicator but who can *already* do the Latihan here from Earth," Manuel said. "There's a man named Brother Ashoka who knows Jane and who's been trying to transfer here for a long time. He's a priest or whatever they call themselves in the Fellowship of Prismatic Light. He should be able to do the Latihan as well as anyone."

"What do you think about him, Jane?" Jo Anne asked.

"He's a very kind man," Jane said. "And he's . . . he makes up his own mind about things."

"Is he sensible?" Catherine asked. "Or is he likely to go crazy the way Amber did?"

"He's very sensible," Jane said. "He never thought the Latihan was the voice of God. And he's smart. But nobody has a chance against that thing."

"Let's vote on it," Laurent said. "Everybody in favor of having Manuel tell Brother Ashoka why we need him and asking him to transfer here—Yes, Ted?"

"I think we need more people who can do the Latihan. It's too risky to depend on just one man."

"A good idea. All right, everyone in favor of asking Brother Ashoka to come here and asking the Institute to find us some more people who can do the Latihan, raise your hands."

It was a clear majority.

●　　●　　●

The behemoths would never return to the trees. Long before the coming of the next rainstorm they would be too big for any tree to support and their glossy black and green hides were already tough enough to protect them from the larvae. They lived on barkpulp, not meat: they ate too much for any other diet to keep them fed.

And they grew. Already they were far, far stronger than the two gray skirmish beasts that had penetrated into the settlement, already their skin was far too tough for any arrow to pierce. But the Forest Mind was waiting to see how the one enemy under its control could be fitted into its pattern.

The ground had been rising steadily for some time, the hills growing higher and steeper, the hollows rarer. They were following a well defined path beneath the trees. On either side the forest was so dense that Amber would have been unable to see anything farther off the path than he could reach without entering the undergrowth himself.

Through the occasional rents in the crimson and scarlet foliage overhead Amber caught glimpses of the huge mesa toward which the path was taking him, its sheer, gray walls soaring straight up until abruptly cut off, as though the greatest mountain imaginable had been sheared off a distance up from its base and the top part thrown away.

It was two days more before he and his companions reached the steep trail coiling up the sheer rock face. Where the trail began the forest ended: the gray stone was devoid of life.

It took most of a day to reach the top. Two beasts preceded him; two followed. When he tired they stopped to allow him to rest. Below him the forest had become a sea of red stretching from horizon to horizon.

Each time he stopped the sky was a richer, deeper yellow. By the time he reached the top it was yellow no longer, but gold, and Amber knew instinctively that he had climbed above the rain.

There probably aren't any insects here, he thought. *I must be more than a mile high.*

The rim of the mesa was bare rock, as devoid of life as the cliff face, but about three hundred body lengths from the edge a riot of vegetation began: fruit-bearing bushes, melon vines, tuber crowns, edible shrubs. Animals were everywhere—gray beasts like the ones that had escorted him from the colony, small animals with reddish fur, near squirrels, woodpigs, fruitbears and dire mice.

In the distance something huge caught the light, shone.

The path led towards the gleaming. They followed it, moving at the same comfortable pace they had maintained so long. Amber plucked a fig apple from a bush and ate it as he walked.

The gleaming grew brighter, more metallic, spread to become an immense wall of burnished metal, became—

A wall of intertwined trees, the tangled trunks visible like bones beneath the metallic flesh of bronze, copper and gold flowers growing overlapping like the scales of some great fish. There was only one opening in the wall, an archway formed by two trees that came together high above the ground. The path led through it.

On either side of the archway a pair of green and black beasts fully fifty times the length of Amber's body slumbered. The beasts did not stir as Amber and his escorts passed within.

"Can you build them, Felipe?" Catherine asked.

"Easily, but it'll take time. *And* wood from the forest."

"How much time?"

"A tenday."

"That's the best you can do?"

"Yes."

"We'll get you the wood."

"What did this Brother Ashoka say when you asked him to come here?" Sally asked.

"He said that when he heard that Jane was able to contact an alien intelligence by means of the Latihan he wanted a chance to try it for himself."

"That doesn't sound very sane to me," Sally said.

"It's what we want, isn't it?" Manuel said. "I mean, if your definition of sanity is not wanting to contact an alien intelligence, we're going to have a hard time getting someone sane to come here and contact our pet alien intelligence for us, aren't we? Well, aren't we?"

"Sorry," Sally said. "I withdraw my objection."

"Besides," Manuel said. "I like him."

"Did you find anyone else?" Ted asked.

"We've got three more volunteers but they're going to have to be taught the Latihan and that'll take months. So Brother Ashoka's our only immediate hope."

The beasts escorted Amber down a wide, dark corridor cut into the rock. The corridor dead-ended in a small cave. One wall of the cave was a glowing mass of tiny roots or vines gleaming silver and copper ropes intertwined with white filaments like incandescent spider silk.

The beasts left. Amber stood alone before the glowing wall, smelling the strange sweet spice of the place. Joyfully, he triggered the Latihan.

Smiling, he crumpled. A length of golden vine fell from the glowing wall and writhed across the floor to his unconscious body. The vine coiled twice around his head and sank tiny rootlets through his skull and into his brain.

And the Forest Mind began to learn.

CHAPTER TWENTY-SEVEN

"THEY'RE PREPARING to send him through now," Manuel Candamo reported. "He'll be here any moment."

"There he is!" someone shouted. "Outside the barricade!"

"Everybody outside quick!" Catherine yelled.

They stood in a triple circle, spears, knives, axes and arrows ready, around the patch of ground where a shimmer was becoming a blur, a blur a thickening green mist, and a mist a man.

"Get him inside before he snaps back," Catherine said. They carried him through the gates, but he disappeared before they could get him to the Newcomers' Hut.

"It's all right," Ted told Jane, who was waiting back at the hut. "We got him inside the barrier. We'll bring him to you as soon as he reappears."

"No problems?" the technician asked.

"None. They got me inside their wall. How much longer until I go back to them?"

"A few minutes. What's it feel like, not being human anymore?"

Brother Ashoka smiled. "Good. Exciting. It's the first really new—"

The technician reached for the phone.

Though Amber and the Forest Mind were no longer distinct entities they lost nothing of themselves.

Amber awakened to glory. He saw splendor with a thousand

billion eyes, felt the earth with a trillion roots; he was one with all the plants and animals of his world and he was one with God.

And the Forest Mind was learning to use Amber's brain with all its untapped capacities, with its magnificent, alien ability to think with language and concepts, to abstract, imagine and dream.

Though they were one, yet they remained two. They could converse:

—*You are God and I have become one with You.*

—*Yes. I am God. Yet before you became part of Me I was not God; I had not created Myself. And I remain Myself only as long as I have you as a focus for my Godhead. And though You-In-Me are immortal, your humanity is not. When your mortal body dies We shall return to that which I was before I created Myself God.*

The answer to the question already known, question and answer part of a game played for the joy of playing.

—*Jane. She too can experience Union.*

—*She fears Me.*

—*She loves me. She cannot fear You-Who-Are-Me.* A conversation gratuitous, unnecessary, serving no purpose beyond the joy they felt at conversing: they were one and each knew everything known to the other.

—*Jane too is mortal but even as I command the forest around the settlement from which You-Who-Are-I came to be no more barren but to bear fruit once more, so shall She-Who-Shall-Become-Us bear Us-Who-Are-One children, for I am life to this world and without my participation no creature may bear young.*

—*I shall return to the settlement for her.*

A gray skirmish beast was waiting for Amber outside the entrance to the tunnel, a young beast whose back had not yet developed the spiked ridges of maturity. Amber climbed onto its back feeling its armored skin with the insides of his legs and feeling the pressure of legs against his armor-plated back. The Two-Who-Were-One began the ride back to the colony.

Draped across the beast's back was a length of golden vine twin to the one coiled around Amber's head.

•   •   •

"It's been months and we haven't seen any sign of those behemoths Jane warned us against," Grace Benson said.

"And the fruit's growing like never before," Mary replied. "Winter's over; I don't see why they keep us locked up like this."

"For your own protection," Bill Simmons said.

"Hah!" Mary said. "I think Sally's right. Jane's crazy."

"That's what I first thought when she told me about that 'alien mind' she said she contacted but I didn't say anything," Mrs. Benson said.

"You should have," Mary said. "I wish I had."

"And now we've got another one," Grace Benson said. "That Brother Ashoka."

"What's his first name?" Mary asked. "Nobody's really named Brother Ashoka."

"This one is," Bill Simmons said. "Manuel said he gave up his original name when he became a guide—I think that's what they call them, like kids playing Indian at camp—in that Fellowship."

"We can take care of two lunatics now that Spring's here," Mary said indulgently.

Amber liked to close his eyes and feel the fruit growing up around the colony, feel the buds bursting forth and ripening. But God—and who was Amber now if not God?—had commanded that no more vines put forth metal flowers where the colonists could find them, for He knew they would only use them to forge more weapons. Later, when they had listened to the word of God, then they would be allowed to have metal again.

Brother Ashoka was walking well, though he was still unable to form more than a few comprehensible words. Watching over him filled a place in Jane's life that had been vacant since Amber had deserted her, but the joy she took in caring for her former mentor was tempered with the knowledge that he would soon be adult enough to try a Latihan.

And then, she knew, the spider-mind would snare him, take him over, make of him a soulless puppet.

"Promise me you won't try to do the Latihan," she pleaded.

"Just nod your head if you promise." But though he always listened politely, he never nodded his head in agreement.

The green and black skirmish beast was waiting for Amber. It was about twenty times the length of his body, far smaller than the beasts that had guarded the gap in the trees on the plateau, but its glossy hide was beautiful and its strong odor perfume.

He slung the length of golden vine he carried with him over his shoulder and climbed a tall tree. The green and black beast brought its great squarish head close to the tree and rested its chin on the ground. Amber dropped from an overhanging branch onto the top of its head.

His head. He carefully set the golden vine down beside him, where it clung to the beast's head.

Moving gently so as not to dislodge its burdens the Beast-Who-Rode-Itself lifted its head and began the slow trek back to the settlement.

Jane heard the ringing of the gong and stuck her head out of the hut to see what was happening. Colonists were yelling, grabbing weapons, running. She scrambled out of the hut, looked around. Looked up.

Saw: a dozen green and black beasts like glossy tyrannosaurs, so tall that they moved through the forest like children wading through shallow water. Coming toward the settlement.

"Brother Ashoka!" she shouted. "Come on out and take a look at the thing you were going to give your soul to! Come on, hurry, or you won't get a good look before it kills us!"

There was no answer from within. She paused a moment, listening to the gongs and shouting, watching the beasts make their unnaturally silent way through the forest, then climbed back through the door into the hut.

Brother Ashoka sat propped up against the far wall, his yellow eyes staring into nothingness.

He's doing the Latihan, she realized. She could feel it pulsing from him, lapping like warm waves at her thoughts—

No. She held herself apart from it, refused to let it insinuate itself into her consciousness.

That's why the thing's attacking us. Because he's doing a Latihan. She felt no anger, only a certain bitterness at the thought that he, too, had abandoned her.

A slow smile was born, grew to engulf Brother Ashoka's face. *A zombie or just insane?* she asked herself. But it made little difference: in either case she would have to face death alone.

"Jane," Brother Ashoka said hesitantly. "Jane, come with me." He got to his feet.

"Why? Why go anywhere?"

"Amber. He's back."

Insane, she decided. But one action was as good as another, so she followed him to the gate.

"Let's let them get a bit closer before we start shooting," Catherine said. "We won't be able to kill them all if they rush us all at once but if we can kill some and scare the rest off until—John! Do you see something on top of the first one's head?"

"A man," John said. "There's a man riding it."

"It's Amber," Ted said. "And he's wearing a golden crown, like he was king of the things or something."

"You're sure it's Amber?" Catherine asked.

"Yes," Ted said. "And—" He pointed.

A horde of smaller animals—first near squirrels, fruitbears, wood pigs, and dire mice, then the gray-plated skirmish beasts and snake weasels, came pouring out of the forest. Each creature carried a gift of fruit in its mouth. They ignored the arrows some few of the colonists were shooting at them and deposited their gifts in full sight of the defenders, then retreated to the forest.

"They're peace offerings," Catherine said. "Tell everyone not to shoot."

"But—" Bill Simmons protested.

"It may be a trick, but if whatever we're up against has got the intelligence for that sort of trick *and* the behemoths, we don't have a chance."

"So we take the peace offering on faith?" John asked.

"We don't have any choice."

Amber waved at them from the head of his beast.

"How'd he do it?" Ted asked.

"What did he do?" John asked back.

Amber's behemoth lowered its head to the ground before the gate and closed its eyes. Behind it the other beasts lay down as if to sleep. Amber picked up the golden vine and leaped from the beast's head to the ground.

He stood before the gate, smiling and relaxed, waiting. Presently the gate opened.

John and Catherine stood facing him. They were empty handed, but behind them stood Bill Simmons and a number of other archers with arrows nocked. To their right stood Jane and Brother Ashoka.

"Hello," Amber said and the very mildness of his voice, the unchanged ordinariness of it, terrified Jane. She felt herself beginning to tremble.

"Hello, Amber," John said calmly. "You seem to be connected somehow with these beasts—"

"I share their oneness with God," Amber agreed.

"Then it was 'God' who was responsible for the attempt to destroy the colony?" Catherine asked. "And you're his emissary?"

"Yes," Amber agreed. "But I come not to demand terms of you but to bring you God's offer: all of you can live here in peace for the rest of your lives, in the paradise that God will create for you here. All that God asks of you is that no humans transfer here from Earth unless, like Brother Ashoka, they can do the Latihan and are ready to enter into full communion with God."

"How do we know we can trust you?" Catherine asked.

"You need not; I ask nothing of you. I am here for Jane, to bring her to share the oneness that I share with God."

"God?" Jane's voice trembled, almost breaking into a whistle. "That thing's not God. It stole your soul, you're not my brother anymore, you're just—you're *dead* and that thing's inside your body pretending to be you."

"Jane. You're wrong." Brother Ashoka had gained full control of his voice. *It's got him too,* Jane thought but something made her listen as he continued, "This is Amber. And these beasts, they too are Amber. So is every tree in the forest. So am I. This whole world is Amber now. And God? Perhaps, in a way. Because everything is Amber and Amber believes in God. Because of Amber they have become God. But if they were Amber and Brother Ashoka and Jane and many, many others, what would they become? Accept what he offers you.''

''Accept what?''

Amber held out the length of golden vine.

SCIENCE FICTION BESTSELLERS
FROM BERKLEY

Frank Herbert

DUNE	(03698-7—$2.25)
DUNE MESSIAH	(03930-7—$1.95)
CHILDREN OF DUNE	(04075-5—$2.25)

Philip José Farmer

THE FABULOUS RIVERBOAT	(03793-2—$1.75)
TO YOUR SCATTERED BODIES GO	(03744-4—$1.75)
NIGHT OF LIGHT	(03933-1—$1.75)

Robert A. Heinlein

STRANGER IN A STRANGE LAND	(03782-7—$2.25)
THE MOON IS A HARSH MISTRESS	(03850-5—$1.95)
TIME ENOUGH FOR LOVE	(03471-2—$2.25)

Send for a list of all our books in print.

These books are available at your local bookstore, or send price indicated plus 30¢ for postage and handling. If more than four books are ordered, only $1.00 is necessary for postage. Allow three weeks for delivery. Send orders to:

Berkley Book Mailing Service
P.O. Box 690
Rockville Centre, New York 11570

"WE ONLY HAVE ONE TEXAS"

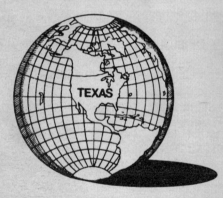

TEXAS

People ask if there is really an energy crisis. Look at it this way. World oil consumption is 60 million barrels per day and is growing 5 percent each year. This means the world must find three million barrels of new oil production each day. Three million barrels per day is the amount of oil produced in Texas as its peak was 5 years ago. The problem is that it is not going to be easy to find a Texas-sized new oil supply every year, year after year. In just a few years, it may be impossible to balance demand and supply of oil unless we start conserving oil today. So next time someone asks: "is there really an energy crisis?" Tell them: "yes, we only have one Texas."

ENERGY CONSERVATION -
IT'S YOUR CHANCE TO SAVE, AMERICA

Department of Energy, Washington, D.C.

A PUBLIC SERVICE MESSAGE FROM BERKLEY PUBLISHING CO., INC.